VOTE FOR QUIMBY

—AND QUICK!

Harry Miles Muheim

★

COLLIER BOOKS

A Division of Macmillan Publishing Co., Inc.

New York

I
AND
VOTE FOR QUIMBY
QUICK!

Macmillan Publishing Co., Inc.
866 Third Avenue, New York, N.Y. 10022
Collier Macmillan Canada, Ltd.

Library of Congress Cataloging in Publication Data

Muheim, Harry Miles.
Vote for Quimby—and Quick.

I. Title.
PZ4.M9495Vo 1978 [PS3563.U37] 813'.5'4 77–28697
ISBN 0–02–587870–0
ISBN 0–02–023120–2 pbk.

First Collier Books Edition 1978

Vote for Quimby—and Quick! is also published in a hardcover edition by Macmillan Publishing Co., Inc.

Designed by Jack Meserole

Printed in the United States of America

This book is dedicated to Jane Curtze Muheim, a handsome and skilled woman to whom I have been attached both legally and affectionately for more than thirty years.

As anyone with half an eye will be able to see immediately, the story is a fabrication, a work of unmuzzled fiction.

The setting is New Jersey, but my familiarity with that state is derived from travelling through it occasionally at a hundred and two miles an hour on the Amtrak Metroliner. Any opportunity to study the real people or the real politics of New Jersey has been precluded by the high speed of the train. Any resemblance to real people or real politics is coincidental.

H. M. M.
December 1977

There is no mystery about good government. It obtains at those times when the men who govern are honest.

—THOMAS JEFFERSON (*1784*)

Let me respond to those who say
that there is no law in Hackensack.
I am the law in Hackensack.

—JOHN L. O'TOOLE (*1884*)

I can govern New Jersey effectively, whether I am in the State House or the state pen.

—HORACE J. QUIMBY (*1984*)

CHAPTER 1

BORN in the Harkness Pavilion, raised on Manhattan's East 83rd Street, educated at Yale, I had always taken a dim and patronizing view of New Jersey. But at the time that my company, Polcon, Inc., became the political consultant for New Jersey's Governor Horace J. Quimby (Dem.), I had to make several trips into that state to target precincts, take polls, confer with jaded local politicians, grasp the issues, and lay out a campaign plan for the Governor's reelection that November. I thought these trips might create a little interest in my heart for New Jersey—perhaps even a budding affection. They did not.

Then one bright morning, when the United States of America had moved into her third century and I was almost halfway through my first, I made a critical decision. Sitting in my bronze-windowed office on the 67th floor of the Sarantopolous Building, looking out across the top of the General Motors Building and beyond the lofty excitement of Manhattan to the low profile of distant, smog-bound New Jersey, I decided that, like it or not, New Jersey was the place for me. When I went to Trenton for my strategy meeting with Governor Quimby that afternoon, I would take out citizenship papers in the Garden State. Only in New Jersey, I had figured, could I actually survive.

"Time for action!" I said aloud, swinging around, flipping on the Picturephone Intercom, and pounding on my free-form mahogany desk, the surface of which had some repetitious striations in the wood grain that seemed to portray human nymphae—over two hundred times.

Emily appeared on my tube. Emily was neat. She was twenty-one, blonde, bright-eyed, beautiful, and her wet-lipped mouth was open wider than it had to be.

"Yes, Mr. Quick?"

"Emily, I'm going over to Jersey and—"

"Your meeting with the Governor is at three."

"I know. I'm also going to set in motion a new chain of events."

"How can I help?"

"Punch up the Times Terminal, will you please, and find out where the Hudson and Manhattan Tube comes up in Manhattan. Penn Station is under another bomb threat."

"Sure," she said. "It'll take just a millisecond."

Emily swung around toward the electronic information machine that I'd leased from *The New York Times*. On command, it brought the whole newspaper, back to the first issue in 1851, right into your office on a screen. It could tell you what Lincoln said at Cooper Union, or what Carl Furillo said when the Dodgers lost the 1952 World Series, or what Mayor Rizzo said when the Fine Arts Commission proposed a mature, sixty-foot Picasso bronze bull for the plaza of the Philadelphia City Hall.

"Do you know the Key Command Inquiry words?" asked Emily.

"I would say U.S. Public Transportation, New York Metropolitan Area, Hudson and Manhattan Tube, Eastern Terminus. That should do it."

"Let's see," said Emily.

I tilted the Picturephone camera to get a shot of Emily's breasts as she punched up the inquiry. They were fun to watch while she did this, or while she threw back her head in laughter, or while, best of all, she ran unfettered through a springtime field of Connecticut clover. I had done a senatorial campaign in Connecticut the year before, and Emily had run miles in clover.

Emily was not the only reason that I had become one of America's leading political consultants. ("At the top of the list this year is Manhattan-based, computer-based political wizard, Thomas J. Quick" [*New York Times*, November 19, 1977]; "A remarkable creator of plausible candidates, even in South America" [*Psychology Now*, Winter 1978]; "Tom Quick, the fastest gun in American politics today . . ." [*American Rifleperson*, November 1981].) But she was one of them. Unlike my three former wives, Emily agreed with my politics (Dem.), she loved the turbulence and excitement at Polcon, Inc., she loved the turbulence and excitement of a sexual encounter—and she balled with abandon, affection, and a sure grasp of the current community sexual standards for the Borough of Manhattan.

"It comes up in Gimbel's Basement," Emily said, turning back to the Picturephone camera. I tilted up.

"What does?"

"The Hudson and Manhattan Tube."

"Oh, of course. Thank you, dear."

"But it's no longer called that. After it went bankrupt in the early sixties, they dumped it on the State of New York for three hundred and fifty-seven million dollars, and it's now called the Port Authority Trans-Hudson System—or PATH. Besides the acronym, they've got a logo, fifty brand new Budd cars with slashed upholstery, and an on-time arrival record of seven percent."

"What's the logo?" I asked, intrigued.

"A smiling turtle."

"Brilliant PR," I said. "How often do they run?"

"Whenever they can assemble a train, they send it out," said Emily. "There's more here about it. The line was attacked by Robert Moses in the winter of 1937 on the grounds that it interfered with the orderly flow of interstate commerce. And furthermore—"

"That'll be enough for now, Emily."

"How come you're not taking the limousine, Mr. Quick? It seems a shame to spend thirty-one thousand dollars for a silver Grand Mercedes, and then to—"

"I'm putting the Grand Mercedes up for sale," I announced.

"No!" she said, drawing in a big, upthrusting breath. "Including the back seat?"

"Of course, Emily."

"I'll miss it," she said, with a look of sad-yet-happy remembering.

"I will, myself," I said. "But I'm moving to New Jersey and changing my whole lifestyle. A Grand Mercedes limousine with a uniformed driver won't fit my new image."

"To *New Jersey*?" she asked.

"Parts of it are lovely, Emily. I'll get along."

"All the more reason for a final fling in the big back seat!" she said enthusiastically.

"I can't take you along today, Emily. This is a business trip."

She laughed heartily, throwing her head back the way Marilyn Monroe used to do. I tilted down. There they were. Jiggling.

"Mr. Quick, you are so wonderfully full of bullshit! *Nobody* can mix business and pleasure better than you. Not even Mick Jagger."

I was touched by the compliment. I've always liked Jagger's work, and once even tried to persuade him to run for sheriff of a small county in northern Alabama. A group of do-gooder Democrats down there had contacted Polcon looking for a candidate who was not cast in the mold of a typical southern sheriff. Jagger seemed ideal. I agreed to consult the campaign, and the committee, Citizens for a Sensible South in the Seventies, agreed to pick up the tab. Mick would have done a terrific job. He would have changed the entire concept of law enforcement below the Mason-Dixon Line. But he was sparring with the Bombay Police Department at the time, and the whole thing never came off.

"Emily, darling, even if I took you, we couldn't drive," I said.

"Why not?"

"The Holland Tunnel is blocked by a raging propane fire. The Lincoln Tunnel is closed while the navy searches for that nuclear torpedo that slid out of the U.S.S. *Whitefish*. And the George Washington Bridge lost its westbound deck last night in a racial confrontation."

"Oh."

"And now, will you please get me Gus Schmiddle out in Oakland?"

"Sure."

In a few seconds, Gus was on the line. I gave him a firm order, knowing that even three thousand miles away, it would be carried out right. Polcon, Inc. has used Schmiddle Litho., Inc. for bumper stickers, billboards, and quarter cards in sixteen campaigns. Gus Schmiddle is the most conscientious and color-true lithographer in America. (I learned long ago from a man named Joseph Napolitan, the dean of Democratic political consultants, that an important part of the game is knowing where the best talent is, no matter how distant or expensive. The best political button company in the world is in Bangkok.)

My order to Gus was for ten thousand bumper stickers. They would be four by sixteen inches in size, and on a dark blue illuminated background would be just two words in hard, bright red: "—AND QUICK!"

I flipped open the brass locks of my Hartmann belting-leather attaché case, dropped in a SONY videocassette and a SONY cassette recorder, then filled the case to the brim with computer print-outs. On top, I placed copies of the *Congressional Record* and the *Wall Street Journal.* It was going to be a crucial meeting with the Governor and his volatile administrative assistant, and all I really needed was the videocassette with the six one-minute spots we had just completed. But I have found that a client is always impressed by a stuffed attaché case. They particularly like the computer print-outs, those endless wide sheets with a million numbers splayed across them—numbers that only the wizardry of the consultant can clarify.

In the outer office, I paused to kiss Emily an endearing good-bye. Our open mouths and intertwined tongues did not reflect any long-term commitment. We had spent a lot of time in First Avenue bars trying to define and redefine our fragile relationship, but basically we just liked to kiss and feel each other. It was childlike, perhaps, but fun. We did other things, too, to signify our mutual affection, and the only thing we'd ever disagreed about in the two years she had been with Polcon, Inc. was sexual congress in which I approached her from the rear. Though this is illegal in twenty-seven states (including the entire Confederacy, of course), I myself have always thought it was a powerful way of relating to a woman, of letting her know that you are there. But Emily was touchy about it, and I did not persist. I've always felt that it's unseemly for a man to do anything to a woman's orifice—any one of them—that she does not want done to it.

Slipping into my nappy Gucci pigskin trenchcoat, I quoted Emily a few lines from Lincoln's Farewell Address at the Great Western Railway Station in Springfield, Illinois, on the morning of February 11, 1861:

"My friends, no one not actually *in* my situation can appreciate my feeling of sadness at this parting. . . . I go now, not knowing when—or whether ever—I shall return."

Emily was laughing, looking up at me with warmth. I loved it.

"Oh, Mr. Quick, you *are* full of bullshit!"

"To His care commending you," I said, holding up my hand in a kind of blessing, "as I hope in your prayers you will commend me, I bid you an affectionate farewell."

I backed out the door, imitating a distant steam-railroad whistle and waving as politicians used to wave from the rear platforms of observation cars as they went whistle-stopping across the heartland of a simpler, more contented America.

CHAPTER 2

I WALKED down the subdued hallway, where deep brown carpeting curved gracefully and ran up each wall to the ceiling, then curved again and ran across the ceiling to a wide bronze strip that was the center line. A string of clear spherical globes were hung from the strip, lighting the way to the elevators with brilliant orange filaments.

Opposite the elevators hung a forceful urban acrylic by Fleugenweilder. Alongside the painting was a small bronze plaque:

BLUESTEEL NIGHTTOWN, 1978
Klaus Fleugenweilder (1944–)
from the collection of
Mr. and Mrs. Aristede Sarantopolous

I would miss the Sarantopolous Building. More than anything else—more than my Mercedes limousine, my UN Plaza apartment, my soft Dunhill jackets, my fantastic alimony payments that left me dead broke at the end of each month—the Sarantopolous Building, lifting me high above the grim street realities of New York, symbolized my success in the seventies. It was a shallow way to look at life, perhaps, but that's the way I was in those days. Shallow, opportunistic, upward-mobile, and mesmerized by the surface glitter of Eastern Establishment life. My friends were all the same way.

When the big building opened early in 1979, it wasn't easy to get Polcon, Inc. accepted as a tenant. Mr. Sarantopolous, a squat Greek distiller who had made a fortune bringing a sticky white liquid called *ouzo* across the Atlantic in his own tanker fleet, had started to assemble the land for the structure back in 1950. It was the block bounded by 59th and 60th streets, by Fifth and Madison avenues. The final big jewel in this real-estate diadem was the Sherry-Netherland Hotel. When Sarantopolous finally acquired that graceful building in a pinochle game, he knocked it flat, along with the rest of the block, and thrust his bronze ovoid shaft eighty-seven stories up into the sky, dwarfing the marble General Motors Building immediately to the south.

Mr. Sarantopolous and his young wife, who was a striking beauty as well as a raving one, knew that fads were the fuel of New York. They were themselves a fad, and so most anxious that their building be "in" in the same way that certain discos and restaurants and *bottiers* and leech-dispensing pharmacies are in. They set up strong criteria for Cornwall, Elliman, and Zoltan, the renting agents. To make it, you had to be a company in the Top 200 of the *Fortune* 500 companies, or you had to have been mentioned constructively in *The New York Times* at least six times in the year before you signed the lease.

For people like David Susskind, it was a snap. But for me, just getting started on success, it was tougher. I asked Emily to go to the *Times* office and strike off my mentions from the microfilm file. There were only five. But one of them described me as "a responsible political mastermind."

That was enough to impress Mr. Zoltan, a kindly, withered old Democrat who said he had once been a responsible mastermind himself.

Instead of pressing the heat-sensitive button at the elevator, I inserted a bronze key into the panel. This key cost an additional twelve-hundred dollars a year, but it was worth the money. In seven seconds, an empty elevator car was delivered to me on the 67th floor. I stepped in, and the elevator —programmed by the key for Personal Express Service— plunged without stopping to the lobby.

I would miss the Sarantopolous lobby, too. It was eleven stories high and contained a full-fledged rain forest—one that made the rain forest in the lobby of the Ford Foundation look piddling. Every half hour, it actually rained. The great macaws took shelter from the computer-controlled tropical storm. Incredible—and refreshing.

Crossing a huge plaza called The Agora, I hailed a cab and hopped in. Instead of an ordinary, crummy New York cab with broken seats and a quarter-inch sheet of grimy Plexiglas designed to keep me from robbing and murdering the surly driver, I found myself in a clean, spacious old Checker.

The interior was filled with sketches of human feet. Not footprints, but feet. Each pair, drawn on a sheet of white bond paper, was almost life-size. They were Scotch-taped everywhere—on the little folding seats, even on the ceiling. I had once ridden in the Manhattan cab with the hands on display, but never before in the one with the feet.

"Nice day," said the driver, turning around with a broad smile to look at me through a sheet of crystal-clear Plexiglas. His voice came through a high-fidelity intercom system. "And where may I take yuh?"

He was not surly. This was disappointing, for I wanted to dictate an important letter en route to the PATH station.

The surly drivers, once they insult you and rip apart the mayor and the fabric of Western civilization, let you alone. But the friendly ones draw you into long, dim-witted discussions, punctuated with the question: "Am I right?" In this case, the conversation would be about feet.

"Gimbel's Basement, please," I said, flipping open the attaché case and taking out the SONY. "I'm in a hurry."

The cab did not move. I looked up to find the driver looking back at me with an extended smile.

"Anybody ever tell yuh, yuh look *exactly* like Jack Kennedy?" he asked.

"Yes, I've heard that."

"An *amazin'* resemblance," he went on. "The shock of hair. The deep-set eyes. The set of the mouth. Smile, will yuh?"

I smiled an annoyed smile.

"Look, driver—"

"Even the smile! Even the *smile*!"

"—I'm in a hurry to catch a train."

"Sure—sure," he said, pulling into the southbound traffic jam on Fifth. We moved along at one mile an hour through the fumes.

"You're a Kennedy relative, that's it!" he said, continuing to inspect me in the rearview mirror.

"No, I'm not."

"You an Irishman?"

"No, I'm not."

"What are you?"

"An American," I said, hoping to cut off the conversation.

"God bless America," he said.

We drove for two blocks in silence.

"Yuh happen to notice the feet?" he finally asked.

"Yes, I did."

"I'm the artist."

"Is that so?"

"Want me to draw yours? Only five bucks."

"No, thanks," I said. "I've got to catch this train, and—"

"Don't take any time. You jus' take off your shoes an' socks, an' I snap your feet with my Polaroid Close Up. Then I sketch the feet at home an' send you the original after I Xerox a copy for the cab."

"Nevertheless—"

"Yuh'll be in the company of a lot of famous feet, mister. There's Johnny Carson's in the upper right-hand corner—right between Fats Domino and Anna Moffo. How about it?"

"No, thanks," I said.

"But pretty good drawin's, huh?" he asked proudly.

"They're fine," I said. "Particularly if you like bare feet."

"I do," he said. "I do. You see, I got this thing about feet that they call a fetish. Ever heard of one?"

"Yes, I have," I said.

"Had it ever since I was a kid," he went on. "Got it from watchin' my mother put on black silk stockin's before goin' out to a speakeasy. Kin you imagine that?"

"I guess one never knows," I observed, "what devious pathways the young human mind will suddenly grasp in an attempt to find an answer to the more pervasive mysteries of life."

"You said it," he replied. "Anyhow, my analyst recommended these drawin's as a good way of dischargin' my hidden anxieties about feet—an' at the same time pickin' up a couple of bucks."

"Seems very sensible," I said. I sat back with a sigh and lit a cigar.

"There's all kinds of these fetishes, yuh know," he said, suddenly slightly defensive. "Not only feet."

"Yes, I've heard that."

"Handkerchiefs, buttocks, heels, armpits, gloves, breasts, panties—"

"I wonder if there's such a thing as a cunt fetish," I asked, hoping to jolt him into silence. It didn't faze him.

"Oh, no, no," he explained. "The cunt don't count. It's got to be what they call a sexual preoccupation with something *non*erogenous."

"You mean a breast is nonerogenous?"

"It's a little difficult to explain to a layman," he said. "But a lot of these guys get pretty far to the left sexually, if you know what I mean. Chains, boots, urine—if you had a fetish, it'd be easier for you to understand what I'm gettin' at. Am I right?"

"I would imagine so."

"I hope I'm not embarrassin' you with these unexpected revelations."

"Not at all," I said. "They're yours, not mine."

"Listen, how come with that face you're not runnin' for office?"

"I'm in politics," I said. "But I've never been a candidate."

"Come to think of it, maybe it's just as well. There'd be a lot of people who'd say you were tradin' on the Kennedy name—or image. Am I right?"

I did not answer.

"But whaddeya do in politics if you're not a politician?"

"I'm a political consultant."

"What the hell is that?"

"I run a company that tells candidates how to get elected."

"Don't they know how to get elected?"

"Only half of them do, as it turns out."

"So what do you tell 'em?"

"First, I tell them whether I think they can win. Then I tell them to focus on the principal aim of their campaign and to decide how their message should be put across in a carefully determined media mix—using private polls as a political tool. That way, I help them strike a balance between direct mail—shooting with a rifle—and television—shooting with a shotgun. Finally, I tell them to be honest once they assume the mantle of public office, for public office is a trust."

"Yuh ever recommend a torchlight parade?" he asked.

"They're out of style right now," I explained. "But whenever we do have a parade or a rally, I urge my candidates to have their signs hand-lettered. Even when they're lithographed, they must *look* hand-lettered–with the capital Ns and Rs turned around."

"What for?"

"It shows on television that people who print letters backwards are for you."

"Is it important?"

"In an election, you need everybody."

"It sounds pretty exciting," he said.

"It is," I agreed. "It wrecked two of my three marriages, but I'll be damned if it's not exciting! Now, if you'll excuse me, I have to dictate a—"

"But wait a minute. Where do you find the politicians?"

"Word of mouth. They call up the office."

"Anybody can call?"

"Only Democrats."

His smile in the rearview mirror suddenly faded.

"Democrats, huh?"

"That's right. Do-gooder Democrats in the Harry Hopkins tradition."

"Who the hell is Harry Hopkins?"

"Franklin D. Roosevelt tried to groom him for the presidency in 1940, but they could never get his suit to hang right."

"Never heard of him."

"Nevertheless, Hopkins turned out to be one of the pivotal Democrats of the twentieth century."

"I used to be a Democrat," said the driver, and now he

was going surly. "I was a Democrat until they let the niggers in."

"That was quite a while ago," I said.

"Yeah. It was Missus Roosevelt let the niggers in. Am I right?"

"I did a campaign for a black woman in Connecticut last year," I said casually. "She's now a member of the United States Senate."

"Shit," said the driver. "They're taking over."

That was the end of our discussion. I flipped on my SONY and started to dictate a mailing to my three former wives:

"Dear Beatrice and April and Elizabeth:

"In reading the Constitution of the State of New Jersey a couple of weeks ago, I came across an item that has caused me to plan some substantial changes in my style of life. If all goes according to plan, I will be able to cut down or even eliminate the bloated monthly alimony payments I must now make to the three of you—on the fifth, sixteenth, and twenty-seventh of each month. Paragraph.

"In spite of my apparent well-being and my repeated mentions by James Reston and Tom Wicker, my CPA tells me that I am slowly going broke. So I am going to beat an imaginative retreat, modify my lifestyle, terminate our basically parasitic relationships, and have a little cash on hand for myself for a change. Paragraph.

"Therefore, by next January third, which is Inauguration Day in the State of New Jersey, please have taken jobs or have taken new husbands. For after that date I will no longer be carrying the stupefying financial burden of our old mistaken marriages. There will probably be court challenges from you on this—particularly from you, Elizabeth—but you might as well know that my attorneys have indicated that my position is impregnable. Furthermore—"

"Gimbel's Basement," said the driver. "That'll be eleven dollars and seventy cents. Here's my card in case you change your mind about the feet. An' please don't leave a dead cigar in the back of the cab."

CHAPTER 3

THE UPPER LEVEL of the PATH station beneath Gimbel's is indistinguishable from any New York City subway station —naked lights, grimy tile, defaced ads for rye bread, blank-faced citizens, sad graffiti—and everything covered by a patina of steel dust that grinds daily from the screeching train wheels and floats invisibly down there forever, causing soiled shirts, damaged eyes, magnetic hair, and an occasional incipient case of black lung.

A blinking electric sign said that the NEXT TRAIN would leave from the LOWER LEVEL. It didn't say when, though, and I recalled Emily's words about the sketchy service. The lower level was a duplicate of the upper—with one stunning exception. Three irrevocably naked girls were dancing down there to the muffled beat of bongo drums and a quiet Oriental melody played on a recorder. The musicians were two young men—also naked. The moment remains to this day happily etched in my memory.

There I was, walking down the iron-edged stairs, thinking about the unfinished letter to my wives. As I cleared the ceiling level, I heard the odd music. In the distance, down toward the darker end of the platform, the dance was going on—three girls moving sinuously through identical gyrations, flanked by their nude musicians. Two amber, battery-powered Coleman lanterns lit the scene. Above them, strung between two steel posts, was a banner:

THE SUBTERRANEAN DANCE THEATRE
JOIN IN IF YOU LIKE!

Eyes riveted, I approached slowly, expecting them all to vanish—*pouf!*—in a flare of powdered magnesium. But they were real. They kept right on dancing. Ordinarily, a New York crowd collects at the vortex of any excitement, but this audience of about thirty stood transfixed, their feet rooted by shock and surprise to the spot. Not me, though. Ensnared as always by the basilisk of sex, I kept moving closer.

There was magic in the scene, ridiculous as it would appear later when the five young people were brought up against some Nixonian strict constructionist on charges of indecent exposure. The judge would surely say that, taken as a whole, the predominant appeal of their performance was to the prurient, shameful, or morbid interests of the people waiting for the PATH train.

To me, though, it was a charming ritual—something you might see in a small temple outside Bangkok. It was also a piece of recent history. These splendid bodies were leftovers from the late sixties, when young people spent vast energies marching and shouting and defacing libraries and igniting branch banks—trying in a thousand jarring, execrable ways to encourage older Americans to embrace a natural, loving, warm human ethic. Failing, they drifted to the right, settled down, tightened up, and went on to law school. But here before me in the PATH station were some remnants of those memorable days, the sensuous New Left, still in action. Remarkable!

The five naked bodies had been painted with polka dots —red and green polka dots, each about the size of a silver dollar. It was the first time I had ever seen a penis with polka dots.

Sizing up the girls, I panned slowly from left to right. They were entirely caught up in the dance, lost in the rhythm and movement, loving it. The girl on the left was a full-bodied, smooth-curving Scandinavian with long blonde hair that seemed to ripple in slow motion, the way that hair does in Clairol commercials. The lovely girl at stage center was fragile and Oriental, and she was the one who sang a strange melodic line as they danced. But when I saw the girl on the right, I forgot not only about the other two, but about everything else on the face of the planet, including the New Jersey gubernatorial campaign.

There are plenty of so-called perfect bodies around town, of course, but this one *was* perfect. She was black—bronze in color, actually—and her calm, oval face was cast with a mysterious, high-cheeked symmetry. Her breasts rose from her body as gracefully as Mount Fuji rises from the Kantō Plain. Her hair—straight, silky, and black—flowed to her hips, where, at the vortex of everything, danced a small, heart-shaped, ebony bush. Her long legs kept to the beat without effort, swirling this splendid form around on heel and toe.

I was mesmerized, but not everybody else was. In the distance, I heard somebody scream; then there was a voice of gravel shouting about a lewd spectacle. Another voice shouted that somebody should call the cops—call the cops—call the cops.

To my right, a handsome middle-aged woman was starting to faint. A boy of fifteen or so was helping her to a bench. Fanning her considerably, he helped her off with her coat, a sleek, beige-dyed, Fouke-processed Lakoda sealskin. I thought the lad was going to place the coat over her like a blanket. Instead, he wheeled and started to run with it.

Though enormously reluctant to leave the Subterranean Dance Theatre, I ran after him. He was fast and shifty, and I could not get quite close enough to clout him with my attaché case. But as he started up the iron stairs, he bounced off a descending fat man, lost his balance, and fell at my feet.

Contrary to the Afro-Hispanic stereotype, he turned out to be an angry Swedish youngster who wanted to know, as he put it, what the fuck I was doing.

"I'm rescuing my wife's coat," I told him calmly, prying it out of his hands. "And I suggest that you get your Nordic ass out of here before I call the cops."

I started back toward the stage. The gravel-voiced man was now shouting epithets at the dancers. People were laughing nervously—cackling. A faint police-whistle sound filtered down from the upper level. The PATH train arrived from Newark with a roar and a screech of brakes. The fragile mood of an Oriental temple had dissolved.

The dance came to a calm halt. The two young men slipped into patchwork jeans and faded blue shirts, concealing their polka dots. Without haste, they doused the amber lights; took down the banner and folded it; then put lights, banner, and musical instruments into a Lord & Taylor shopping bag and walked off.

The dancers had turned upstage to the long loose dresses that lay on the platform where they'd been dropped as the dance began. Their moves were exceedingly cool. Clearly, they had melted into crowds before.

Then suddenly the Swedish kid—avenging his earlier defeat—dashed from behind me, roaring with laughter. He snatched the black girl's dress from her hands and continued running at full speed down the long dim platform, his laughter recoiling off the walls.

The other girls kept dressing as though nothing had happened. My girl, pausing for only a second to scoop up her boots from the platform, took out in full, naked pursuit. I found myself running after them. I could not stand the idea of losing sight of her.

She ran with fleet grace, but was no match for the speedy Swede. Epithets roared from her mouth as she ran. Some were familiar ones from the ghetto, like "motherfuckuh!" and "jive-ass sack of shit!" but there were others I had never heard before. They were deep tribal imprecations in a strong unknown language, rolling out of her as though she were casting an ancient spell. The spell, however, didn't work. Suddenly, she tripped and fell. The kid clattered up some dim, distant steps and was gone.

The last thing she shouted after him was in perfect, clear English:

"You little honky prick!"

Breathing heavily, her body shiny with sweat, she remained for several seconds propped on her arms, her head down, defeated. Then she raised her head and saw me standing there.

"You out to get me or help me?" she asked quietly.

"To help," I said. "I thought you might need a coat for the getaway."

I held it out to her. Police whistles, civil commotion, the voice of the lady screaming about her coat—all these sounds were echoing from back down the platform, but the girl was at ease.

"I must be getting slippy in the head," she said with a smile. "Who *are* you, mister?"

Deliberately, she swung her long legs around and began to pull on the tall, green suede boots.

"I'm one of America's leading political consultants."

"Then this must be a little out of your line," she said, zipping the boots, then holding out both hands for me to draw her up to her feet.

"Not at all," I said. "In politics you have to be ready for anything."

The momentum carried her into my arms, where, glistening and moist, she lay her head on my shoulder. The high heels of the boots made her taller than when she'd been dancing—just the right height for her head on my shoulder.

"Thanks, Mister Charlie," she said in a low and easy voice.

"You're welcome, whoever you are."

"Victoria. Victoria Woodhill."

I held her gently, feeling her heart pound, making sure that my surprise did not interfere with my savoring. But angry people were moving toward us on the dim platform. There was no time for a real exchange of affection.

"Victoria, I'm Tom Quick. And since we're both in trouble, I think we should get the hell out of here."

"What trouble are you in?"

"I just stole a coat."

"Where we going?"

"Trenton, New Jersey."

"Terrific," she said. "I've never been to Trenton."

I held the soft light-brown coat for her to slip into, then I flipped her hair so that it cascaded down the back. The coat, fitting to perfection, came down right to the tops of the over-the-knee boots. All the bright polka dots were hidden.

"I just knew you wouldn't bring me the wrong size, Tom," she said, laughing and slipping her hand into mine.

"Let's go, Victoria."

I swung her around, and we started away from the PATH train, climbing the stairway at the darker, far end of the platform.

At the top of the stairs stood a cop. He was young, fat,

sweating, earnest, and stunned by her bronze, sexy symmetry.

"Excuse me. I'm Officer LaDue. Badge seven-two-three-four."

"Yes, Officer?"

"We're looking for some people who were doin' a nude dance down there on the lower level. You see 'em? Stripped?"

"I'm afraid not, Officer," I said.

"They got red and green polka dots all over their bodies, and the broads dance naked while a couple of queers play the bongo drums an' toot? See anything like that?"

"I'm afraid not, Officer," I said.

"I'm sure we'd have remembered it," said Victoria.

"What you two doing coming up this way?" he asked, his brow creased with suspicion.

"We just got off the first car of the PATH train, Officer," I said, "and we're proceeding to my office in the Sarantopolous Building." I had already taken a card from my wallet. "I'm Thomas J. Quick, a political consultant. We've been in New Jersey at a meeting with Governor Horace J. Quimby."

"A political consultant?" he asked, turning the card over as though there might be an explanation on the back.

"Yes. Polcon, Inc."

Suddenly he smiled.

"With that face, I suppose you do pretty good."

"I try my best, Officer."

"But who's the girl?" His face had returned to its earlier suspicious setting.

I gently moved her a step closer to him.

"Victoria, may I present Officer LaDue. Badge seven-two-three-four. This is Victoria Woodhill, a member of the Polcon staff. Victoria is a specialist in—in the politics of intuition."

"How do you do, Officer LaDue?" said Victoria, extending her hand graciously. Her voice was quiet, low, elegant.

"My pleasure, ma'am," said the cop, touching the visor of his cap. "I'm sorry to have detained you."

"Not at all," said Victoria. "Mr. Quick and I appreciate the importance of law and order. Good luck to you, Officer LaDue."

Exchanging the smiles of conspirators, we walked the length of the upper level. Loud arguments and explanations filtered up through the gratings from below.

"You not only *look* like him," said Victoria. "You even walk like him—and you finger that button on your coat the same way."

"You remember Kennedy that well?"

"I was just a little kid out in Nevada, but I remember his walk from the TV set. It was in the bar where my mother worked. He always leaned forward, and his fingers were always checking to make sure that his coat was buttoned."

"Very observant for a little kid."

"My father taught me to *see* things," she said. "He was a Kawaiute Indian, and he said that Indians had to keep their eyes open or they'd get stepped on."

At the Seventh Avenue end of the platform, we went down again to the lower level, to board the other end of the waiting PATH train. The doors slid closed as we walked into the empty car, and in a moment we were headed west through an ancient, crumbling concrete tube toward Newark.

"Tom?"

"Yes, Victoria."

"Thanks."

"You're welcome," I said.

For a while we rode in silence, with me looking at her matchless bronze profile, and with her smiling a faint smile and looking straight ahead.

"Victoria—when I saw you dancing there, I felt about

you what Irving Thalberg once said men felt when they saw Garbo. You ever heard of Greta Garbo?"

"I saw her last week in *Ninotchka* at the Thalia."

"Thalberg said that Garbo was the kind of woman who, once seen, would give a man no rest. She would make him feel that his life was empty and incomplete, that he was unfulfilled as a human being—if he did not have her."

She turned her head slowly to size me up. A bright full smile broke across her face.

"And that's the way you feel about me?"

"Exactly."

"Boss!" She said the word with a deep, drawn-out vibration.

"What the hell does that mean?"

"I learned it from my mother. It's an old African expression of approval. It translates as 'Sheeeeeeeetit!' "

I put my arm around her, drew her to me, and we kissed down there under the Hudson River. It was a first kiss, but there was nothing tentative about it. Victoria knew exactly what to do. I did, myself. And when it was over, I sat back in amazement and said, trying for the same intonation: "Boss!"

CHAPTER 4

In Newark, we caught the Metroliner, and in its comfortable parlor car—the Metroclub—we rocketed south at a hundred and two miles an hour toward Trenton, the historic capital of New Jersey.

I liked the Metroliner. In the general physical deterioration of America, it was one of the few things that continued to work. Occasionally, of course, as Penn Central officials and Amtrak bureaucrats and track-maintenance supervisors and gandy dancers gave less and less and less of a damn about what they were doing, there would be several horrible deaths aboard a Metroliner as it slammed full-speed into a derailed tank car full of concentrated liquid ammonia. But mostly they arrived intact.

"Did you notice the dancer in the middle?" asked Victoria. We were facing each other in our revolving seats.

"Not as clearly as I noticed you."

"She's the leader of the Subterranean Dance Theatre," Victoria explained. "Xuantherese—from Thailand. She's also an artist."

"Does Xuantherese paint the polka dots?"

"She stamps the circles in a design all over us, and the

rest of us fill them in on each other. Like little kids with a coloring book!" In laughter, too, her face had the warm dignity of cast bronze.

"You always go out with polka dots?"

"Yes. Xuantherese says that the polka dots hypnotize people—unnerve them—exhilarate them. Nobody screams right away to restore reality."

"*I* was hypnotized," I said. "I still am."

I leaned forward confidentially, putting my hands lightly on her knees. "My God, Victoria, where did you get that body?"

"I just grew into it, Tom," she said. "It was easy."

"And your face—" I reached up to cup her chin. "It has the symmetry of a face on an Aztec coin."

"You make me sound like something on display at the Metropolitan."

The steward paused and asked if he could take Victoria's coat. She told him she was quite comfortable with it on. We ordered drinks.

"You dance every day?"

"No. About once a week—whenever Xuantherese gets the urge. She has some sexual complexes that she works out in dancing."

"You, too?"

"No, said Victoria. "I work out my sexual complexes in bed."

"That's neat," I said, sitting back, smiling, as a couple of scenarios skitted through my head. "And how long has the Subterranean Dance Theatre been going on?"

"It started out as a protest against Nixon and the Vietnam war. But it was so much fun that we just kept going after the war was gone. And Nixon, too."

"You ever try to get a grant from the Ford Foundation?"

"We've been to all of them. But they all send back the same letter saying that their federal tax exemption is not broad enough to cover our particular artistic activity."

"How do you describe it in the application?"

"As a hit-and-run attack on frozen minds."

"The minds in Manhattan are frozen?"

"From the jump. But then we come along—and strip and dance—"

"I saw it. I saw it!"

"—and we're a crazy combination of everyday street reality and the forbidden!" Victoria explained enthusiastically. "We're out there, vulnerable, naked, but also *free*! Everything is on the line. And it turns out it's *not* forbidden! Most of the time, we get away with it!"

"Then it's a contribution to mental health?" I suggested.

"And also a chance to raise some hell!" she added. "That's important, too." She paused for a second. "My father was a hell-raiser out West, Tom. I liked my father."

The steward came with our drinks. I tilted my seat back, lifted my glass to her. She winked. It was a delicious moment, sitting back, sipping a cool Manhattan in the warm company of a girl like this.

"What do you do when you're not dancing?" I asked.

"I'm a four-hundred-dollar call girl."

"And worth every penny, I'll bet."

"I'm no flat-backer, Tom. I put out my best."

"How long have you been in that line?"

"Since I graduated from Vassar. I'm putting away a stash in case I decide to go back for my master's."

"You have a pimp and everything?"

"No. I decided when I got into The Life that I'd do better with an accountant than a pimp. It's working out fine."

CHAPTER 5

THE YELLOW CAB at the Trenton station had a little vertical billboard on its roof, urging everybody to vote for Bradford J. Bassett, the certified Republican, for governor on November 5.

"Quimby's opponent," I said to Victoria, indicating Bassett's powerfully benign picture.

"Biggest jowls I've ever seen," said Victoria, observing Bassett critically.

"If jowls were popular in New Jersey, we'd be in bad trouble."

"How do you know they're not?"

"It was a subliminal question in our last Polcon poll. People across the state are suspicious of paving contractors and of jowls."

"Then if Bassett were a paving contractor—"

"He *is*, Victoria. One of the biggest. The ecologists complain that he's paved over more than seventy-seven percent of the arable land in the state."

"Is ecology big in New Jersey?"

"Not as big as paving."

I sat closer to Victoria than was necessary in the back seat of the cab. Happily, she responded. She laid her muscular dancer's leg hard against mine, all the way from thigh to ankle.

"One thing you'll find," I said, drawing her torso closer, "is that New Jersey politics is full of surprises."

"I had a feeling it might be," said Victoria.

We kissed again—this time a deep, scorching, exploratory kiss. It didn't represent any long-term commitment between us, but certainly it might have given a stranger that impression. Victoria's hand began to run gently along my left thigh, and just as I was ready to return the compliment, we were interrupted by a grim voice from the front seat.

"I gotta warn you folks that miscegenation is illegal in New Jersey."

Unhindered by any sheet of Plexiglas, the seam-faced, red-necked driver had swung around with an arm over the front seat. He was looking angrily at me, hornily at Victoria.

"You're wrong, driver," I said calmly. "I read the entire New Jersey Constitution just last month. It says nothing about color, nothing about sex!"

"This isn't miscegenation," said Victoria, running the moist point of her tongue around the edge of my ear. "This is just a taste test."

"What *cheap* motel you want to go to?" asked the driver, his voice thick with racism and jealousy.

"Take us to the State House," I said.

"Goin' to visit the Governor, I suppose," he said with clumsy sarcasm.

"As a matter of fact, we are," I said.

"Hah! Well, yuh better get there fast. He may not *be* the Governor very long."

The cab moved ahead with an angry jerk.

"What do you mean by that?" asked Victoria.

"The jury is out, folks. That's what I mean."

"Governor Quimby is running under a handicap this time," I explained to Victoria. "He's been on trial for the past five weeks. He's alleged to have taken thirty-seven million dollars in kickbacks from a big paving contractor."

" 'Alleged,' my ass," said the driver.

"That's three hundred and seventy thousand big bills!" said Victoria, incredulous.

"They're claiming that he was bribed by his opponent, Bradford J. Bassett," I said.

"They'll get Bassett, too!" said the cab driver enthusiastically. "Those two thought they had the whole thing sewed up perfect. Would they squeal on each other? Hell, *no*! But you know what they forgot? They forgot a disgruntled former employee! He blew the whistle on 'em!"

"Disgruntled former employees are the most dangerous people in American politics," I pointed out. "I always tell my candidates that if they're not going to be scrupulously honest after they take the mantle of office, then they should be careful about who they get sore at them."

"Did you tell Governor Quimby that?"

"Of course. I tell all of them. It's in my Basic Candidate Information Kit."

"Then you admit he took the money!" shouted the driver.

"I don't admit anything," I said. "The jury is still out, and the Governor confidently expects to be vindicated."

"That's what they all say," retorted the driver, tossing the words angrily back over his shoulder. "But if Quimby gets out from under these bribery charges, the Republicans got a bigamy charge and a sodomy charge to toss at him before the election! How about *that*!"

"Rumors," I said. "Just rumors. American politics has always been full of cheap, sexually oriented rumors—like the one that Thomas Jefferson had syphilis."

"I heard it was really true!" said the driver with an eager leer. It was as though he was discussing a current rumor rather than an item over two hundred years old. "And I've heard *plenty* about Quimby, too. *Plenty*! The stuff about how he likes young girls, an' the stuff about—"

"But I like young girls myself," I said, my arm firmly about Victoria's waist. "For example, Miss Woodhill here is—"

"Just twenty-three," said Victoria.

Her fingernails continued to scratch gently along the inside of my thigh. This action had created a rush of blood to the area, draining it from my brain, making it hard to focus on the discussion.

"Yeah," said the driver, "but Quimby's supposed to dally with them in a closet under the main staircase of the executive mansion—the way that Harding used to do in the White House with Nan Britton."

"There's no closet under the main staircase in the White House," I said.

"A hell of a lot *you* know about it!" he hollered. "Nixon turned it into a rectory for Billy Graham."

"Even though you don't approve of the Governor's sex life, driver, what do you think of his political achievements in general?" I asked.

"Let me put it this way, bud," he said. "In my opinion, there's never been a governor in the whole history of New Jersey worth a shit."

"He'll be glad to hear that you haven't singled him out."

I smiled at Victoria as she moved closer for another entangling kiss. What was she doing this for? Was she rewarding me for rescuing her? Had she actually grown fond of me—a fondness that would ripen and grow as the years went on? These questions were surging through my mind. But raising them would have been ridiculous. The plain old animal passion suffusing the back seat of the cab could in no way be improved by talk or clarification.

We pulled up at the State House. I told the driver to keep the flag on the meter up.

"What for?"

"We don't meet with the Governor until three. I want you and Miss Woodhill here to wait for five minutes while I take care of another matter. When I come out, we'll run over to the Four Star Printing Company on Ashley Street. You know the place?"

"Yeah. Bunch of crooks."

"I'll be in with the crooks at Four Star for another five minutes, and then we'll come back here."

"Hold on, bud," said the driver, with a whine. "Hold on. You're gonna make me lose money sittin' around and *waitin'* like this. There's a city ordinance says I don't have to wait any more'n two minutes for anybody on a single fare."

"Don't worry, I'll put a dollar on top of the meter and the tip."

"Hah! A dollar! A lousy, crummy dollar!" he snarled. "Do you know what the dollar closed at this afternoon in Zurich for Christ's sake?"

Victoria leaned forward, putting a gentle hand on his arm.

"Driver, don't worry about a thing," she said graciously. "If you get restless while we're waiting, I'll come up there in the front seat and blow you."

"Oh, my God—" said the driver, suddenly muted and frightened as his rich fantasy veered toward hard reality. His hands started to tremble.

"That's kind of you, Victoria," I said, "but I don't want to put you to any trouble."

"It's no trouble, Tom," she said reassuringly. "That used to be my speciality on Eighth Avenue. Car jobs—for northbound commuters—during rush hour. It was just before I matriculated at Vassar."

On the second floor of the State House, I entered the office of Mrs. Penelope Potter, Registrar of Candidates. Working with this ancient, congenial woman, I quickly got two things done.

First, I stated that my legal residence was at No. 7 Old Powderhorn Lane in the township of Prospect in Hunterdon County, New Jersey. Though I'd never been inside that building, I did own it, and I'd been advised by counsel that it was legal for me to do this. I had paid fifty-five thousand dollars for the house ten years before, and my first wife, Beatrice, and our two teenagers, Ben and Belinda—handsome children except for their crooked teeth, which still required enormously expensive orthodontia—lived there at my expense.

Second, after paying a fee of one hundred dollars and turning over to Mrs. Potter a nominating petition of two hundred actual signatures of New Jersey citizens, I announced to her that I, Thomas J. Quick, was declaring myself a candidate for Lieutenant Governor of the State of New Jersey, running as an Independent in the November 5th general election.

"You got here just in time, Mr. Quick. Today's the last day for filing."

"I was late deciding," I said. "But I'm in the race to stay."

"Just sign here and here and here, and you'll be a candidate."

While I signed, she looked me over carefully.

"You planning a big campaign, Mr. Quick?"

"No. A modest one. But I hope to be a plausible candidate."

"You've got the *face* for politics, I'll say that," she said. She kept sizing me up. "You know, if I'd liked that young Jack Kennedy better, you'd get my vote."

"He was a fine President," I said.

"But entirely too classy for me," she pointed out. "Too suave—too rich—too elegant. I think we need *homey* officials."

"Like who?" I asked.

"Well—like Mr. Nixon was in the early days. Remember how homey he was when he gave the Checkers speech and when he nailed Alger Hiss to the wall? That's a quality I like."

"But he didn't stay homey in the stretch," I said.

"No, that's true. He tightened up. And more's the pity. He surrounded himself with those Christian Scientists out of the world of advertising, and they quite inadvertently did him in, Mr. Quick."

"Well, that's one way to put it."

"Yes, indeed. Somehow the key people in the White House lost sight of Man's oneness with God, and so, unhappily, they veered away from their Natural Perfection."

"I've never heard Watergate described so elegantly, Mrs. Potter."

"Even a fine civil servant like Henry Peterson veered away from perfection," she said, pursuing her theme.

"I plan to avoid those pitfalls," I said.

"I'm glad, young man. But you know who would have made the best president of all? Even homier than Harvey Firestone or Luther Burbank?"

"Who?"

"Thomas Alva Edison! There was a man who understood what made things tick."

"I've heard that."

"I drove out to his lab in West Orange one afternoon in 1920 to try to persuade him to go for the nomination against Mr. Harding. But Mr. Edison was too busy extracting rubber from goldenrod to think about the presidency. I came back to this office a very disappointed young lady."

"You were here *then*?" I asked

"Oh, yes," she said. "I'm the last remaining Woodrow Wilson appointee. I've seen five generations of larceny in New Jersey. Five generations of men who confidently expected that they would be vindicated when all the facts were known."

She stuck out a firm, bony hand to shake mine.

"Good luck, young man. Keep your nose clean. And run as your own man."

"I will."

"It won't be easy, Jack. Your first press conference, they'll ask you about Camelot or they'll try to hang the Bay of Pigs rap on you. You'll see."

"Thank you, Mrs. Potter."

I walked down the wide marble steps to the first floor, feeling the good feeling that comes with pulling something off properly. Mrs. Potter's words proved to me that I'd planned my noncampaign for Lieutenant Governor exactly right.

CHAPTER 6

ON THE WAY to the Four Star Printing Company, the cab passed a big billboard with Bradford J. Bassett's bloodhound face and his campaign slogan, which I'd not seen before. It was:

HONOR—WEALTH—CONTENTMENT—HEALTH

Not bad. It was rhythmic, Republican, and vague enough for every situation. Exactly the kind of slogan you come up with when you can't think of anything brilliant.

"That's the fourth Bassett billboard I've seen," said Victoria. "But none for Quimby."

"We're not using billboards," I said. "Quimby's name has the best recognition factor in the state. Even pitted against historic New Jersey figures, the only ones who top him are Woodrow Wilson and James Fenimore Cooper."

"What about television?"

"I've shot a bunch of non-task-oriented TV spots."

"What are they?"

"Television spots that evoke feelings with a minimum of facts. In one minute."

"Tell me one."

"Well, for example, we took Quimby out and set him walking with a boy on the banks of the New Brunswick River where it looks unpolluted. The boy was twelve and barefoot. Then back in the editing room, we laid a narrator's quiet voice over the scene, saying: 'Horace J. Quimby came to this land as a boy, and he saw that the land was good. He wants to keep it that way for tomorrow's Americans. His own grandchildren—and *yours*, too!'"

"Was it really the Governor's grandson?"

"Sure. You can't fake stuff like that, Victoria, or the FCC raises hell with you."

"How many grandchildren does he have?"

"Only the one. He lives with his divorced mother in Rome. We had to fly him in."

"You flew him all the way from Rome for a one-minute spot?"

"Yes. And it wasn't easy. The kid was a son of a bitch to work with. Didn't speak English, and kept nipping on a bottle of Soave Bolla. He lurched through the scenes and spoiled the best take by throwing up on the Governor's coat."

"He was probably just nervous."

"Exactly, Victoria! You're right. The boy was entirely out of his element in New Jersey. If I had to do it over, I'd fly the Governor to Rome and shoot it from a high angle on the banks of the Tiber."

"But how did it come out?"

"It was saved in the editing room."

"By you?"

"No, by a young Cuban woman who's the most skilled political film editor in New York. The way she edited out the lurching and the fright and the anger and the throwing up—it was remarkable! There's not a speck of vomit. The kid looks sober and decent and natural. So does the Governor. Victoria, the spot is going to be a smash."

At the Four Star Printing Company, I told the pretty girl receptionist with the tight Capri pants and the full lips and the hair wound on pink plastic rollers that I wanted to talk to Eddie. She said to go through the swinging doors and all the way back of the shop. The man on the left would be Eddie.

I walked back through the smell of ink and the clatter of presses to find a skinny man in a printer's apron clicking type into a stick from a font.

"You're Eddie?"

"I'm Eddie."

"Eddie, here's an envelope with two thousand dollars in fifties."

He took it, stuck a fingernail under the flap, ripped it open, and extracted the money—all with his left hand.

"Gotcha," he said. "What do you want?"

"When you print the second-line ballot strip for November fifth—the Lieutenant Governor strip—I want the name "T. J. Quick" to appear on the ballot directly beneath the name of Governor Quimby."

"Gotcha."

"That's Q-U-I-C-K. He's an Independent."

"Gotcha."

"You want to write it down? T. J. Quick."

"I never write anything down."

"Well—can you *do* it?"

"I took your money, didn't I?"

"You understand? I want the vertical combination to be QUIMBY—QUICK."

"Gotcha."

Eddie, a dextrous man, had already finished counting the money with his left hand. He folded it once and stuffed it in his shirt pocket.

"This is a firm order, Quick?"

"Why wouldn't it be?"

"Sometimes you amateurs come in to try to change the order. Suppose the Governor turns up guilty?"

"He plans to run anyway."

"You'd ride in on the coattails of a guilty man?" he asked, a touch of disapproval in his voice.

"Eddie, you're in no position to discuss ethics."

"Gotcha," he said, with a nod. "But lemme tell yuh, if there *is* a change, it'll cost yuh another two grand."

"Gotcha," I said.

"When we draw straws here at Four Star to see who gets what spot on the ballot, we do it under *strict* official supervision. We gotta be sure whose straw we're drawin'. An' we gotta have enough cash on hand for payoffs."

"Thanks, Eddie," I said.

I walked back through the grimy shop, smiling. Both my maneuvers had worked. A friend of mine with connections had once told me that you could get *anything* done in New Jersey for two thousand dollars. Except get a man or a woman shot dead, stuffed into the trunk of a Cadillac Eldorado, and disposed of in concrete in Raritan Bay. That cost five.

Back in the cab, Victoria was relaxed in the back seat, smoking a little cigar, reading a pocket book of Kafka short stories. She had found both in the pocket of the sealskin coat.

"Kafka is so great!" she said. "All that business about waking up and not knowing where you are. I really dig that. The girls at Vassar never understood him."

"My wives were all from Vassar," I said. "I went to three tenth reunions over the years. It's not easy to picture you up there."

"You don't believe I was?"

"Oh, I believe it, Victoria," I said. "I just can't picture you in that Daisy Chain Celebration."

"I *enjoyed* it," she said. "I'd never *seen* all that middle-class shit before!" She laughed at the memory. "But mostly I went up there to learn the language."

"What language?"

"English."

"Oh?"

"Right. You see, my first language was Kawaiute."

"It's still actually spoken?"

"Oh, sure. All around the reservation—up in northern Nevada. And my second language was ghetto. After my father was killed, my mother took me back to Harlem. But even as a little kid, I could see that I'd never get anywhere unless I learned the high-priced tongue."

"Well, you did it, Victoria. Aside from those tribal phrases, you sound as elegant as Mrs. Averell Harriman."

As the cab rolled along, Victoria threw open the coat. "I found an identification label, Tom."

I got a glimpse of the owner's name embroidered in silver thread under Ben Kahn's name, but mainly my eye was caught and held by the single, splendid, polka-dotted breast that had come into view. With many women who have not yet borne a child, the nipple remains hidden in the areola and can only be coaxed out with an affectionate touch. As Victoria read the label, I reached out affectionately:

" 'Property of Mrs. William P. Winstead,' " she read. " 'One Thousand Old Bent Willow Road, Short Hills, New Jersey. Return Postage Guaranteed.' And let's see, Mrs. Winstead's Zip Code is—"

"Never mind her Zip Code, Victoria," I whispered. "Never mind—"

Victoria closed the coat back over my fond hand. Once again we began to kiss in a pioneering way. Once again, as

Emily had pointed out, I was mixing politics and pleasure. Once again, I was drifting off into the moist timelessness of sensuality, losing all perception of the outside world.

Victoria pulled back for a moment, laughing a low, sinuous laugh. "Tom Quick, I've got your nose so wide open, you could run a truck through it!"

"What the hell does *that* mean?" I asked, stopped short.

"One of those tribal phrases," she said, touching a fingertip lightly beneath the tip of my nose. "A black metaphor of passion. It refers to the flaring nostrils that show passion—as on a bull."

She kept laughing and tickling my left nostril. In all my life, nobody had ever tickled my nostril this way. It was remarkable—an ordinary tickle that turned out to be a surprisingly prurient gesture. Taken as a whole, I'm sure the Supreme Court would have held that it had no serious artistic, social, scientific, or political value. Still, I liked it. I *loved* it! And, as usual in the arena of sex, I could not get enough of it.

"Incredible!" I murmured, flaring my nostril even wider. "This started out as a business trip."

CHAPTER 7

THE GOVERNOR'S OFFICE in the State House in Trenton has the dignified reality of an old Frank Capra movie set. The ornate scrolls of the woodwork have been stained over the years to a deep, rich brown, and the nonstatic nylon carpeting has been exactly matched to the wood. A blazing chandelier of Austrian crystal suspends from an eighteen-foot ceiling, lighting soft green walls that are hung with paintings of some of the anonymous men who have held this office since New Jersey became the third state in 1787. The only governor ever recognized is Woodrow Wilson, whose pinched Presbyterian face looks down from the north wall. And Mr. Wilson's old rolltop desk and stand-up telephone—property of the New Jersey Historical Society—are tastefully enshrined in one corner.

The governor's contemporary desk, with a gold-tooled leather surface as big as a Ping-Pong table, sits opposite the heavy double-entry doors. Behind this squat symbol of power is a large window overlooking a park. In the center of the window is a stained-glass version of the Great Seal of the State of New Jersey. The motto, translated from the Latin, says: SONS AND DAUGHTERS OF FREEDOM, PASS NOT BY, BUT

TARRY HERE ON THE BANKS OF THE RARITAN, FOR IT IS HERE THAT YOU WILL FIND YOUR DESTINY.

Flanking the window are two flags—the American and the New Jersey.

No governor ever fit into this seemly room better than Horace J. Quimby (Dem.). He was a big bear of a man, with silver hair, a warm smile, a courtly manner, and a fluid grace. Horace Quimby was determined to put people at ease, no matter how awful the facts or how abrasive the antagonists. Almost every day, he would stand in the midst of a total sociopolitical shambles in this room and reassure everybody with Abraham Lincoln's fine old line: "Let us confidently hope that all may yet be well."

Having a relaxed view of statecraft, Governor Quimby never hesitated to oil the machinery of government with Jack Daniels bourbon whiskey or a wide variety of other brands. During his tenure, two huge brown-leather sofas had been placed along one side of the office, facing a low, polished-marble coffee table. On these sofas, the Governor sprawled to consider his future, to think about the state, to conduct informal meetings, and from time to time, when the press of other business had subsided in the late afternoon, to ball attractive young women whose names were not on the Official Appointments List, and who arrived on the service elevator. When all these things were not going on, the sofas were occupied by jaded politicians and hangers-on.

In July, before accepting the assignment as consultant to the Quimby campaign, I'd asked his administrative assistant, Rocky Bettenhauser, to let me look through the press book. I wanted to get familiar with Quimby's major administrative achievements during his eight years in office. There were none. He had worked hard in favor of off-track betting, legalizing numbers, and registering prostitutes. He had proposed legislation limiting the amount of

Lasix you can administer to a racehorse to keep his nose from bleeding. And that was about it.

Yet the press book showed something else. Though Horace J. Quimby didn't know much about governing, he surely knew how to campaign. There was no such thing as a campaign season for him. It was *all* campaigning, even in the week following his reelection. From High Point to Cape May, from Passaic to Phillipsburg, the Governor always *showed up*. Whenever a school opened, whenever a section of the Interstate Highway System opened, whenever a supermarket or a large storm-drain sewer was dedicated, Governor Quimby would be on hand to tell the people how glad he was to be there. Then he would say a few words suitable to the occasion.

He also had the courage to show up at negative events, at fires, floods, mass murders, plane crashes, and major bankruptcies. And he came to the smoldering scene of every New Jersey riot—prison or campus or street—within hours. Looking solemn, indicating the need for an immediate rebuilding of the buildings as well as the human spirit, he would confidently hope that all would yet be well.

Having looked him over carefully, impressed by his brilliant PR, I concluded that Horace J. Quimby could indeed campaign himself into a third term. I liked him, even if he lacked the quiet profundity of men like Justice Douglas or John Deardourff. I took the job. Five days later, along with Bradford J. Bassett, Quimby was indicted on three counts: bribery, concealment, and the receiving of a kickback.

Promptly at 3:00 P.M., the appointments secretary threw open the double doors for Victoria and me to enter. As we walked into the big room, the Governor got up and came around the desk, his face warmed by a big smile, his eyes fixed—transfixed—on Victoria. Time had diminished the

Governor's interest in the dull mechanics of deficit state government finance and his interest in his wife (who had progressed during his tenure from a shrew to a shrike to an all-out virago), but time had not diminished his interest in fast horses or beautiful young women.

"Victoria Woodhill," he said, after the introductions, "let me say quite frankly that you are breathtaking."

"Thank you, Governor," she said, the bronze face smiling, the eyes direct. "You're the first governor I've ever actually met."

"Then how do I look to you?" he asked, chin up, looking merrily off to the side the way Roosevelt used to do.

"Like a governor in a movie," she said.

"Excellent!"

Moving in from the sofas were two men coming for a closer look. One was Rocky Bettenhauser, my principal antagonist in the Governor's camp. The other man I did not know.

"Miss Woodhill," said the Governor, "may I present my administrative assistant, Mr. Buford "Rocky" Bettenhauser, and Mr. Pierre LeCrum, who is the Democratic County Chairman of Charon County down in southern New Jersey."

Victoria held out her hand, saying that she was charmed. Rocky shook it perfunctorily. LeCrum kissed it.

"The LeCrum family first came to America from France with the Du Ponts," explained the Governor with a chuckle. "But they couldn't keep up the pace, and so in 1796 they crossed the Delaware into New Jersey and became Democrats."

"How interesting," said Victoria. She was graceful and demure and melodious—quite unlike the girl who, a short time before, had run screaming naked through the PATH station, bellowing: "Motherfuckuh!"

"And Rocky here," said the Governor, sounding like the narrator in a travelogue, "Rocky is from the far western part of New Jersey. From the lovely and historic town of Phillipsburg, which looks across the shimmering Susquehanna to our sister state, Pennsylvania."

"How interesting," said Victoria.

"Most people understand that New Jersey is a long state, north to south," the Governor's voice rolled on, "but they have no idea of its breadth. It's a *very* thick state, Victoria."

"I had no idea."

"And now, my dear," said Quimby, his big eager hands going to her shoulders, "let's take off your coat and get you a drink and—"

"Thank you, Governor," she said smoothly, laying her hands gently atop his. "I'm quite comfortable. But I will have the drink."

"Jack Daniels and water?"

"Perfect."

"Tom? A drink?"

"How about a touch of sweet vermouth on top of the Jack Daniels, Governor?"

"One Manhattan, coming up."

Guiding Victoria to Woodrow Wilson's desk, Governor Quimby rolled back the rolltop with a rumble. Two dozen bottles of the finest booze stood there, flanking Mr. Wilson's historic L. C. Smith typewriter. The pigeonholes, once stuffed with early drafts of the Treaty of Versailles, now held embossed paper napkins and yellow plastic stirrers with the Great Seal of the State of New Jersey on one side and the Governor's name on the obverse.

Rocky and LeCrum and I moved toward the sofas. It was time for action.

"I suppose you've brought the TV spots," said Bettenhauser, his round, sour face reflecting his dislike of me and his persistently troublesome stomach. Rocky Bettenhauser maintained his No. 1 position in the Governor's entourage by attacking anybody who came close, even a friend.

The attack took the form of a massive disdain for everybody's work, for any idea that was not his own. In dealing with a horse's ass of this calibre, I learned long ago that you must attack in the opening sentence. Deliberately, I lit a long cigar, then dropped the videocassette into the Betamax.

"I brought the spots, Rocky," I said quietly. "These are rough tapes with no opticals or titles or effects, and let me assure you in advance that you're going to think the entire package is shit."

"Nothing new about that," he said.

"No, there isn't. But don't be misled by your shallow perception of the role of television in a modern, state-level campaign."

"Come on, Tom. Come on." He belched. "Hit the button. Show the spots."

"Why don't we wait until the candidate gets here?" I suggested. "I think he might be interested."

We looked across to Wilson's desk, where the Governor was chatting delightedly with Victoria, a kind of loud, tumescent tone in his voice. Victoria was standing much closer to him than was necessary, and her hand lay easily on his forearm.

"—and since leaving Vassar I've been in a very special kind of counseling in Manhattan," she was explaining.

"What outfit you with?" asked Quimby.

"Oh, it's *very* small. Danou Associates, Inc.—"

"I'm planning to bring Victoria onto the Polcon, Inc. staff, Governor," I spoke up from across the room. "She'll be our specialist in the politics of intuition."

Rocky Bettenhauser leaned over toward me.

"This is a typical cheap Polcon trick," he said in a gravelly whisper.

"What is?" I asked, falsely innocent.

"You brought that black broad here to distract the Governor from the business of an important meeting—from the fact that you haven't done a damned thing in this campaign, even though it's damned near election day! You brought him a toy to play with."

"She *is* a toy, all right," agreed LeCrum, who also seemed tumescent, even at a distance of thirty-five feet.

"You're wrong, Rocky," I said. "I brought Victoria along simply so that I do not lose sight of her."

"Couldn't you have left her in the cab?"

"No," I said, suddenly confidential. "The driver wouldn't wait more than five minutes, even though she offered to blow him."

"Obscene," said Rocky. "Obscene!"

The Governor, with Victoria on his arm, was now crossing the room, carrying my drink and his own. LeCrum already had one.

"Drink for you, Rocky?" asked Quimby.

"No, thanks, Governor," said Rocky, "I have to remain sharp for this encounter."

As the Governor sat down on the opposite sofa next to Victoria, Rocky started to cut me up.

"Let me tell you, before we see any of your television stuff, Quick," he said, "that the Governor is quite disappointed with your handling of the campaign."

"The Governor is here," I said. "Why don't we let him speak for himself. Governor?"

"Uhhh—yes. Yes." The Governor tore his eyes away from Victoria for a moment to glance at me. "Uh—it's mostly Rocky's concern," he said. "But I'd appreciate it if you'd give him a good listen now, Tom. He's explained this to me a dozen times."

"But it seems to me, Governor, that we should be taking our cue from *you* on this. I realize that an AA is an important figure in a political hierarchy, but the administrative assistant is *not* the candidate."

The remark was designed to stir Rocky up. It did.

"Goddamn it. Quick! It's almost the end of September, and there's been no campaign at all! The Governor's great strength—as I told you when you were putting together that thick Campaign Plan—is not that he can govern but that he can *campaign*."

"That was my line, Rocky. I wrote it in the preface to the Campaign Plan."

"Okay—okay, let's not quibble."

"I'm not quibbling. It's an important idea in this campaign, and it was mine."

"But where *is* the campaign, Quick? Where is it?"

"My original recommendation still stands," I said. "The Governor is free to reject it, but I say that we cannot campaign effectively—we cannot campaign *at all*—until the jury returns and the Governer is vindicated in that courtroom downstairs."

"I confidently expect to be vindicated when all the facts are in," said the Governor, looking at Victoria, with just a trace of anxiety.

"The facts *are* in, Governor," said Rocky. "And the jury is out."

"I'm sure they'll see the truth," said Victoria. "How long have they been out?"

"Seventeen days," said the Governor. "It's a record."

"And here we sit," Rocky pressed on, "paying you half of a one-hundred-thousand-dollar fee for *nothing*. All you've released is that simpleminded bumper sticker—VOTE FOR QUIMBY."

"Sometimes simplicity is the best way to go, Rocky," I said. "You remember when Robert Montgomery was hired to be the TV consultant for Eisenhower? You know what he told Ike? It was very simple. He told him to pause for one second at the commas and two seconds at the periods. He told him to try to work a verb into every sentence. And he told him to stop saying, "Eeeeeeuuuuuuuuuhhhhhh," when stalling for time. With that help, Ike became—for the first time—intelligible on television and eligible for a second term in spite of a leaky aorta."

"Not funny," said Rocky.

"No, but illustrative," I said, sitting forward and quickly growing intense. "Look, for Christ's sake, the Quimby campaign is all set. But it is predicated on the Governor's *innocence*."

"What do you have besides these TV spots?"

"Everything, Rocky. *Everything*. Television, AM radio, FM radio, black radio, force-feed radio, storefronts, sound trucks, the beeper, phone canvassers, volunteers, feedback endorsements, computers, telenews, newspaper layouts, rallies, meetings, motorcades, speeches, buttons, bumper stickers, streamers, skywriting, posters, quarter cards, pins, pennants, and a torchlight Victory Parade through Trenton with the Goodyear blimp announcing the results overhead."

"No direct mail?" asked Rocky.

"Cut the shit, Rocky," I said, "we've already talked about that. Direct mail is of no value when the candidate is the best-known public figure in New Jersey."

"That's true," said Quimby to Victoria. "I am."

"And I can see why," she said, smiling at him and touching him again on the arm. "But isn't it nice, Governor, the way that Tom here has thought of *everything*?"

"Thank you, Victoria," I said, beaming at her. "I've got a clincher, too, Governor. We'll need a sign-painter."

"I thought I ruled out billboards," said Bettenhauser.

"You did, Rocky. And it was a wise decision. But I'm not talking about a billboard."

"Well?"

I paused, looking across at LeCrum.

"I don't like to be suspicious, but is it all right to talk in front of Mr. LeCrum here?"

"But of course," said LeCrum, bristling a little.

"Pierre's okay," said the Governor. "He just came by to report that if I'm *not* acquitted, he's going to have trouble holding the machine together down in Charon County."

"*Mais oui*," said LeCrum sadly. "Everyone he and she is threatening to cut off the rice pudding."

"Rice pudding?" asked Victoria.

"Yes, my dear," said Governor Quimby. "Rice pudding is what we call the illegal four percent kickback that a jobholder pays our political machine each year. Without rice pudding, there would be no machine."

"They won't pay it if you're in jail?" asked Victoria.

"No. Pierre claims they'll lose faith if I'm incarcerated. But I've been telling him that I can run this state effectively, whether I'm in the State House or the state pen."

"How could you *ever* do that?" Victoria asked.

"Simple, my dear. Modify the rule about a convict sending out only three letters a week. Allow unlimited phone calls instead of three a week. Move a couple of these leather couches into my cell. Set up the adjoining cell for my Appointments Secretary—"

"Will the Director of Prisons go along with this?" I asked.

"If he doesn't, I'll fire him," said Quimby.

"Well, Polcon is ready to ride it out with you either way, Governor," I said. "But the entire concept of the campaign will have to be changed if you are running as a convicted felon rather than as a free man."

"And I suppose that'll cost more money?" asked Bettenhauser disdainfully.

"You're goddamned right it will, Rocky," I shot back at him. "We'll have to persuade the citizenry that this democracy called New Jersey is *so* fair-minded, *so* altruistic, *so*—"

"That's enough, Quick," said Bettenhauser, rubbing his abdomen with both hands. "Let's get out of this negative area. It upsets my stomach."

"Very well."

"What's this so-called clincher?"

I turned back to the Governor.

"Are you aware, Governor, that the rest stops on the New Jersey Turnpike are named in honor of New Jersey's most famous citizens?"

"I didn't realize that," said Quimby.

"They are, indeed," I said. "Thomas Edison, Woodrow Wilson, Joyce Kilmer, Clara Barton, Grover Cleveland—"

"That's a splendid idea," said the Governor. "It helps give our citizenry a sense of New Jersey identity, and, God knows, that's something we need. For years, Victoria, we've been crushed between the volcanic vanity of New York and the historic disdain of Philadelphia. Who was Joyce Kilmer?"

"He wrote 'Trees,' " said Victoria.

"Of course. Of course," said Quimby. "A lovely song."

"It began as a poem," said Victoria gently.

"Of course. A lovely poem."

"What the hell's all this got to do with the *campaign*?" asked Rocky irritably.

"A new rest stop is being added in the southbound lane just below New Brunswick," I explained. "Late in October, assuming you are acquitted, Governor, the Quimby Campaign will announce the results of a statewide popularity poll showing citizen preference in the naming of the new rest stop. A week before the election, you'll win the poll hands down. The new facility will be called The Horace J. Quimby Rest Stop. You'll be at the dedication, of course, and—"

"I'll be happy to be there," said the Governor. "That's *real* campaigning, Tom."

"While yet in office, you will have become a historical figure—almost a legend in your own time, Governor," I said.

"How do we know he'll win the poll?" Rocky persisted.

"Have a little faith, Rocky. The man sitting opposite you is the best-known, best-liked man in the state. And he will continue to be—if acquitted."

Rocky leaped up and began to pace. All the rest of us seemed pretty well composed, but there was a film of sweat on Bettenhauser.

"But why—*why* hinge the whole damned campaign on the acquittal?" he shouted. "It's not all that important. In the past two decades three hundred and twenty-seven public figures in this state have been indicted and tried. Even when they plead guilty, they stay right on the job! All through their trials they stay right on the job! And nobody can ever remember whether they were acquitted or not. Why can't you make the campaign more—more ambiguous?"

"God damn it, Rocky," I said, raising my voice to match his. "An election can embrace ambiguities, but it cannot bridge the gap between innocent and guilty!"

Rocky was standing over me now, fat, nervous, loud, sweating.

"Quick, I don't like your campaign. I don't like your concepts. I don't like your attitude. And I don't like *you*! You might as well know that I've recommended to the Governor that he dump Polcon, Inc. at this meeting, and cancel the last half of your fee!" Then he belched.

It was a touchy moment, considering my personal election plans and my flaky financial status, but the one thing a political consultant must never do is look fazed. "You must always be ready," a pottery buyer from Macy's once told me, "to piss ice water."

"Then let us ask the Governor to respond to your recommendation, Rocky," I said coolly. "I have an international reputation in this field that cannot be dimmed or demeaned by your ill-informed view of my work. And, frankly, I see no reason to bring my skills to a place where they are neither understood nor appreciated." I swung around to face Quimby. "Governor?—"

Suddenly Victoria stood up.

"I *am* a little warm now, Governor. Can you tell me where to hang my coat?"

"I'll take it for you, Victoria, and—"

As he spoke, Victoria uncinched the sealskin belt, and the luxurious supple coat fell from her shoulders into the Governor's hands. The silence lasted for several seconds as the tall, naked, polka-dotted, bronze, booted girl smiled down on the open-mouthed Chief Executive of New Jersey.

"—and—and hang it up—hang it up—hang it up—over in—over in the closet," he stammered.

"Thank you, Governor," she said, smiling. "And while you do that, I'll freshen my drink just a little."

Her retreating figure—smooth, parabolic, fluid, with the nates bouncing just a touch as she walked across the thick carpet—precluded any further discussion of my future in the Quimby Campaign.

"*Sacre bleu!*" whispered LeCrum.

"Tasteless," muttered Rocky Bettenhauser.

"*Splendid!*" observed the Governor.

I said nothing, but the Governor's flushed awestruck face made it unlikely that I would be dropped from the campaign now, particularly with Victoria's coming onto the Polcon, Inc. staff.

As Victoria passed the big double doors, they were thrown open, and Al Divver, the Governor's driver, the most intelligent and Jersey-wise man I had come across in the campaign, burst into the room. "Governor, the. . . ."

He saw Victoria, who had stopped with a kind of wide-spread, straight-on stance to greet him, standing as the women used to stand in the Flash Gordon comic strip. Struck totally dumb, Al Divver just kept looking up and down and across her body—up and down and across—up and down and across—like a surveillance TV camera in a discount drug store. He finally came to rest on her vortex.

The Governor, having recovered his aplomb, came over to introduce them.

"How nice to meet you, Mr. Divver," said Victoria. "Can I fix you a drink?"

Al Divver, a powerfully loquacious man who spoke out of the side of his mouth (he could have been played beautifully by the late Jimmy Gleason), was still staring fixedly at Victoria's neat, heart-shaped bush. He could not summon speech.

"Al here," said the Governor, filling in amiably, "drives me everywhere, and is one of the most politically astute men in New Jersey. Al never misses a name, and he knows precinct voting records like some people know the batting average of Pee Wee Reese. You should see him nose a heavy Caddy limo through a hostile crowd without hurting a soul!"

"I always like to meet an important man behind the scenes," said Victoria, beaming at Al. Divver was still gulping air, like a gaffed carp.

"Al is also from one of the most historic spots in all New Jersey," Quimby went on. "When Alexander Hamilton was searching for a place to establish the infant American iron industry, he journeyed to the Great Falls of the Passaic River—in what is now the city of Paterson—and there he—"

Victoria shifted from the widespread Flash Gordon stance, now bringing her boots together with a little squeak. That broke the spell for Divver.

"Governor—Governor—excuse me, but the—the jury is back. The judge would like you down in the courtroom. Nice to meet you, ma'am."

The Governor turned back to us at the sofa. He was once more flushed red, but his manner stayed cool.

"Come along, my friends. We'll find out now."

"May I come, too, Governor?" asked Victoria.

"Of course, my dear," he said. "But don't forget your coat."

The Governor walked quickly out of the big room. Al Divver, after one more confirming look at Victoria's snatch, followed him. I could hear him muttering as he went:

"It's trimmed—for Christ's sake. *Trimmed!*"

On the way downstairs to the courtroom, Victoria spoke in a low voice as she walked by my side.

"Let me pull your coat to something, Tom."

"Pull my coat?"

"Tip you off. The Governor's collar is too tight."

"What?"

"The collar on his shirt is too tight. Makes him look as though he's choking. If you do any more filming with him, buy him a blue shirt half a size bigger."

"I'd never noticed," I said.

"I see it with my johns all the time," she explained quietly, as we followed the Governor and Divver and Rocky and LeCrum down the broad marble staircase. "Men never like to admit that their necks are not the same size as when they were in college. So they go around for years with crepey turkey necks sticking out of tight collars."

I felt my collar.

"Not you," she said. "The Governor. But the next time you see Ronald Reagan on TV, take a look at *his* shirt."

"Too tight?"

"Oh, no! He's one of the few American politicians who's solved the turkey-neck problem. Reagan's collar sits so loose and so low on his neck that it looks like the yoke of an ox. The knot of his necktie is halfway to his belly-button."

"Jesus H. Christ, Victoria. You see *everything!*"

"Just like my father," she said, smiling.

The big courtroom, on the first floor of the State House, was jammed. As we walked in behind the Governor, there was no place for us to stand but at the rear of the big center aisle.

The judge was a small, hunched figure behind the high bench. They'd had to bring him down from Beemerville because all the other judges in town were old friends of the Governor. He nodded to the Governor and to Rocky, and they sat down with two attorneys at the defendant's table.

The matter was over quickly. The judge turned to the foreman of the jury to ask if they had reached a verdict. The foreman stood up and said that they had. The judge asked if there was a verdict on each of the three indictments.

"There is, Your Honor."

"What are those verdicts, Mr. Foreman?"

"On the first count of bribery, we find the defendant guilty. On the second count of concealment, we find the defendant guilty. On the third count of receiving thirty-seven million dollars in kicked-back cash, we find the defendant guilty."

I looked at Governor Quimby. His face had gone to a bright red color. He stood up as requested by the judge, and he was told that sentencing would be in one week. One of the Governor's attorneys stood up with him to announce that an appeal would be filed immediately.

"Under the New Jersey Crime Act," said the judge, "I cannot order you removed from office until your appeals have been exhausted, Governor."

"I understand, Your Honor," said Quimby.

"Therefore, I release you on your own recognizance and ask you to return to your office upstairs and to continue with the governance of this state."

"Thank you, Your Honor," said Quimby. "I appreciate your consideration."

It was the first time I'd ever seen Horace J. Quimby in

public without his glad-to-be-here smile. His face still burning, he turned and walked toward us down the aisle of the dead-silent courtroom. As he got to Victoria and me and LeCrum, he paused and said quietly:

"Let us confidently hope that all may yet be well."

Rocky Bettenhauser, also looking stricken, followed him out of the courtroom. On the way back upstairs to his office, Gov. Horace J. Quimby (Dem.) dropped dead on the wide marble staircase. It was a massive heart attack.

CHAPTER 8

I TOOK a second Manhattan from the Metroclub steward and swivelled my chair away from Victoria. It upset me to see her weeping, and I had enough on my mind.

Pushing the button to recline the seat, I sat back, closed my eyes, and tried to get things straight. But all I could do was summarize what had screwed up. Everything had. The Quimby Campaign, like the Governor, was dead. My great plan to ride quietly into office behind him was dead. My brilliant retreat to income-sheltered anonymity as the Lieutenant Governor of New Jersey was dead. The last half of my payment from the campaign—fifty thousand dollars —that was dead, too. Angrily, I sat forward. The seat popped up behind me.

"Damn it, Victoria!" I said, almost shouting at her. "When I walked out of the Four Star Printing Company this afternoon, I felt like Martin Luther King. Free at last. Free at last. Thank God Almighty—free at last!"

"From what?"

"From my three former wives," I said, spinning the seat to face the window. "The piranha fish of my pocket. They cost me nine thousand dollars a month! And I set this whole thing up brilliantly so I could *legally* dump them. Then Quimby falls dead and knocks down my whole politico-financial house of cards. Son of a bitch!"

The outburst was not like me. I even spilled my Manhattan. There I was, mouthing off in public instead of looking calm and opaque and pissing ice water, like all first-rate political consultants.

"Shouldn't you be sadder about the death itself?" Victoria inquired.

"I'm devastated, for Christ's sake!"

"He seemed like a lovely man," she said, wiping away a tear. "Such warm, firm hands—"

"But withal, *guilty*!" I said grimly. "And deceased. Oh, I'm sad enough, all right."

"But sad for *yourself*, Tom. You sound—you sound shallower than I thought you'd be."

"You're right, baby. But my shallowness is linked to my survival. I've moved up fast in the world and I've never got far enough ahead financially to get profound or broad-visioned."

"You mean you've never sworn eternal hostility to every form of tyranny over the mind of man?" she asked.

"I've never had the time for that stuff, Victoria."

"Maybe you'll be different if greatness is ever thrust upon you."

"I hope so. I sometimes think it would be neat to be great. But in the meantime—"

"I'll tell you something," she said, beaming her lovely symmetrical smile at me. "Even shallow—I like you."

"I'm damned glad you came along," I replied, turning my seat back toward her, taking her hands in mine, kissing her lightly. "I wonder—I wonder why it's so easy to say things to you."

"Because there's nothing at stake, Tom. We'll get off this train at Penn Station, and—*pouf*!—that'll be it."

"Jesus, I *hope* not," I said.

"We'll see," she said, the smile faint.

The steward brought me a new Manhattan on the rocks. Victoria sat back deeply in her seat, tucked up her legs, snuggled into the coat, and we rode in silence for a while. The drink tasted good.

"What *was* the house of cards?" she asked.

I thought for a moment, and I could feel a smile cross my face as my admirably complex scheme came back to me. I have always been fond of my own material.

"Let me put it this way, dear. It's not easy to retrench in America. Once you're started on a career, once the upward thrust begins, once *The New York Times* finds out who you are in a nation of two hundred and sixty million people—you're stuck. Because once you are in the public eye, you have to keep getting bigger and better all the time. If you pause even for a moment—if you stop growing and smiling and exuding confidence—then you fall off the Great American Ferris Wheel and die."

"It's exactly the same in whoring," said Victoria.

"The whole thing is a poop-out," I added. "Staying successful, Victoria, is more exhausting than *getting* successful. And what the government doesn't take from me, the wives take from me."

"A hundred and eight thousand dollars a year," she said.

"How'd you know the figure?"

"I multiplied."

"Of course. Well, one day right after I took the Quimby assignment, I was looking through the New Jersey Constitution to see if it could be broken down into some good radio spots. Suddenly, I came across something else. Right there in the Constitution, I found a way to beat a graceful retreat from the public eye! A way to slip into obscurity."

"How?"

"By becoming the Lieutenant Governor of New Jersey!" I said.

"Man, that *is* obscurity."

"Nobody ever knows who he is. It's like the vice-presidency used to be."

"But you couldn't really hide," she said.

"True. But professionally, I'd have said I was getting a new slant on the political process. And privately, I'd have told my wives that my fifty grand annual salary was mine and mine alone."

"Wouldn't they sue?"

"They couldn't! That's the great thing I found in the New Jersey Constitution, baby! Article Seventeen, Clause Six, Line Nine. 'The monies received for services by public officials holding statewide office shall not be subject to attachment, garnishment, or subject to litigation in any court of the State of New Jersey.' "

"But they could sue in another state."

"Impossible. My attorneys have assured me that the New Jersey courts would *never* permit the Lieutenant Governor to be extradited for something like this. So I could have kept the cash and screwed them!" I paused to consider. "Except for the orthodontia on Ben and Belinda. I'd have kept that going."

Victoria looked puzzled.

"Then why not just go ahead and run? What's it got to do with Horace J. Quimby?"

"I had that worked out, too," I said, laying down my next card. "With this face of mine, I could never win on my own."

"Why not?"

"As soon as my face showed up in the paper, the people who liked Jack Kennedy would accuse me of cheating, of stealing the old image. And my campaign would run into terrible trouble with the family. The Kennedys have never liked anybody muscling in. They're worse than Rocky Bettenhauser about that."

"Muscling in on what?"

"Look, Victoria, there's a whole new generation of Kennedys playing touch football and writing books and climbing mountains and looking exuberant—all by way of taking another crack at the presidency. Well, the last thing those kids need is somebody hanging around to remind the voters of their fabled Uncle Jack. They want to make it to the White House on their own."

"But what could the family *do*?"

"Plenty. They'd throw in all their heavyweights against me. Salinger, Lem Billings, Chuck Spaulding, Red Fay—maybe even McNamara. They'd descend on New Jersey with the contacts and the clout and the brilliant PR that could defeat me."

Victoria was puzzled.

"Tell me one thing, Tom. How do you win an election if you don't tip the people off *somehow* that you're running?"

"*That* was the trump card in my house of cards. But I can't play it with Quimby gone."

"Tell me the trump," said Victoria, sitting forward like a conspirator.

"Ballot position. *That's* the trump! That's what I'm talking about."

"Never heard of it."

"Victoria, most of the time—except for the biggies—people vote for candidates they've never seen or never heard of."

"That's what I do," she said candidly.

"Right! Well, listen to this. Back in '73, the day after President Nixon's second inauguration, Polcon was hired by a skeptical old Democrat who was thinking of running for governor of Arkansas. He wanted to find out why the voters were such suckers for fake piety that they would elect—and then *re*elect—a man of Mr. Nixon's shifty-eyed stature."

"What was the answer?"

"The responses were so angry and erratic that we could never draw a conclusive profile. But coincidentally, we came up with something else. Something remarkable! We found, Victoria, that if a voter does not know anything about a person who is running on the *second* line of a ballot, his tendency is to vote for the candidate whose name is directly below the well-known person he voted for on the top line."

"Ahhhhh! You mean that an unknown Thomas J. Quick right beneath the well-known Horace J. Quimby would—"

"I'd have got eighty-six percent of the votes that Quimby got."

"Without campaigning at all?"

"Except for *one* last-minute bumper sticker."

"Stone-brilliant," she said. "But can't you stick your name beneath somebody else? Bradford J. Bassett?"

"Bassett will be guilty himself within forty-eight hours."

"But other people will be running—"

"Jesus, baby, will they ever," I said, slumping in my seat as I envisioned the cornucopia of half-assed, amateur candidates who would now come forth to announce their narrow, self-centered campaigns. "Tomorrow morning, the woodwork candidates will show up."

"Who?"

"Whenever the corrupt political machines break down—it's about every twenty years or so—the amateurs come out of the woodwork to take a crack at running the state. Last time it happened was in Hudson City back in 1973."

"I was still out in Kawaiute country."

"The O'Toole machine had been running Hudson City for twenty-seven years. Just like Frank Hague in Jersey City. Then just before the '73 election, old Michael Sean O'Toole and his handpicked mayor were convicted in federal court on a twenty-million-dollar kickback scheme using Model Cities money. Inside two days, the whole machine fell apart. Inside a week, thirty-nine candidates had announced for mayor."

"Who won?"

"A naturalized Italian dentist. The same thing is going to happen in Trenton tomorrow. And the most sophisticated polling technique in the world cannot tell me which of thirty-nine candidates to ride on."

"I hope you won't withdraw, Tom."

"Not a chance. I'm in this race to stay."

I spun to face the window and the ancient industrial grimness of trackside New Jersey. The dismal view matched my mood exactly. With a big sigh, I sat back in the seat.

"Sometimes, damn it, I wish I'd been more like Albert Einstein. My mother would have liked that, too."

"Einstein wasn't in politics."

"That's exactly what I mean. Einstein used to sit quietly in a room over in Princeton, thinking things through. All he had was a blackboard. Every few years, he would come out of the room to explain something about the universe. And whether he was right or wrong was provable, Victoria. *Provable*! There was no interpersonal crap involved. No political pressure. No ass-kissing. *No Rocky Bettenhauser*! When Einstein came out of that room and announced that light from the stars bends when it travels around the sun, they waited for a solar eclipse, and they proved he was right. Einstein didn't even have to attend the eclipse. He was already back in the room."

"You'd be lonesome, living like that," said Victoria.

"Rocky Bettenhauser," I said with a deep, gut derision. "My God, he's a *major* political figure in New Jersey, and a man with no skills at all. *None*! All he does is look pompous, belch, and give the impression that he has already heard everything you tell him. If you went into Rocky's office to tell him that the sky was falling, Rocky would nod thoughtfully and tell you that he'd been speaking to Chicken Little just that morning, and he knew all about it. Aaaggggggg-hhhhhhhh! *Politics!*"

I spun the chair another quarter-circle, facing now away from Victoria, trying to pry the whole mess out of my mind and figure on the next move. After a little while, I felt two cool hands rubbing slowly along the sides of my neck. I looked backward and up. Victoria's face was looking at me over the back of the chair—upside down, but still symmetrically beautiful.

"You know what you need?" she said quietly.

"A viable candidate with a good administrative assistant."

"Something more than that. You need to get your mind off politics." She kept rubbing the neck.

"Okay. I'll get into air-conditioning—or aluminum siding."

"I mean just for a few minutes. The Subterranean Dance Theatre took your mind off politics."

"Victoria! You're going to dance naked in the aisle!"

"Watch me, Tom. And thirty seconds later, follow me."

I smiled.

"Shall we synchronize our watches?"

"Start counting."

Victoria spun my chair, kissed me lightly on the forelock, then turned and walked down the aisle toward the rear of the car. Half the seats swung in a 180-degree arc to watch her deliberate, fluid progression. At the end of the car, she disappeared into the starboard restroom. I sat up with a start.

Thirty seconds later, I rose nonchalantly from my chair and walked in the same direction. Nobody paid any attention to my passage. I tried the door handle of the restroom, expecting it to be locked. It was not.

"Come in, baby," said the liquid voice. I did.

Inside was a remarkably sensuous scene—topping even the PATH station. Victoria Woodhill was smiling at me from her perch atop the Monel Metal sink. Her lovely behind was cradled perfectly in the oval of the basin. The Alaska sealskin coat had been hung neatly on a hook above the toilet, and Victoria was, for the third time since we'd met that morning, stark naked. But this time, things were specifically and erotically directed toward me.

The heel of her right boot was hooked through the semicircular handhold built into the far wall. As the door slammed with me inside, she instantly snaked out her left boot, deftly clicked the sliding lock with the heel, then hooked the heel firmly over the door handle.

I stood there between her graceful, bronze, up-cocked legs, returning her smile, admiring her powerfully provocative split position, wondering at the creativeness that had gone into this moment, and reaching out to touch her.

Nothing was more specific or erotic, though, than what she said as she leaned forward to run her tongue again around my ear.

"Fuck me, Tom." That was all. It was a simple, imperative sentence, and it got my mind off politics.

"Victoria—" I said. "Victoria, I—" I was planning to say more, to speak with rising passion, to set the stage, to comment on the basic mystery of evanescent relationships between men and women. But I didn't. Instead, with all deliberate speed, as they used to say on the Warren Court, I stripped away everything I was wearing.

Victoria was laughing her low laugh as she watched me.

"Oh, that's so very cool," she said with admiration. "Most men just fish it out and stick it in."

"Not me," I said. "I figure that when you exchange affection, it's a total tactile experience." I ran my hands lightly down the whole lovely length of her.

"Why the scar?" she asked, drawing a slim red fingernail along a thin, foot-long horizontal scar that she'd found below my rib cage.

"Sub-total gastrectomy," I said. "Ulcer. First marriage. Advertising. Big agency. Years ago. But I don't want to get into that, Victoria—"

"You're right, Tom. Get into me."

We kissed. It must have lasted for ten miles. Incredible! And then, after dropping slowly to my knees—in a somewhat worshipful attitude, perhaps, but then why not?—I placed my face gently against the fleece of her aromatic black bush. The aroma was surprising. Fresh strawberries. But I said nothing. The fact is that I've always been fond of strawberries.

Very slowly, I placed my tongue deep inside her. I could hear her humming faintly the old Jerome Kern tune, "Look for the Silver Lining." After a bit, when I found the spot, she stopped humming and started moaning, low and quiet. Sometime later came the moment when I stood and embraced her and kissed her and entered her—and found my testes banging on the cold Monel Metal of the basin. But, somehow, I did not mind a bit.

"Victoria—Victoria—Victoria—" I whispered.

"Welcome, Tom," she said, smiling the goddess smile, holding me in her warm triple embrace.

The speeding train lurched, throwing me off balance. I grabbed her ankles. We did not lose contact, but drew quickly back together, and then Victoria placed her handsome head on my shoulder, just as she had done in the PATH station. Now there was plenty of time for savoring, as I stood there, swaying and bumping and rolling with the punches of the train. Victoria kept moaning, and then began to repeat the phrase "Ohhhhh, Tom—" over and over. It was neat. By now I'd completely lost sight of the fact that the day had been a professional and political disaster.

Gradually, a delicious thing became clear. In most sexual intercourse, and particularly when it is done vertically, the man has to put at least some reasonable effort into it. But we found that in doing it vertically aboard the Metroliner, it was the *train* that did the work! I simply stood there, my mouth pressed to hers, our tongues entwined, my hands holding her ankles for balance—and the speeding train provided a hundred movements with unexpected nuances that I could never have created myself.

And so I remained locked to this splendid polka-dotted bronze woman with the Aztec face, while the Penn Central Railroad—a division of Amtrak—transported us in rapture all the way home.

CHAPTER 9

NEXT MORNING, buoyed by my vivid memories of Victoria Woodhill, I crossed the suave sandalwood lobby of UN Plaza, nodded to the white-haired Irish doorman who held open the four-hundred-pound glass door, then started walking to work along 55th Street, whistling a happy tune. I was carrying Mrs. Winstead's coat in a clear plastic bag.

The orange sun was at my back, shining directly westward on 55th. The autumn daylight was crisp and amber and pure. The American flag on the oblique flagpole sticking out of the Leonetti Van and Storage Company whipped and snapped in the hard breeze. The turning earth had once again fulfilled the motto on the west wall of the lobby of *The New York Times*:

> Every day is a fresh beginning,
> Every morn is the world made new.

This going-to-work time is Manhattan's finest hour. The autumnal midtown streets are like vast, energetic television commercials. Everybody in sight is successful. There are no shaky old people, no whiny kids with runny noses, no incontinent winos. On the contrary, the bright and busy people look as though they have just finished a cup of the finest decaffeinated coffee and found it indistinguishable from the kind that has caffeine. They look as though their underarms have been sprayed with a high-pressure dessicant, as though their headaches, low-back pains, and residual irregularity have been eliminated as effectively as the wax buildup on the vinyl kitchen floors of their smart, high-rise condominiums. I look that way myself. Reality, anxiety, and confusion do not set in until we get to the office.

On this day, reality set in sooner. I had walked up Madison Avenue to 59th, and as I turned once again westward, I could see a great smog storm blowing in from New Jersey, rolling across the Hudson to ruin Manhattan's weather for the day or the week. In the early sixties, smog used to come in high and quietly, simply putting a sick gray enamel across the sky and stinging the eyes. But in the last quarter of the twentieth century, much to the dismay of the few environmentalists who were still alive, the unsolvable phenomenon of the smog-spill from the overworked, obsolete refinery had become one of the two hallmarks of the American petroleum industry. (The other was unconscionable greed.)

Smog now arrived in great tumbling gobs—a greasy fog that would never really be dispersed because it was linked to America's mobility. Smog lights on cars grew larger as clogged catalytic converters spewed more and more unburned hydrocarbons out along the American Road, but nobody could make the final wrenching decision to turn off his internal combustion engine—for America was a nation on the move, and had been ever since Jefferson sent Lewis and Clark westward in 1803.

Triggered by the smog, a personal miasma settled over me. It could not be dispersed, even when I entered the cheery atmosphere of the Sarantopolous rain forest. Reality had struck hard. My man, Governor Quimby, was gone. He was gone far beyond my poor power to add, as Lincoln had once put it, or detract. And now, up on the 67th floor, I had to find quickly another candidate on whose coattails I could ride secretly to victory over there where the smog was coming from. My head started to ache, something it seldom did.

"It must have been quite a day, Mr. Quick," said Emily, bringing coffee in my large mug labelled Proprietor.

"It was—it was," I said, tilting back in the chair, rubbing my temples.

"I know you're upset by the Governor's death and all," she said, running her fingers through the smooth fur of the coat as it lay on my desk, "but is this for me?"

"No, dear. I stole it."

"From whom?"

"From Mrs. William P. Winstead of Old Bent Willow Road in Short Hills. Call a messenger, will you please, so we can return it."

Emily, usually a model of high-speed efficiency, did not move. It was clear that, having been denied the coat, she wanted the explanation.

"It's hard to explain if you weren't there," I said. "But there was this naked girl in the PATH station, and I—well, I stole the coat to cover her up."

"She'd been raped?" asked Emily.

"No, no. But you see, at the very end of her dance, just as she was—"

"She was dancing naked?"

"That's right. With some friends."

"In the *PATH* station?"

"That's right."

"Mr. Quick, are you on coke again?"

"Not at all. She's a member of the Subterranean Dance Theatre. Emily, have you ever been obsessed—sexually obsessed?"

"I don't think so, Mr. Quick," she said after a moment's consideration. "I can take it or leave it, as you know. Though usually I take it."

"Yesterday, I got myself obsessed."

I threw open the coat to show Emily the faint red and green circular marks that Victoria's skin had left on the brown satin lining.

"She was all polka-dotted, and—"

Victoria's succulent aroma wafted up, enveloping me in memory, stopping speech.

"She was all polka-dotted and what?" asked Emily, her inflection thudding downward.

"—and I took her to Trenton," I said.

"What on earth for?"

"She'd never been to Trenton. Emily, I could not stand to lose sight of her. That's all."

"You said it was going to be a business trip," said Emily. Her tone was suspicious, a note that only a wronged woman can hit right.

"But it was," I said. "Victoria turned out to be very businesslike. She subdued a red-necked cab driver. She charmed the Governor. And she made a perfect diversionary maneuver just when Rocky Bettenhauser was ready to fire me."

"Where did the obsession come in?"

"It started the first moment I saw her dancing. It built up all through the day. And it exploded on the Metroliner on the way home."

"Tell me what she looks like."

"Not now, dear. I've got to pry her out of my mind." I pounded on the desk. "It's time for action. I need a new candidate immediately."

Saying no more, Emily slid the front page of the *Times* across the desk. It carried an article outlined in black Magic Marker by the clipping service:

Special to the New York Times

TRENTON, N.J.—The body of the late Gov. Horace J. Quimby (Dem.), who dropped dead yesterday shortly after his conviction on three criminal counts, will lie in state for six hours in the rotunda of the State House at Trenton beginning at noon today, it was announced by Assemblyman J. Hunter Mattoon (Rep.), Chief of Protocol for the State of New Jersey.

"There was some question about whether or not we should so honor a convicted felon," said Mattoon when reached by telephone at his Rippling Falls estate, "but the members of the legislature, polled by telephone last evening, indicated that since Governor Quimby had not exhausted all his appeals, he should be presumed to be innocent and displayed with candor, if not exactly with honor."

In a related matter, Mrs. Penelope Potter, veteran Registrar of Candidates here, announced last night that between the time of Governor Quimby's collapse at 3:45 P.M., and the close of business in her office, eleven candidates for governor had declared themselves and been assigned places on the ballot. More are expected.

"The New Jersey Supreme Court has instructed me to keep the Roster of Candidates open for another forty-eight hours," Mrs. Potter said. "The Court has also authorized a runoff election if no candidate receives more than forty percent of the vote on November 5th."

Political observers here in the capital predict that these rulings will trigger the candidacies of a large group of political novices, spurred on by the old hope that the corrupt Democratic machine, a fixture in this state ever since Andrew Jackson was swept into office in 1830, is once again dead.

"Emily, please call Mrs. Potter," I said. "We've got to get the names and addresses of the candidates."

"Yes, Mr. Quick. You want their bios, too?"

"If she's got them. I've got to find a new candidate who's halfway viable."

"That's one thing you could say about Governor Quimby,"

Emily observed sadly as she punched up the phone number. "Until he fell over dead, he was viable."

Mrs. Potter came on the line to report first that Bradford J. Bassett (Rep.) had just been found guilty on three counts that were mirror images of the Quimby counts. He had resigned from his candidacy, saying that the evidence against him was a tissue of lies, predicting calmly that he would be vindicated on appeal when *all* the facts were finally laid before the court.

"Why is it, Mrs. Potter," I asked, "that nobody in America sounds cleaner or more confidently noble than a politician who has just been convicted?"

"I've never been able to figure that out. But keep your nose clean, Jack, and you won't have that trouble."

While Mrs. Potter gave Emily the names and addresses and biographies, I called Al Divver at his old clapboard house in Paterson. I thought maybe he could help me.

"Al, I want to express my condolences about the death of the Governor," I said. "He was a good man."

"Thanks for callin', Tom," said Divver. "The Governor was basically misunderstood, but then who the hell isn't?"

"What about your job, Al?"

"I'm gonna drive the Governor on his last trip tomorrow. To Mt. Olivet Cemetery. Then I'll be at liberty."

"Al, I've got to find me a candidate over there," I said. "And also, we'll need a campaign driver. You interested?"

"That's thoughtful of yuh," he said. "But the Machine'll take care of a job for me. I'm puttin' in for a rest-up."

"A what?"

"A rest-up. It's a job the Machine gets you when you're between real jobs. Like bein' a lifeguard at a playground with no swimmin' pool."

"Not too taxing, eh?"

"Right. Mornings, you figure the horses at Monmouth Park. Afternoons, you go to the track."

"Listen, Al. I need the winner in this election. You have any idea at all who it might be?"

Divver laughed his thin, side-of-the-mouth laugh. It was the sound of a man who has a lot of mileage on him.

"Who knows, for Chrissake. I wish I could help you, but when the woodwork candidates come out, it's anybody's guess."

"Who you figure the Mafia candidate will be?"

"I'd say Six Fingers Tarantina. But he doesn't have enough real warmth for politics."

"I'm leaving right now to look over the field, Al. I'd still like you to drive for us."

"Get somebody up to my standards and maybe I'll do it."

"Suppose I went with a woman candidate?"

"Then you kin forget Al Divver."

"Some women are terrific, Al."

"Personally, sure. But, politically, their period interferes with their judgment."

"Men can have bad judgment, too."

"But at least it's not affected by the phases of the goddam moon!"

As we hung up, Emily reached suddenly across the big desk to cover my hands with hers.

"Is Victoria pretty?"

"Jesus."

"Is she built right?"

"Jesus."

"Has she got the legs you like?"

"Jesus."

"Does she look like me?"

"No, dear," I said gently. "Victoria is a tall, bronze Aztec goddess. Half black, half Kawaiute Indian—in green boots."

"Kawaiute?"

"It's a small Indian tribe in Nevada."

"I suppose she makes jewelry for a living?"

"No. She's a four-hundred-dollar call girl."

Her hands tightened over mine.

"Mr. Quick, she'll drag you down."

"She may, but on the other hand—"

"She'll drag you down just like Nana did in that Zola novel."

Suddenly, I reached for the phone and started punching up numbers.

"Emily, it's the chance you take when you're obsessed."

"You're calling her?"

"That's right."

"You said you were going to pry her out of your head."

"*You* brought her up again." I kept punching. "But what the hell, it's impossible."

A lovely French voice came onto the line.

" 'Allo. This is Madame Danou, and this is *aussi* a recording. Thank you for calling Madame Danou's call house. But sadly, I must tell you that at this hour, all our *filles de joie* are in retirement. Our house of pleasure opens again tonight at the stroke of nine."

She sounded immensely sensuous, as though she were playing a scene with Ronald Colman.

"Please wait for the beeping tone," she went on, "and then give your name, the name of the girl you desire, the hour, and the particular *pièce d'amour* you have in mind. This week only, we are having an around-the-world special. There is nothing like it. *Au revoir*—"

The beeping tone sounded, and then I asked quickly that Victoria Woodhill keep the whole night loose for Tom Quick. I hung up. Emily was looking sad and hard at me across the desk. Her chin was quivering, the way that Judy Garland's used to do.

"I—I guess I've been hoping that one day you'd be suddenly obsessed by me," she said.

"But one never knows, Em, what devious pathways the human mind will take in an attempt to—"

"Yet if that's not to be, then maybe this Victoria Woodhill is the answer for you."

"Only time will tell. But if you'll type up that list of candidates now, I'll be off."

"She *is* the answer," Emily went on, her lips thin. "After all, if you couldn't make it with three Presbyterian wives from Vassar, and if you're unwilling to commit to a fervent young Unitarian like me, then maybe a half-Indian, half-black heathen whore is just right for you!"

"*Emily*! You're being spiteful at a time when my emotions are completely out of control."

I sighed and put my face down into the coat.

"Christ, Mr. Quick," she said. "They've been out of control for years. Ever since your mother told you it would fall off if you played with it."

Yet within a few seconds, she had come around the desk to knead the tense muscles running along my shoulder blades—a place from which a set of nerves shot right up the side of my neck into my headache. That felt good. I lay my head on its side and spoke quietly.

"Emily, come with me to New Jersey! Okay? We'll look over the candidates. We'll make a day of it and have a nice dinner and won't come back till late. It'll be just like old times in the big back seat!"

"Thanks, anyway," she said, and her voice still had the quaver, "but the big back seat will never be the same again."

"Sure it will."

"No, it won't, Mr. Quick. You've—you've passed on to another field of clover."

CHAPTER 10

PLUNGING toward the street in my Personal Express Service elevator, I decided not to take the Grand Mercedes. A twenty-seven-foot limousine with a brushed-aluminum roof, a cranberry mohair interior, and a polarized Sky-Vue window would be too noticeable. What I needed was a low-profile, undistinguishable vehicle that would fit in anywhere in New Jersey. I rented a mauve Avis Chevy Nova.

I had only forty-eight hours now to check out the candidates. Since I was going to have to lay another two grand on Eddie over at Four Star Printing, I wanted the best ballot position that money could buy. My hope was that I could quickly find the *one* candidate who would be, like Franklin Delano Roosevelt, the very embodiment of the office.

Thirty minutes later, in the utilitarian city of Secaucus, I drove up in front of a grimy bar wedged in between a defunct tannery and a hopeless hotel. A sputtering neon sign announced that it was Sal's Place. On my list of candidates, this was the state headquarters for the candidacy of Salvatoro Wyncyncynski, the proprietor. According to Mrs. Potter's bio sheet, "Sal" had become a popular local folk hero after trying to create a uniformed vigilante group to keep this part of the city lawful and orderly on his own terms —particularly at night when sneakered black people, with their lower visibility and higher sprinting rates, could, according to Wyncyncynski, get away more easily from the scenes of their nefarious crimes.

Inside the front window of the bar were two smaller neon signs—Miller's High Life, and Open. I went in. It was grimy. Behind the bar, a two-hundred-and-fifty-pound man in shirtsleeves was making political promises to four pasty customers who had either arrived early or stayed all night. Clearly, this was the candidate.

"Remember how they used to have a code word for them blacks?" he was asking. They nodded in unison. "Well, I'm gonna have a code word for everythin'! A code word for welfare. A code word for pornography. A code word for busin'. A code word for Arabs, an' another one for Jews. A code word for perverts, an' one for commie perverts. Even gonna have a code word for the Pope. I'm gonna call him 'Papa.' "

As I stepped up to the bar, his face creased with concern at the arrival of a stranger. Sal's Place had only regulars.

"You're one of them reporters come here to size me up," he said flatly. "Well, I ain't talkin'! You guys from the captive fag Eastern Establishment press are always writin' that I said somethin' that I never said."

There was a long pause while I lit a cigar.

"See?" he said to his customers. "A skinny cigar. One of them damn fag cigars."

"I'm not a reporter," I said. "And it's unwise, Mr. Wyncyncynski, to make a sexual judgment based on just a cigar."

"What the hell you want?"

"A Miller's High Life."

Still suspicious, he drew me a draft as he went on with the explanation of the code words. As it ended, he was pointing a thick finger across the bar at me and saying that when he announced his candidacy in Military Park, all his friends who stood with him here in the bar would be standing with him out in the world. And *they'd* know what he was talking about.

"An' it's no small bunch, either, mister. Believe me, it's *no small bunch.*"

Wyncyncynski did not know, of course, how big the bunch was. But I did. A recent Polcon poll for the late Governor Quimby had shown that big, disaffected, second-generation single males, with living mothers who implore them to keep speaking Ethnic in the home, comprised only 0.5 percent of the total New Jersey registered voters. It was not the basis for a landslide.

"Mr. Wyncyncynski," I asked, "have you listed for your supporters—even in code—the three main points of your campaign? In order to be a plausible candidate you ought to consider the—"

"I only got one," said Sal.

"Which is?"

"To keep the blacks in their place, an' to do it quiet an' half-legal, so nobody kin bitch. Unnerstan'?"

I did. I also understood that Sal Wyncyncynski was not the candidate for me. I didn't underestimate his local clout. Like Mussolini, he would have ironclad control over his followers. But he was no Franklin D. Roosevelt. I needed somebody with a lot wider appeal. I drained my grimy stein and left.

Half an hour later, I pulled up in front of a trim little house in Somerville. It was covered with gray asbestos shingles. Not a single one was cracked or broken. A small sign in the front window said:

HEADQUARTERS—MS. VIRGINIA SMITH (DEM.)
ELECT THIS WOMAN GOVERNOR *NOW*!

A little, frizzy-haired woman of about sixty bounced out of the front door, slammed it, and came fast down the steps, two at a time.

"Ms. Smith?" I said.

"That's right, brother," she said.

"My name is Tom Quick. I'm a concerned citizen searching for the best candidate for governor."

"It is I," she said crisply.

"Why do you say that?"

"I am the only candidate who can lead the Garden State out of the fog of female sexual repression."

"But there's more wrong with this state than female sexual repression."

"Perhaps. But that problem is the foundation stone on which all others rest."

"You mean that fuel shortages, polluted rivers, and skyrocketing medical costs all begin with female sexual repression?"

"To name three," she said.

"Could you trace the logic of that for me?" I asked.

"Sorry. I'm on my way to address some sisters at a coffee."

"Can I come along?"

"It's a coffee for sisters, brother."

We had now progressed to her Saab at the curb.

"What's the first piece of legislation you'll sponsor as Governor?" I asked.

"A bill to approve open lesbian relationships—including marriage—between consenting New Jersey female adults."

The wiry little lady paused with her head cocked to see how I would react.

"But Ms. Smith," I said. "Isn't that using the majesty of the state for a narrow personal purpose?"

"What did you say, brother?" she asked, thrusting her face close to my face.

"I'm suggesting that you are using a historic political entity—the *polis* itself—for a narrow private purpose."

"Let me respond to that," she said.

Her face stayed so close to mine that I did not see the cocked fist of her right hand. But I felt it when she suddenly drove it into my stomach.

"Ooooooof!" I said.

For a few seconds, she danced around me defensively, fists up, as graceful as Gene Tunney in the old Stillman's Gym. When she saw that I was not going to counterattack, she leaped into the Saab, laid a patch, and was gone.

In the low rolling hills up above Parsippany, I arrived at the estate of Luigi ("Six Fingers") Tarantina, an under-the-table Mafia figure who had recently surfaced and become a public figure after an altercation in a Union City clam bar.

A tough-looking man in a knit suit opened the big iron gate, and I drove the Nova up a curving road to the top of the hill where a Bastille-type house loomed. Tarantina was waiting for me in an olive grove at the side of the house. He looked like an overweight Valentino as he sat in a white, knobby wrought-iron lawn chair, pouring himself a glass of Ruffino chianti. He did not shake hands, but gestured for me to sit opposite him in another knobby chair across the knobby table. He filled my glass, too. As he talked, Doberman pinschers nipped around my calves, and plaster garden statues of chubby little Italian boys urinated into the Greek Revival fishpond.

Tarantina, a man of the underworld, was close-mouthed about where he'd been. He also was close-mouthed about where he was going. When I asked him about the three main points of his campaign, he just grunted. I wasn't even sure he had heard me. I asked again.

"I'll show 'em," he muttered quietly, pou g himself another glass of wine. "I'll show the bastards—

"I take it that you're running for governor to make a point with some specific group?"

"You're damned right. I'll show them bastards."

"Who?"

"*All* of them!"

"As you move ahead into your campaign, Mr. Tarantina," I said, trying to keep the discussion alive, "what would you say is your principal advantage?"

"Anybody knows that. In any big argument down in Trenton, I kin let a contract to *nail* the other guy."

"You mean that as the governor of New Jersey, you might actually have a state senator killed?"

He smiled a smile of great internal enjoyment.

"It'd sure whip that fuckin' legislature into line."

"Have you mentioned this advantage to the Fair Campaign Practices Committee?"

"I don't give a shit about them."

"But Professor Samuel Archibald, their executive consultant, is sure to take a dim view of outright murder as a political technique in a mature democracy."

He downed his wine and stood up.

"Get out of here, you."

"I take it the interview is over?"

"It's over."

I stood up and put out my hand for a handshake.

"Mr. Tarantina, I want to thank you for this opportunity to exchange views with you and to tell you that—"

"Get out."

He turned and walked toward the great black masonry house, still muttering—like an ungrammatical Richard III—about retribution. The dogs saw me to the Nova. Tarantina stood in the vestibule, watching me leave, and I concluded as the gate slammed behind me that Al Divver had been right about him. There would be strong subterranean pressures all through urban New Jersey on behalf of Tarantina's strange candidacy. Six Fingers would be endorsed over fettucini in many places. But unless there was a hit man stationed inside the green curtain of every voting machine in the state, I knew he would never make it to Trenton. Never.

There was just time before lunch to drive to the Paramus Shopping Center to size up Ms. Myrtle Bruce, a lovely conservative Democrat. Ms. Bruce, a cool woman of about fifty, was standing next to her Buick Estate Wagon, speaking quietly into a hand microphone with the assurance of somebody who owns not only the wagon but the estate, too. Her voice emerged from two high-fidelity Beltec speakers mounted on the roof of the car, and, like everything else about her, it was rich. When she leaned back against the Buick, hiking her Halston shirt dress up just above the knee, she was so neatly relaxed that she might have been at a tailgate luncheon just prior to the Maryland Hunt Cup. Time and life had made her sensuous rather than scrawny, an achievement I admired. There was no question that she was a plausible candidate.

"Let me answer, my friends, a question that has just been put to me by Ms. Patricia Windsor of Short Hills," she said. "While I do believe that *all* women will eventually become a part of The Movement for Our Freedom, I think also that we cannot allow The Movement to be distorted by narrow self-interest—by those intense, driven women who are always out there holding down their end of the bell-shaped emotional curve.

"I want to be specific about this. Candidates who base their entire campaigns on total sexual freedom are taking attention away from other important issues—equal wages, day-care centers, job accessibility, assertiveness training, military combat duty, the retranslation of the Bible so that God appears as a woman in fifty-two percent of the references to Him or Her, and the search for a nonsexual singular pronoun, which already exists in the Armenian language. For myself, I don't want to see an election as important as this one hinge on the narrow issue of lesbian sexual mechanics."

The audience of six middle-American homemakers with shopping carts was jolted by her candor, but they stood their ground, nodding, and waiting to hear more.

"Women who do this—women like my energetic opponent, Ms. Virginia Smith—are, it seems to me, using the grandeur of the state for a narrow private purpose."

I could see myself working for Ms. Bruce. I asked what the three main points of her campaign were. She turned with a glint in the smoky gray eyes.

"Why, I have many more than three. You see, men, having constructed the whole machinery of Western civilization to their own advantage, must be opposed on *all* fronts simultaneously. We must neutralize administratively the biological fact that most men, when they want to, can beat most women up. And that is why in the Bruce Administration, fifty-four percent of the state employees will be women—reflecting exactly the state's population ratio. And the office of Lieutenant Governor *must* be filled by a woman or we shall be shafted by chauvinism before we begin."

The women applauded, little realizing that I had just been jolted out of my strong ballot position directly beneath her.

A portcullis having been dropped on my candidacy here, I left.

CHAPTER 11

Looking disconsolately around for a pleasant place to eat lunch, I could find nothing but aluminum diners. Nowhere in the world are there more aluminum diners than in New Jersey. They are clean, but also loud and drafty and mechanical—and they always give me the feeling that when I emerge I will be in Albany.

I finally spotted a gleaming new Holiday Inn. Being partial to their beef stroganoff, I went into their Old English Dining Room and ordered it. Then carrying my Manhattan to the long bank of phones against the lobby wall, I checked with Emily at the office. Mrs. Potter had called to give her the names of an additional ream of candidates who had signed up during the morning. There were thirteen of them. I would never be able to see them all.

When I got back to my table, the steaming stroganoff had arrived, along with a bottle of Miller's. I plunged in. Holiday Inns International had just that year achieved their standardized worldwide stroganoff. Each morning, eleven tons of it were cooked and frozen in a computerized plant in Nashville, Tennessee, then shipped by air to participating Holiday Inns across the span of the free world. It was not a distinguished dish, but it was a consistent one. From Baltimore to Bangkok, it was a stroganoff with no surprises.

After lunch, as I paused to light a cigar in the lobby, another candidacy was being announced on the one o'clock television news. I paused to take a look. Mr. William Spavin was the candidate. He was a hearty, thoughtful man, making his announcement from the dayroom of the State Hospital in Clabberville, where he was a mental patient. Mr. Spavin was lucid and persuasive. His idea was to run a campaign based on what he called "Insane Liberation." As governor, he planned to eliminate all involuntary commitments to mental institutions.

"We are beginning to see," said Spavin, hunching himself confidently toward the camera the way that Ironside used to do, "that *we* are not necessarily the sick ones. The sane are also in bad trouble, as you will see if you look at the front page of any newspaper. I have cabled Dr. R. H. Laing in England, and have invited him to become my campaign manager and speechwriter. I am in this race to stay."

Spavin was concerned and constructive, but the base of his political strength—incarcerated people in New Jersey mental institutions—was even narrower than Sal Wyncyncynski's.

"For Christ's sweet sake," I said to myself, sitting down in a fake Barcelona chair, "where is the candidate who can *encompass* the people? Where is the candidate who can unfurl the banner to which, as George Washington put it, we all could confidently repair? Where is the candidate who can stand up to the intense, selfish, astronomical expectations of an angry, fragmented America? Has the traditional idea of a nation held gracefully together through two centuries of constitutional self-restraint been exploded by Jack Kennedy's murder, by Lyndon Johnson's death-dealing thrust into Vietnam, by Richard Nixon's Haldeman slash Ehrlichman, by Gerald Ford's incomprehensibility, by Jimmy Carter's endless, vacuous smile?"

As a skilled and high-priced political consultant, I really should have had the answers to my questions. I did not.

Though I was in a hurry and in a dither, Victoria Woodhill kept floating back to mind. I returned to the bank of phones and called Mme Danou's. After her seductive recorded speech and the beeping tone, I asked that Victoria call me back within ten minutes. Within two minutes, the phone rang. It was Victoria. Her liquid voice brought back fond memories. I could feel my nostrils flaring.

"Tom! I've been thinking about you all morning!" she said. "Did you find a replacement for Quimby?"

"No," I said. "So far the best thing about the day has been the stroganoff."

"I went all through my book of New Jersey johns," she said. "But I don't think *any* of them are right for governor."

"That's kind of you, Victoria. I appreciate that."

"And I got your message, Tom. The night is yours."

"That's neat! Madame Danou said there was an around-the-world special."

"I've got something in mind even better."

"There's nothing better than that."

"Yes, there is. Pick me up at nine. We're going to New Jersey."

"Not again!"

"Trust me on this, Tom. You know politics. I know pleasure. I'll be ready at nine."

After breathing heavily into the phone a couple of times, she hung up. My headache had disappeared.

By three o'clock, I had seen the following candidates, and my headache had returned:

An Asbury Park sewer commissioner.

A Parsippany Indian, who was running to enforce the

claim that his tribe owned all New Jersey marshlands down to mean high tide.

The Mayor of Pemmican, New Jersey.

A heavy-drinking columnist for a defunct Newark newspaper.

A man named Bertram ("Banjo") Miller, more promising than the others, even though he was doing thirty years in the New Jersey State Penitentiary for stealing a 1952 Ford.

Miller was a man of broad outlook leading a narrow life. His campaign plan, which he'd been working on for a decade as a jailhouse lawyer, was quite professional. In addition, he had that level gaze so necessary in films and politics—the gaze of Spencer Tracy, Eugene V. Debs, FDR, and Robert Redford. Miller was quick to point out, tapping his fingers on the mesh that separated us in the visitor's room, that he was entirely beyond temptation. No other candidate could say that. It was a plus.

I could see myself working with Banjo Miller. He would be an unusual, yet plausible, candidate. But when I put a call to the New Jersey Director of Prisons, requesting some release time for Miller so that he could campaign, I got a flat turndown. The Director knew that Banjo Miller was a model prisoner who would probably be a model governor. But, unlike Horace J. Quimby, he did not believe that the state could be effectively governed from the pen. That being that, I left.

"The trouble with you, Whitey," said candidate Kabu Makabu across his big oval Danish desk, "is that ever since the day that those two Portuguese captains sold twelve black African males into slavery in Lisbon in 1451—ever since that day on which the whole institution of African slavery began—you have not understood what black men *want*. All we want is to be treated like white men. Like you. Once we get the power, we will be!"

"That's true," I said, "but—"

"You never have a stranger size up your *skin.*"

"That's true," I said, "but—"

"You never look at the palm of your hand and wish you were colored all over the way your palm is. You got the winning color, Quick, right down to your balls."

"Mr. Makabu," I said, "do you want to win the election or make a series of emphatic social points?"

"Both," he said.

"Suppose you can't have both," I said.

"Read Lenin."

"I've read Lenin. But Lenin never had to run in New Jersey. All he had to do was stir up a bread riot and storm the Winter Palace. It was easy."

"I'm prepared to take measures like that," said Makabu quietly. "I'm prepared to ride to Trenton in a sealed train."

"But it's not necessary," I said emphatically. "You could win this election gracefully instead of grimly."

"How?" he exploded, leaning across the desk, drilling me with angry eyes. "Just say how, Quick."

"There's nothing to it. All you have to do is put together a coalition with a cool white lieutenant governor—a coalition that would reach out and embrace the whole community."

"And piss away my only real strength?"

"Come on, Mr. Makabu," I said. "You think blackness is your only strength because you used it to get a piece of the Jersey numbers game from the Mafia."

"That's your line, not mine."

"And it's true. My Polcon poll last year showed that you got a piece of the numbers only because the white runners were scared shitless to go into black neighborhoods."

"That's not black strength?"

"Sure, but it's piddling. Now that you've set up your own political party, you've got a chance to become a black statesman. Something more than a loudmouth with a linoleum knife in your back pocket."

"I don't have to listen to this jive."

"This jive is politically valid," I said. "You can't spend your whole life massaging the people who already think you're right. You'll turn out to be a black Wyncyncynski. What you *want* is to be a black FDR, a pivotal Democrat."

"Maybe—maybe," he said after a momentary pause. "But for now, I got to stick with my black brothers. The ABP. The Angry Black Party! After I win—after we're not so angry anymore, we're going to change the name. The ABP will become the American Black Party!"

"Brilliant PR," I said, standing up. "TWA did the same thing once, and it worked out fine. Here's my card. Phone me if you change your mind."

"Not a chance."

"I can put you into a coalition with an excellent honky who'd be an outstanding lieutenant governor—and a credit to his race."

"Not a chance," said Makabu. "These coalitions with honkies have already set us back five hundred and thirty-three years."

I left.

Late in the afternoon, with hopes sagging, I drove into the little resort town of Flensburg. (Pop. 1,227. Elevation, 6 ft. Founded 1814.) A crowd of about fifty people had gathered in front of the Flensburg firehouse, where a small reviewing stand had been erected next to the driveway. It was solidly built of new two-by-fours. Red-and-blue bunting was festooned all over it.

The sky was blue in Flensburg. It had turned out to be an Indian-summer day. The Atlantic shimmered off in the distance. The old firehouse had a new coat of white paint, and the engines stood red and burnished in the driveway.

The small-town crowd was congenial. Everybody knew everybody else, and there were lots of little kids running around in shorts and blue sneakers. It could have been the opening scene of a Disney movie. My hopes were revived. The setting was promising.

A half-dozen reporters sat at the press table, but, of course, there was no television coverage. New Jersey did not have her own commercial TV station then, and the TV news directors in her two contiguous states—New York and Pennsylvania—had never bothered to learn the quagmire of her politics. So the only thing ever reported on television from New Jersey were axe- and sex-murders, smog storms, racial explosions, multi-vehicle crashes on the New Jersey Turnpike, and the Miss America Contest.

When Mr. William ("Smokey") Carson (Ind.) mounted the speaker's platform to announce for governor, his neighbors gave him a good-natured hand even before he spoke a word. Carson looked promising, too. He was in his late twenties, tall, handsome, windburned like a golfer, a man with a pleasant, almost shy smile. I picked up his bio sheet from the press table. It explained that he was one of the two paid, full-time members of the Flensburg Volunteer Fire Department. To underline the main theme of his campaign, Smokey appeared in his complete fireman's running gear with hat, coat, turned-down boots, and a yellow tank of oxygen strapped to his back. A shade theatrical, I thought, but still plausible.

Smokey's speech was brief and straightforward. He simply announced his name, said he was running for governor of New Jersey as an Independent, and added that the main plank in his platform would be to keep the traditional, historic volunteer fire department system in the Flensburg Fire District—a system that had its origins in a leather-bucket brigade in Swedesboro in 1798—intact. It was a *good* system. The audience applauded, particularly the volunteer firemen in their fatigues, who stood in the wide doorways of the firehouse.

Then Carson recalled for the audience some notable fires that he had helped to put out—notably the Hirschfield holocaust—and said that as governor he'd be doing the same thing on a political level. The audience applauded again, and he threw the meeting open for questions.

There were three routine questions from the reporters. How old was he? When did he decide to run? Why was he running as an Independent when he'd been formerly registered as a Republican? Smokey Carson handled these gracefully. It was the fourth question that exploded the conference. It came not from a reporter, but from a young man standing in the audience.

"I understand from the crowd down at the candy store, Smokey, that you're queer. Would you care to comment on that?"

Everybody in the audience stiffened a little. The congenial Disney atmosphere vanished instantly.

"Why do you ask?" inquired Carson, his warm smile still fixed on his face.

"Because if you are, it's only fair that the electorate know it. We don't want any *nolo contendere* on a point like this."

"I agree with you," said Carson. "The fact is that I was planning to make a complete financial disclosure. And there's no reason not to make a sexual disclosure, too."

A hush fell over the crowd. The firemen moved into a small knot just inside the firehouse.

"The answer to your question," Smokey continued with aplomb, "is, Yes. I am a homosexual." There was a long flat pause. "Are there any further questions?"

The audience was dead still.

There were no further questions. It was the first time in the whole span of American history that a man had announced for governor and come out in the same speech. A low muttering began to emerge from the firehouse.

"If there are no further questions," said Smokey Carson, "let me add one thing, and let me add it categorically. I see nothing disabling in having an acknowledged homosexual as the chief executive officer of this state. The gay community, as you know, is developing political clout all across the country, and we contend that there is no connection whatsoever between private behavior and public service."

"I'm not so sure, Smokey," said the young man who had asked the question. "Whom will you take to the inaugural ball?"

"That's simple," replied Carson. "The person I take will be a human being who has—"

He never got to finish the sentence. A powerful blast of water, shot from an unseen hose inside the firehouse, knocked him right off the stand. Carson stood up and was immediately knocked down again as three firemen, manning the hose, emerged from the firehouse and started for him. The audience, wet and dismayed, fell back. The hose continued to play out as a knot of firemen, his former colleagues and buddies, pursued the stumbling, soaked Carson down the middle of the street. Others joined in the pursuit now, suddenly jeering at him, pelting him with stones as he got hosed down again and again, and shouting—as had Henry VIII—that Smokey Carson had been engaged in the detestable and abominable vice!

But Carson was game. With his oxygen tank askew and his boots full of water, he continued to get up again and again and to stand his ground. He also continued to discuss the issues, though in a fragmentary way.

"Nevertheless!" he would shout from time to time, "I am in this race to stay!"

I had reached the nadir of my disappointment. Driving

with my newest headache back to Manhattan, I tried to imagine a less likely candidate for the governorship of New Jersey, upon whose popularity I could myself ride to power, than a just-out-of-the-closet fireman from Flensburg. I could not.

CHAPTER 12

BACK at the UN Plaza, I tried to relax. Sitting in front of the picture wall, I put away three Manhattans while looking out over the lights of Manhattan. Then I went and soaked for two hours in the Jacuzarium of my sunken Levantine marble tub. By nine o'clock, as my driver brought the Grand Mercedes limo to a stop in front of the shiny art nouveau facade of Victoria's building on East 71st Street, I was feeling looser and better, even though my underlying problems remained unsolved.

The etched glass door was swung open, and Victoria appeared suddenly, a shining, burnished idol. Pausing for a moment in the bright amber light under the canopy, she stunned the doorman, a delivery boy on a three-wheeler, a man walking a borzoi, the borzoi, and me.

Her hair no longer flowed to her waist, but was tightly braided into long rows that were then wound into a tall, perfect cone. She wore a short black mink coat, open over a short vermilion suede dress—and vermilion boots identical to the green ones of the day before. She smiled her classic smile. It lit up half the block.

Recovering, the doorman sprang to open the rear door,

and Victoria came into the car and into my arms in a single floating move. Once again, it was that fragrant moment when slavering anticipation is fulfilled. We fell into a searching kiss. When the kiss was completed, the car was emerging from the Lincoln Tunnel.

"I tell you one thing," I said. "Sexual obsession is one of the last great excitements left in all Christendom."

Confirming my opinion, Victoria smiled, lay back across the big back seat, and suddenly swung her bright red boots up into my lap.

"Victoria, are you under the impression that I'm a boot man as well as a leg man?"

"From the jump. So I wanted you to know that I have eight pair of these from the Soho Cobbler—Fire Engine Red, Skydive Blue, California Lemon Yellow, Ghirardelli Chocolate—"

"That means I'll see you eight times before we drift apart?"

"At least eight times before we go *pouf*!"

"How come you're so sure about all this?"

"Because most people grab my behind when we make love," she explained with a smile. "But you wouldn't let go of my boots."

"It was a matter of balance," I said. "The Metroliner was jiggling. We were going a hundred and two miles an hour. Furthermore, your behind was in the sink."

"That's just evasive jive, and you know it," she said, laughing the low-pitched laugh, swinging the boots out of my lap, and kissing me on the tip of the nose.

"Victoria, you've seen through everybody else—including Ronald Reagan. Why not me?"

"We learned about you at Vassar."

"Me specifically?"

"No, you generally. You had a powerful mother and a low-risk father. The imprint was fixed before your fourth birthday. And the whole thing is an unconscious reaction formation to your need as a kid to be passive to your threatening father."

"That's exactly what Dr. Fessenden used to say," I said. "We talked about it three times a week for five straight years."

"That's a lot of explaining."

"Even then, it was never completely clear."

"And it never will be," said Victoria. "Sex can't be *explained*, Tom. It can only be enjoyed."

"I like you, Victoria," I said, holding her close, kissing her lightly. "Everything is right up front with you."

"Because I'm a Kawaiute. We were never any good at concealing things."

"When I walked down into that PATH station, I never expected to find a—"

"Pardon the interruption," said the driver on the intercom, "but just where in New Jersey are we going?"

"It's the incorporated village of Whoopeeton," said Victoria. "On I-70, just beyond Paterson."

"Thank you, Miss. I've never heard of it."

He clicked off the intercom.

"Me neither," I said.

"It's one of those new towns," she explained.

"Like Reston or Columbia?" I asked.

"Not exactly," said Victoria with a sly smile. "It's more like the Casbah."

"What?"

"It was founded by a friend of mine from Texas. Belton Waco Jones. He formed a syndicate one morning a few years ago, and the syndicate founded Whoopeeton."

"Why would a syndicate from Texas found a town in New Jersey?"

"Belton Waco Jones got an awful jolt at the time the

Burger Court made that hard ruling on American sex," said Victoria. "Remember? The court held that any sex-for-money transaction in the United States had to abide by the contemporary sexual standards that are the norm for the community."

"I was jolted myself," I said.

"Of course you were. Belton and his syndicate members are just like you, Tom. Bright and hard-working people who are also sex-crazed. They'd fuck a snake."

"But the Burger Court didn't ever say what a community *was*," I said.

"Right, Mr. Charlie! And that's the loophole they jumped through. They decided to incorporate a town with private sexual standards set so low that there would be true public freedom! Whoopeeton, New Jersey!"

"I can't imagine why I've never heard of the place," I said.

"Neither can I," said Victoria. "It's your kind of town."

The sign at the exit from I-70 said:

WELCOME TO WHOOPEETON
A PATENTLY OFFENSIVE COMMUNITY
One-bedroom Condos from 77 Thousand

Downtown Whoopeeton was a blaze of bright, jiggling neon—a small, tasteful Las Vegas. The largest building on the main street had a huge neon sign emblazoned across the whole facade, proclaiming that it was The Palace of Pleasure. This was our destination.

In a big brown leathery office, Victoria introduced me to Belton Waco Jones, Resident Manager. Clearly, he was from Texas. He stood up to about six four and came around from behind his desk, his right arm held out in a large arc as he moved to shake hands. From his Stetson to his boots, he was dressed in light powder blue, and even before he spoke, his body language was saying: "Welcome pardner!"

As his right hand shook mine with an amiable death grip, his left hand shot up to clamp me by the shoulder. His handsome face, bending over close to mine, was crinkled like a topographical map of the San Jacinto Mountains. It was like being greeted at the White House by Lyndon Johnson.

"Welcome, pardner! Sheeeeeit, Ah'm glad tuh see yuh! Glad yuh could take the tahm tuh come visit with us. Lemme show you the *place*."

I noticed that, like many Texans, he was gimlet-eyed.

With the pride that can come only with success, Belton Waco Jones guided us out into The Palace of Pleasure. We walked past a long line of waiting, smiling, eager-faced men, past a ticket window, and then we boarded an endless train of slowly moving seats. Jones continued to talk as the shell-like seats carried us into a dim tunnel, and as sensuous music began to drift out of the little speaker built into each headrest. The orchestra, heavy on the woodwinds, was playing "In a Persian Garden."

Jones's voice rumbled out of the dimness.

"This unusual buildin', Tom, is the old 'Futurama,' which, you may remember, was the big General Motors exhibit at the New York World's Fair. The most successful exhibit in the whole history of Western man, according to the BS of the PR boys at GM."

"I never knew that," I said.

"Anyhow, mah syndicate bought the equipment lock, stock, an' barrel. Took it out of storage in Flint, Michigan, an' set it up here."

"You mean we're going to emerge from this tunnel and see that same old splendid America of the future?" I asked in amazement.

"Oh, no, no," said Belton. "We kept the basic design, but we changed all the exhibits. We also changed the name from 'Futurama' to 'Sexarama.' But GM took us to court on that one, claimin' plagiarism an' bad taste. So we went ahead as The Palace of Pleasure—which has a nice lilt to it."

The moving seats emerged from the tunnel into the exhibition area. Belton was right about the displays having been changed. Instead of the diminutive, perfect Cleveland of the future, we found naked people on exhibit. Full-sized, real, naked people. Doing things to each other. Reaching out to touch the parts of the human body associated with pleasure. I was flabbergasted.

We moved slowly past a series of living dioramas—living room and bedroom and bathroom and playroom and dungeon settings—settings in which the whole spectrum of human sexual response was taking place. For a moment I thought of Masters and Johnson and all the PhD. theses that would eventually flow from this place. But then I stopped thinking and got back to mindless *looking*.

"You're bug-eyed, man," said Victoria, as we passed an intricate group of seven entwined people.

"You're damned right," I said. "I've never seen linkage like that anywhere. Not even in Hong Kong."

"It's a nice way to meet people," said Belton.

Victoria hummed a few bars from the song "Get Happy."

"Look at the way that big girl is twisted around that little guy," I said.

"We try to run a *friendly* place," explained Belton.

"—and watch the hands of the cat coming in from the left," explained Victoria. "He looks like he's going to—"

"Look at the fourth lady's ass!" I shouted. "If she moves an inch to the right, the whole pyramid will collapse, and the guy on top will—"

But we had passed on to another diorama. This one contained a lovely girl chaining some chap to a masonry wall. Totally tumescent, he seemed to be enjoying every minute of it.

"Wait a minute, Belton," I said, swinging around to look at him in the dimness. "Who *are* these people?"

"The girls are on the staff," said Belton. "The guys are jus' plain citizens, out for an evenin' of harmless merriment."

"How do they get onstage?"

"By payin' thirty-five dollars for a half hour of pleasure."

"And they don't mind?"

"They love it," said Belton. " 'Course, if you ain't an exhibitionist at heart, then you kin take this ride for only five bucks. It's all been priced out."

As the moving seats moved on, I sat back in relaxed amazement. I looked at Victoria. She smiled, clearly happy with how the evening was going. When I looked back into the next diorama, an absolutely stunning naked girl was in the process of seating herself on the face of a man who I believe was J. Willis McGee, the Democratic Chairman of Arcane County.

At the end of this bizarre journey, Belton Waco Jones invited us into the Red Velvet Bar. Lighting up our cigars, he explained that he'd started out in Houston as the local distributor for Dare-to-Be-Terrific, Inc., an extremely successful operation that taught success by cassette. Then one night, just when he was ready to move up to regional distributor, he read the Burger Court sex ruling. Seeing instantly what a terrible impact the Chief Justice could have on his life, he immediately went into action. By late that evening, sitting at the dining room table, Belton had conceived The Palace of Pleasure concept. Next morning, he resigned his job and founded the syndicate with four friends. They called it Dare-to-Be-Horny, Inc.

"But the concept had to be developed, designed, proved out, an' marketed jus' right, y'understand?" he said. "Yuh couldn't jus' put The Palace of Pleasure anywhere. An' you sure as hell couldn't put it in Houston, with all them Baptists around. So we flew up here one afternoon, an' founded Whoopeeton as kind of a *settin'* for the palace. But now they're *both* successful. Why, Ah tol' the boys yesterday that we're gonna make as much this year from condominiums as from condoms!"

Belton laughed happily at his prepared joke.

"What's the future look like, Belton?"

"Bright. Bright! We're franchisin' new Palaces almost as fast as Burger Chef. Openin' up fourteen new locations next month, from North Carolina to Nevada. An' we jus' got a trainin' program goin' for resident managers—like the Holiday Inns train their innkeepers in Nashville."

"That's the place they make the stroganoff!" I added.

"We try to be imaginative," said Belton.

"You are—you are!" I assured him.

"You think that's imaginative, Tom," said Victoria, laying a hand on my arm, "just listen to Belton's next big kinky idea. What a wrinkle *this* is!"

"Thank you, honey, for bringin' that up," said Belton. "Because it will prove to Tom here that Ah'm an able planner as well as a good administrator."

I could not imagine why Belton Waco Jones wanted to prove that to me, but I listened anyway. The whole place fascinated me. Belton tossed down another straight shot of bourbon, and then he explained that The Palace of Pleasure was now having the same basic trouble that plagues every successful new American company. As soon as success arrives, so does the Teamster's Union—to organize the help, to drive up the costs, and eventually to drive the business out of business. The Teamsters were now attempting an organization drive at the Palace, pushing toward an NLRB election.

They wanted to represent all the young, hot, naked girls on the staff.

"The *Teamsters?*"

"Yeah," said Belton. "They ain't as hidebound as they used to be, Tom. But we're gonna git around 'em. We're plannin' to phase the girls out."

"Stone-brilliant," said Victoria.

"Yep. No more callin' in sick," said Belton. "No more high turnover, no more piecework, no more featherbeddin', an' no more VD."

"Yet it would seem that the girls are critical to the success of the Palace," I suggested.

"Yeah," he said with a quiet grin, "but it ain't necessarily so. We just got ourselves an R and D contract with the company that made that life-size Abraham Lincoln for Disneyland. You know, the one that delivers the Gettysburg Address? Well, this is a little outfit in San Diego, an' they claim that they kin make for us—out of somethin' called polyvinyl—a lovely, life-size, movin', breathin', talkin', humpin' young woman with a Control Basic Data Computer in her thorax. Jus' right for our purposes. 'Cordin' to the specifications, she's gonna be softer on the outside and smoother on the inside than the real thing."

"Won't the customers complain?"

"Naw. We'll phase the girls out so gradual that they'll never know the difference."

"How many words are in the polyvinyl vixen's vocabulary?" I asked.

"A hundred an' seventy-five," said Belton.

"Is that all you need?" I asked Victoria.

"All you really need is two," she said.

"That's what Ah figured," said Belton. "Hell, if they kin make a fake Lincoln who can stand up an' deliver the whole Gettysburg Address, they oughta be able to make a fake girl who kin lie down an' say 'Fuck me!' "

Victoria and I laughed and applauded his graphic demonstration. Then Belton laid his card on the table.

"An if *that* don't qualify me to be the governor of New Jersey, Ah can't imagine what would."

I stopped applauding, not sure that I'd heard right.

"What?"

"Ah gotta confess that Ah brought you two here under false pretenses tonight," said Belton. "But when Victoria called me to make a reservation an' she tol' me about this Mr. Quick who was lookin' for a governor, I figured what the hell, he might as well take a look at me."

"You, too?" I asked. "Is there anybody in New Jersey who *doesn't* want to be governor?"

Victoria was upset.

"Belton, damn it. We're not supposed to be mixing politics and pleasure tonight."

"Ah'm sorry," he said, "but this seemed like a fine chance to be seen in a good light. Ah'm anxious to make a career change, and Ah'd make one *hell* of a governor."

"Well—you have to admit that he looks like a governor," said Victoria, seeing Belton in his new role.

"Actually, he looks like a president," I said.

"How 'bout it, Tom?" asked Belton, leaning toward me anxiously. "Ah'm successful—rich—a good administrator—an' *mighty* restless. Frankly, Ah don't want to spend the rest of mah whole life franchising fuckshops across America."

I looked at his eager, craggy face, then took a long belt of my Manhattan.

"Belton, I'm sure you'd be great on the campaign trail, but let me lay it on the line."

"Sure."

"A whole slew of rich, successful businessmen have gone into politics, but look at where they came from. Shapp came from electronics. Metzenbaum came from parking lots. Percy came from Bell and Howell. Rockefeller came from

Pocantico Hills. Stroop came from Midas Mufflers. But so far as I know, none of them has ever come from a mechanized theatrical bordello."

"Ah could be a pioneer."

"Belton, we know from long experience that sex can be retailed and wholesaled," I said. "And now your syndicate is proving that it can even be franchised—like cheeseburgers."

"That's pioneerin' for you!"

"But sex in America has never been politicized. Sex and politics just don't go together—as the administration of Warren G. Harding so clearly proved."

"Ah thought times had changed," said the big man, a shade plaintive.

"Not that much," I said.

"But Ah keep readin' in *Business Week* an' *Screw* about the sexual revolution. Ain't it goin' on?"

"Sure it is. Ten years ago, you could never have opened this place. But Belton, use your head. This state is full of Christians, for Christ's sake. In the southeastern counties—Charon County, Flugel County—there are even Mennonites! Christians in New Jersey outnumber Jews four to one. Buddhists, a hundred and seven to one. I've got all the figures on the Polcon computer."

"But what do they signify?"

"That all the other groups together don't outnumber the Christians. With your background, you're just not a plausible candidate. You're beat before you announce."

"Ah won't get a single Christian vote?"

"Not a chance."

"Why not?"

"Because the basic tenets of Christianity are chastity and continence."

"Mebbe so," said Belton confidentially, "but them Christians are in here fuckin' and suckin' all the time."

"Of course they are," I said. "But people don't live morally, Belton. They only vote morally."

"He's right," said Victoria. "I vote that way myself."

"It's the first thing a political consultant must learn," I explained. "The American people are not pious, but they are complete suckers for anybody who *seems* pious. You remember Richard M. Nixon?"

"Ah do."

"The most pious President ever to come down the pike. In '72, he won the greatest landslide in history. And yet out of more than two hundred and sixty *million* people in this country, only the Managing Editor of *The Washington Post* really saw him for what he was."

"Ah'm proud to say that Nixon never took *me* in," said Belton quickly. "Never voted for him once. An' you know why?"

"Because you'd studied the Jerry Voorhis campaign?"

"Hell, no. Because Ah could never envision him *screwin'*. Ah'd never vote for a man Ah could not envision in heated sexual congress."

In all my years of polling, that was a response that had never before shown up. I made a note of it to add to the Basic Candidate Information Kit. Benson drained his drink, stood up, put out a big decisive hand.

"Ah got to check the register, folks. So glad you could come out, honey," he said to Victoria. They kissed. "An' Ah'm sorry mah little scheme didn't work," he said to me. "Ah had really hoped to get into public service."

"Belton," I said, as we shook hands, "you're *in* public service."

"Come see us again, now that you know the way."

The Grand Mercedes rolled back toward New York at an illegal eighty miles an hour, its antiradar device scanning ahead, its split rear axle absorbing all the bumps, smoothing out everything but my basic problem. I felt low and tense about not having a candidate, but, on the other hand, Victoria Woodhill was close and fragrant and warm.

"How come the Christians started a religion based on not doing what everybody likes to do best?" she wondered aloud.

"Search me," I said.

"And how come it's lasted for two thousand years?"

"Search me," I said.

"Just think—twenty centuries of wanting to do it and not doing it."

"Let's not talk religion, Victoria." I drew her close, slipping my hands gently beneath her minimal dress. "Lift the brushed aluminum panel in your arm rest, and press the lighted green button."

"What for?"

"You'll see."

I quickly learned, first from my left hand and then from my right, that Victoria had absolutely nothing on at all under the vermilion suede.

"Press the button," I said. My breath was starting to come just a shade faster, and I figured that Victoria would be delighted when the push of the green button converted the rear compartment of the Mercedes into something most unusual. But she did not press it. Her eyes were looking at me in the dim interior. They were luminous, but now serious. No light of fun, no smoky sex. No hell-raising.

"Tom, where are you going to find a candidate?"

"Somewhere in New Jersey," I said. "Sometime tomorrow before four o'clock. But I can't find one tonight, baby, so press the button."

"Don't you have any idea at all who it is?"

"I know exactly who it is."

"Then tell me, and I'll press the button." Her slim finger was poised above it.

"The perfect candidate is a man. The Franklin D. Roosevelt of New Jersey."

"Is that all?"

"Hell, no, Victoria." I freed my hands for a moment to count off the ideal qualifications. "First, Mr. Perfect is a Protestant who was born in an old, colonial New Jersey town. Second, his birthplace must still be standing so it can be turned into a museum in case he goes on to the presidency. Third, Mr. Perfect was educated in the New Jersey public schools, then entered Rutgers after fighting the last six weeks of World War Two at Fort Dix. Fourth, he plays golf or tennis or something well enough to make a TV spot that proves he's got vigor. Fifth, he's married to a Jewish girl from Oregon, a Miss America runner-up, an ecology buff, and a friend of Gloria Steinem. Sixth, he's a Moose or an Elk. Seventh, he's got a profile that will look good on a coin—"

"You don't need all that jive," said Victoria calmly. "And you don't need a Mr. Perfect. Know what you need?"

"What?"

"All you really need is another man named Quimby."

The sentence was a sledgehammer. It stunned me. I caught my breath in admiration, just as I had when Victoria had spoken that other pithy sentence: "Fuck me, Tom."

It was one of those classic ideas that make everything fall instantly into place and even change the course of history. It was Newton under the apple tree. It was the Wright Brothers starting their engine at Kitty Hawk. It was Einstein writing to tell Roosevelt that we ought to make ourselves "an atomic device." Of course! Another man named Quimby would *do* it! It was the best-known name in New Jersey, and such was the moribund level of political concern in the state that thousands of voters would never even notice that it was another guy running. The entire campaign could take off as planned—instantly.

We would not have to change the blue bumper stickers with the sharp red letters that had already appeared on thousands of cars all across the state saying: VOTE FOR QUIMBY.

And best of all, from the standpoint of *my* campaign, another man named Quimby would preserve the vital alliteration that I was counting on to sweep myself into office. That had been the ridgepole of my original house of cards, and now I tipped my hand to Victoria about it.

"We'll get a Quimby, Victoria! First thing in the morning, we'll get one. And after another visit to Four Star Printing, I'll be on the ballot right beneath him, *exactly* where I belong."

"Right on—way to go!"

"Then you know what happens? The night before the election, hundreds of volunteers are going to fan out all across New Jersey from the local Quimby headquarters."

"What for?"

"Each time they find a car with a bumper that says VOTE FOR QUIMBY, they'll stick on one of *my* bumper stickers. They're being printed on the Coast tonight. My sticker will be placed against the right edge of the Quimby sticker so the final result looks like one long red-and-blue sticker, saying: VOTE FOR QUIMBY—AND QUICK!"

"Classy," said Victoria. "But if you're going that route, why did you pass up billboards? You could reserve a thousand side-by-side billboards everywhere in the state, and do exactly the same thing with the same timing."

It was another damned sledgehammer. I struck myself directly on the forehead with my open palm, the way that the middle stooge of the Three Stooges used to do.

"Jesus H. Sweet Christ!" I exploded. "Why didn't I think of that?"

"I don't know. You're supposed to be the political wizard."

I held her close with a new note of appreciation.

"Stick around, Victoria. It's going to be a great campaign. And I have a strong feeling that we can use you."

"I'm here," she said. "And available."

It was remarkable, unprecedented, neat. My obsession, my naked dancer in the subway, my perfectly formed bronze woman with the cone of black hair and the dress with naught beneath it—this kid suddenly turns out to have as much political savvy as the late, legendary mayor of Chicago. Boss!

"Shall I press the green button?" she asked.

"Not now," I said. "We've got to stop in Newark for coffee and start looking up Quimbys in the phone book."

CHAPTER 13

AT NOON the next day, four hours before the filing deadline, I drove into the little coastal resort town of Misty Harbor, New Jersey. On Dingle Street, my driver stopped in front of a white clapboard house. At the curb was a neat metal sign: MARTIN J. QUIMBY, A.S.C.E. This would be the ninth Quimby I had seen. The first eight were not of the right calibre.

I walked up the path toward the house. Instead of a garden, the house was entirely surrounded by a bed of flat stones—each about the size of a silver dollar. I remembered from the Occupation days that Japan was full of stone gardens like this, but I'd never before seen one in the U.S.A. On the side of the house, a little bronze plaque said that this was the PAOLA QUIMBY MEMORIAL ROCK GARDEN. There was something austere about the setting. I wondered if the occupant would be that way, too. He was not.

The door was opened by a wiry little man whose eyes glinted bright behind rimless glasses. He wore a red wool shirt and was carrying a surf-casting rod.

"Mr. Quimby?"

"I'll be damned," he said, sizing me up. "JFK as a door-to-door salesman!" He laughed at his own line. "Yes, I'm Quimby. Come in."

He held open the door, and I walked into the living room, which was heavy and Italianate and out of the thirties. A Spartan table radio, shaped like a gothic arch, stood on a table, playing "For All We Know."

"My name is Thomas J.—"

He was still at the door, sizing up the Grand Mercedes.

"You come in that car?"

"Yes, I did."

"What is it?"

"A Mercedes-Benz."

"What's the roof made of? Hammered pewter?"

"No. Brushed aluminum."

"Most garish damned car I ever saw in my life. You must be with the Sells Floto Circus or something."

"Not exactly. You see, I'm a—"

"What'd you say your name was?"

"Quick. Tom Quick."

"You realize, Quick, that Americans, with five percent of the world's population, consume forty percent of the planet's raw materials? With men like you in your Mercedes-Benz right out in the lead."

"Mr. Quimby, I didn't come here to have you attack me."

He broke into his sharp laugh.

"Hell, that's right. What *did* you come for?"

"To see if you'd like to run for the governorship of New Jersey."

"Me? The governor?"

"Right."

"That's the damndest thing I ever heard of." He smiled, seeming to enjoy the idea. "Why me?"

"We need another Quimby to take the place of the late governor. And we don't want to fracture the rhythm of the campaign with a new name."

"What if I come up with policies that are different from his?"

"Actually, he had so *few* policies," I said, "that that won't be a problem."

Quimby cocked a skeptical eye at me.

"Listen, Quick, is this an attempt to deceive the voters of New Jersey?"

"No. It's an attempt to use the lassitude of the voters to the eventual advantage of the Democratic party. But we'll run you as an Independent. And we'll tell the precise truth about you to anybody who wants to listen. And if you win, you'll be on your own."

"Damn!" Quimby's eyes twinkled behind the glasses. He took an almost boyish delight in the moment. "I'll do it, Quick! I'll *do* it!"

"One question," I said. "Are you clean?"

"Plenty clean enough to be the governor of New Jersey."

On the emphatic words, he made a kind of chopping gesture with his right hand—the exact same thing that Teddy Roosevelt and Truman and JFK used to do. I seemed to be on the right track.

"You don't have some hidden problem like Agnew or Eagleton or Beltramo?" I asked. "Something that could blow the whole campaign out of the water?"

"Not a damned thing." He laughed again, with obvious anticipation. "It'll be a real kick in the ass to run for public office, Quick. I've been hollering at politicians on television for thirty years. Now people will have a chance to holler at me! You want a cup of coffee?"

"Not now, thanks. It's time for action. I've got to get you over to Trenton and sign you up with Mrs. Potter."

"What about the authentic signatures of two hundred New Jersey citizens who want me to run?"

"Just give me your Christmas card list, and my staff will have the signatures by four o'clock."

"Fine. I'll break down my fishing rod, and we'll crank up the campaign."

Mr. Quimby sat back expansively on the cranberry upholstery of the big back seat, looking over the interior of the Mercedes.

"This thing paid for?"

"Yes, it is."

"How much did it cost, Quick?"

"A little over thirty thousand."

"Does it guzzle gas?"

"Of course not. It's a Mercedes."

"You must do pretty well."

"Pretty well," I agreed. "How about a cigar?"

He looked the cigar over carefully.

"Skinniest damned cigar I ever saw," he observed.

"I get them from Paraguay," I said. "I did a campaign down there last year."

"Too rich for my taste, Quick. I'll just have a Hav-a-Tampa." He took one from his pocket and peeled off the cellophane.

We lit up. A wreath of smoke surrounded his head. He sat there relaxed, quite unfazed by the turn that his life had taken.

"Where'd you find me, Quick?"

"In a computer profile of New Jersey Quimbys. But I need a lot more background on you, Martin. I want to get out a bright, three-color brochure even ahead of the radio and TV stuff."

I reached forward to punch up the cassette recorder built into the same panel as the TV set.

"Let's see now—you're sixty-five—you're a retired civil engineer—"

"That's right. My whole career was spent in the City Engineer's Office of Brandenburg, New Jersey. I built bridges, sewers, streets, pedestrian overpasses—everything."

"Those'll be good for TV spots. The monuments you built."

"They're modest monuments," said Quimby. "So don't overdo it."

"Don't worry. We'll strike the right note."

"Many of the contractors were crooks, of course, so I spent a lot of time with them in bars, urging them to be honest."

"We can make some nice radio spots about that."

"I could never get through to them *ethically*, of course, but I learned how to scare them into compliance."

"How?"

"I'd explain to them that in civil engineering, it's easy to tell if you've done the right thing or not. It's not like psychiatry or soybean futures. You build a lousy bridge and you know what happens? The goddamned thing falls down. Then the state sues, and you can even go to the pen on a negligent homicide rap." He chuckled. "I used to scare the shit out of them."

"You commuted to Brandenburg all those years?"

"Oh, no. Five years ago, I retired, and that's when we moved to Misty Harbor. But that little house had been our family's weekend place for years. I remember I heard Roosevelt's first fireside chat there on the Spartan. Unhappily, the year after I retired, my wife Paola—an Italian gem I met one summer evening on a tour of the Statue of Liberty—died." Quimby paused, looking for a long time at the passing landscape. "I missed Paola. I still do. She was one of the most ardent women of the first half of this century, Quick. And a Wilsonian Democrat, to boot. Did you notice the stone garden?"

"Yes. And the plaque, too."

"When Paola was alive, our house was surrounded by a real garden! It was magnificent. She spent her life growing and tending the flowers, and she had the touch. The house was always full of fresh flowers everywhere—just like the White House when you take the tour." He paused again.

It was clear that the memory was strong. "But after—after she was gone, I found that I couldn't stand all the farting around that you have to do to keep a garden going. You ever garden, Quick?"

"No. I was raised on East Eighty-third Street."

"Well, the damned weeds—the weeds are always right there *just* beneath the surface, ready to spring up and defeat you. Like ignorant people, they're *everywhere*. So when the gardener dies, the garden dies, too. I found that out. Rather than let it run down, I sent to Japan for a carload of those flat stones to spread around. That way, I get plenty of time to fish, and there's also a nice memorial to Paola. And—"

He turned to me with a squint and a little shrug. "Well, that's it, Quick. The story of my life. I'm not sure there's enough for a three-color brochure."

"Children? Grandchildren?"

"One daughter. One grandson. Nice kid. He's eleven. They live down in Flugel County."

"You're a Wilsonian Democrat, too?"

"I was. I became a Democrat the night that Roosevelt nominated Al Smith. I was nine years old. But after the New Deal, the Democrats ran out of ideas."

"I'm not so sure I agree with that."

"Listen. The last decent idea they had was when FDR sat on the fantail of that destroyer in the Black Sea and told King Ibn Saud that since the water table of the Sahara was only twenty-five feet below the surface we could send over a couple of thousand Worthington pumps and make the desert bloom like a rose. Just like we'd done in the Imperial Valley."

"I never knew he said that."

"He did. And let me tell you, the world would have turned out a lot better today if Harry Hopkins had followed up on the promise."

"But Hopkins was sick with an ulcer."

"Goddamn it, Quick, that's no excuse!" Quimby chopped at the upholstery as though the matter had happened yesterday. "A man as smart as Hopkins should have followed up, no matter what. Public men are pivotal people, and sick or well, they can't just sit there with the pivot up their ass, doing *nothing*!"

"I'm glad you're here, sir," said Mrs. Penelope Potter to Quimby after he had signed the Register of Candidates. "We need a man in the State House who does not suffer fools gladly, who knows how to give short shrift, and who can keep his nose clean."

"Thank you, Mrs. Potter. I hope I can measure up to your sensible expectations."

I took the candidate across the street to the Acme Bar and Grill to toast our success.

"To a generally constructive future!" said Quimby, clinking his stein of Michelob against my Manhattan. I want you to know that I expect to win, Quick. But win or lose, I'm going to have a *pisswhacker* of a time!"

He drained half the stein joyfully.

"Martin," I said, after a pause, "you haven't asked me what I'm doing in this."

"It'll come out," he said with an easy shrug. "Everything comes out in a bar."

"I'm one of America's leading political consultants, Martin. I want to consult your campaign."

"What the hell does that mean?"

"I was Horace Quimby's consultant. By combining his name and his momentum with your dynamic presence, we'll sweep the state. Inside four years, I can make you a pivotal Democrat widely mentioned for higher office."

"A political consultant, eh?" He had turned tentative

now. "Is that a recognized trade or profession—like brain surgery, say?"

"It's not as structured as brain surgery. But we do have a trade association, and we're working on an international code of ethics, and within a year, we'll—"

"What percentage of the people you've worked for got elected?" he asked, his head cocked sharply to one side.

"Sixty-one percent."

"That's a better survival rate than in brain surgery," he said. "But are you really legit, or are you just farting around on the fringes of life, trying to make a buck?"

"Absolutely legit, Martin," I said, handing him a Polcon, Inc. card. "My firm is in the Yellow Pages."

"A whore can get in the Yellow Pages," said Quimby. "How do you work?"

"Political consulting is a small but growing industry," I explained. "It had its roots in the population explosion, the growth of television, the easy money of the early seventies, the precision of the computer, the speed of the jet plane, the reduction of long-distance telephone rates, and the erosion of traditional political party structures. Plus, of course, the longtime American faith in experts."

"Must be an awful lot of horseshit in it," he said quietly.

"There is," I agreed. "But I cut through it. I don't build on it."

"Okay. Cut through some."

"The whole process is in my Basic Candidate Information Kit," I said. "I've got a copy here for you. Polcon, Inc. gives each candidate a sales package of calibrated emotional, ideological, and symbolic materials. It's a package that will make you plausible. It's a package that is helping to shape the new politics all across America."

"Say something concrete," said Quimby.

"Okay. I'll take complete control of your campaign and

of you. I'll have complete access to you, day and night. Your speeches, your television and radio, your state fair and supermarket appearances—the whole tone and torque of the campaign will be set by Polcon, Inc. By me."

"I won't buy that. I've never given complete control of me to any man—or woman. Not even Paola."

"There's so little time, Martin. We can't vacillate on this for more than the next ten minutes."

"I'm not vacillating. I'm telling you. You've got to come up with something better than complete control."

"Okay—money. Polcon will provide you with two hundred and fifty thousand dollars to make the race."

"Strictly aboveboard?"

"Strictly."

"How will you get it?"

"There's close to half a million in the Horace J. Quimby Campaign account. Al Divver, the late Governor's driver, knows all the thousand-dollar donors personally. He'll phone them and ask them to transfer their contribution to you."

"Suppose they don't like me?"

"Al won't put it on that basis. He'll tell them to think of it as a memorial to their old friend."

"This Divver sounds like a valuable man."

"He is. I'm trying to persuade him to drive for you, too."

"Okay, you're on," said Quimby, suddenly beaming. We shook hands on it. "Where are the Quimby headquarters?"

"You'll have two. One in Newark. One in Trenton. They open tomorrow."

"And my announcement speech?"

"In Military Park—in Newark—the next morning."

"I'll start writing it tonight."

"You'll need a speechwriter."

"Nonsense."

"Remember to keep it short. If you keep the announcement under one minute, then the networks have to run the whole thing. If they run longer, then they edit the film—and *they* control what you say on TV."

"I'll try to keep it short. I'll also have another beer."

I ordered another round and then laid the next point on him immediately.

"Martin, you have to know right up front that I'm planning to become the Lieutenant Governor in this election, riding in quietly on your coattails."

"Strictly aboveboard?" He was looking at me with the cocked eyebrow.

"Not strictly."

"You're sure you're not setting me up for a Haldeman slash Ehrlichman?"

"Not at all. No matter what happens, it can't touch you."

"I appreciate your honesty in bringing up something dishonest. But I'm going to keep an eye on you."

"All you have to do is trust me."

"I trust you because I need you. But you'll bear watching. You see, Quick, the only thing tougher than keeping a governor honest is keeping the people around him honest. The toadies, the minions, the sycophants, the administrative assistants—they all want to keep kissing the governor's ass on his way to the presidency. They'll do *anything* to win his favor. They bear watching. You ever heard of Eurydice?"

"Who?"

"Eurydice. As the grandmother of Aristotle's most famous pupil, Alexander the Great, she was a maker and breaker of political rulers."

"I've never heard of her," I said.

"Eurydice was charged with having assassinated her king-husband, Amyntas, to be free to frolic with her son-in-law, Ptolemy, and then with assassinating her son-king, Alexander, so that she and her son-in-law-lover-consort could seize the throne."

On the word "seize," he made the chopping gesture.

"What's this got to do with me?" I asked.

"Eurydice wasn't in the Yellow Pages," said Martin Quimby, "but I see now that she was one of the world's very first political consultants. She bore watching."

CHAPTER 14

NOTHING, with the possible exception of an orgasm, is more temporary than the headquarters of a political campaign. The carpet, left over from a previously defunct office, has dirty pathways worn around vanished filing cabinets. The rented furniture does not match. The desk drawers stick. The identical poster-sized picture of the smiling candidate is taped up everywhere, reminding the volunteers of what he looks like and covering holes in the plaster.

Behind the temporary desks sit temporary people, each using the campaign to pursue his or her own private dream of a pivotal place in American politics. And right up to the very night of the election, the place is full of telephone men constantly rigging, installing, checking, and testing the temporary lines—trying to achieve that ideal situation in which everybody in the campaign can be in instant, constant touch with everybody else. They never make it.

Rocky Bettenhauser, economizing after the death of Horace J. Quimby, cancelled the rent on the headquarters I'd rented in the Prudential Building. Now, overnight, I'd had to find another place. What I found was a former J-Mart store on Bagley Avenue in Newark. The J-Mart people had left in disarray two days before, leaving all their store fixtures intact for the auctioneer. We had no pictures of the new Quimby to catch the eye, so there was nothing to catch the eye but placards in slip-in metal frames on empty counters, pointing out Today's Great Unadvertised Bargains in Spandex bras, power drills, pink plastic curlers, epoxy glue, and swivel bar stools.

I'd summoned my hired experts to meet the candidate and set the course of the campaign. Now, at 9:00 A.M., they were huddled over in one corner of this great rectangular cavern—next to the water cooler and the styrofoam cups and the coffee urn and the bottle of Jack Daniels. I was proud of them. Within twenty-four hours, they had arrived, some from across the Hudson River, others from across the world.

From Manhattan had come the film producer, the Cuban film editor, the radio producer, a world-famous time-buyer, a graphics designer for the logo, a politico-theatrical tailor who had worked for both Sinatra and George Pitt, a makeup girl, a hair expert, a black voice-and-diction coach, and two associates from Retrieval Associates, Inc., a computer firm that dealt only in software.

From Budapest had come my temperamental Hungarian lighting man. (According to *Time*, he had just lit an Italian Communist so imposingly in Milan that the man had actually become the Premier of Italy.) Gus Schmiddle, Vice-President of Schmiddle Litho., Inc., was on hand from Oakland, California. And the captain of the Goodyear blimp had driven in from the hangar at Lakehurst, New Jersey.

At nine-fifteen, Al Divver would arrive from Misty Harbor, driving the candidate. He had accepted the job after a midnight meeting with Quimby. Al liked the candidate, but he was not enthusiastic about driving Quimby's Toyota Corolla. There was nothing at all wrong with the Toyota, he explained to me on the phone. It was just that he liked heavy vehicles. His own car was a restored Pierce Arrow. All his political driving over the years had been behind the wheels of great black Cadillac limousines. Earlier, during World War II, Al had driven Sherman tanks.

On the dot at nine-fifteen, I went outside to greet them. I knew that Al would not be late. One of his great campaigning assets was his intense concern with keeping the candidate on schedule. As I got to the curb, the Toyota was just pulling up. Quimby thanked Al for the ride, then popped out of the car with a smile.

" 'Morning, Governor," I said.

"Anything you say, Quick," he replied, touching two fingers to his hat brim in a little salute. "Let's go."

He moved quickly, one step ahead of Divver and myself, into the headquarters. He was leading the parade, as a natural candidate always does. This was good. I knew then that even though Martin Quimby was rather short, he would never get lost in a crowd.

Then he did something else reassuring. Walking down the wide store aisle, he slipped off his overcoat without breaking his stride and handed it, along with his hat, to the nearest person—Divver. Al looked at me, nodding approval. In politics, as in the theater, there are some things that cannot be taught—like getting rid of the overcoat without breaking the rhythm of the developing scene. Warren G. Harding, though deficient in many other respects, was unbeatable in this event.

I introduced the candidate to the experts. Quimby gracefully shook hands with everybody, looking them up and down through the bottom of his bifocals, getting the names exactly right—another good sign. Then they pulled their chairs into a loose circle to hear his opening remarks. There were none.

"We won't bother with any horseshit from me," he said bluntly. "Not at this point, anyway. I'm an instant candidate, as you know, but my candidacy is in no way uncertain or halfhearted or dim-witted. I'm running out of a sense of duty, of hope, and of fun. I expect to win. But win or lose, I'm going to have a *pisswhacker* of a time! And I am now ready for your recommendations."

The experts, a generally loquacious bunch, were caught off balance. I was myself. There were several seconds of silence and a few shifting chairs.

"I don't want to hear that you haven't had enough time to study the situation," Quimby warned them. "There's never enough time to study *anything* in America. Why, the whole New Deal was put together one weekend out at Herbert Bayard Swope's place at Sands Point. That's the kind of speed we want here! So let me have some quick reactions. Hard reactions. Come on—come on—"

Sam Scalese, the small, swarthy showbiz tailor, stood up. His impeccably creased chocolate suit with the white piping followed every move and gesture with unwrinkled ease. The most impressive thing about Sam was always his suit.

"You're not fat, Mr. Quimby," he said, "but you've got a slight potbelly, and a Scalese suit is not cut to drape over a pot."

"That's not enough to take me out of the race," said Quimby.

"No, but I wanted to warn you that you'll have to wear a Mandate girdle while out campaigning. Absolutely necessary."

"How about if I campaigned in my own suit?" asked Quimby, turning to me.

"It'll never work, Martin," I said. "You'll be going up against a Republican. Regardless of his political qualifications, he'll be impeccable. They always are on the state level."

"And your suit," said Scalese, "is an antique."

"But *very* comfortable," Quimby shot back defensively,

hunching the grey herringbone fabric up and down a couple of times with his shoulders. "And it *fits* me. It even fits my pot."

"It fits because the cloth is tired," said Scalese. He stepped forward, pinching the fabric of the sleeve. It stayed wrinkled. "See? The fabric is pooped. Dead. You need a springy new blue worsted with a little drift toward Cardin."

"Toward whom?"

"Pierre Cardin. He's a Frenchman. I'll give you a pinch in the waist an' a little graceful flare in the cuffless pants. Sort of bring you up to date."

"Mr. Scalese," said Quimby, "I've watched these middle-aged politicians on television, frantically trying to follow the whims of fashion. And I could never see the point of putting a personally conservative man like Ed Muskie into a pinch-waisted glen-plaid suit with wide lapels and two vents in the back. He's clearly a single-vent man."

"But *you* could carry it off, Martin," I suggested. "You're zippier than Muskie."

"I don't know," said Quimby, shaking his head, thinking about it for a moment. "A man with rimless bifocal glasses and a flare in the pants?"

"I was also going to recommend that the rimless glasses go," said Scalese.

"You're the optometrist, too?" asked Quimby.

"Sam here," I explained, "has been brought in to study your *entire* visual impact, Martin. He's an expert in coloration, harmony, modernity, drape, body language—the total impression a man makes when he steps out in front of five thousand people to earnestly solicit their vote."

"Now *there's* something I can use," said Quimby.

"What?"

"That phrase. I like it. I'll use it. 'Ladies and gentlemen, I earnestly solicit your vote.' "

"We haven't got much time," said Scalese, a shade edgy

now. "How about a tan gabardine suit with a vest, and contact lenses?"

"Nothing doing," said Quimby. "I've worn glasses since I was ten. I'm not going into contact lenses now."

The Hungarian lighting man interrupted to say in a heavy Hungarian accent that contact lenses give you excellent peripheral vision, which is always useful in an angry crowd.

"There's something else to consider," I added. "Rimless glasses are damn difficult to deal with when they come to make a statue of you. Teddy Roosevelt and Wilson and Truman—they all had a problem with that."

Quimby burst into a laugh of great delight.

"I'll be damned, Quick. You *do* look out for your clients! I'm not even elected, and you're already planning to make me into a goddam statue!"

"Every candidate has a political progression deep in his heart," I said. "At Polcon, we make it quite specific. Take your case. First, you get elected statewide. Then you move to Washington as a New Jersey senator. From there to the vice-presidency, and from there to the presidency. Then comes a statue in Trenton and another one in some Third World country where you've shored up the shaky, right-wing government with half a billion dollars spent under the Quimby Doctrine. In that country, they'll also commission a statue, and you will appear on a large golden coin. Finally, as time goes by and you're perceived as a true statesman, your face will appear on a large-denomination American bill."

"Remarkable," said Quimby, not rejecting any of it. "Remarkable."

"I like my candidates to know where they're going, Martin, so they can solve the rimless-glasses problem early."

"How about a blue gabardine three-piece suit and light-sensitive aviator glasses?" asked Scalese, persistent.

"That's brilliant PR, Sam," I replied. "Martin, you'll turn out to be a mixture of Gary Hart and Carmine de Sapio. Hopeful youth and hard-nosed professionalism—all in one Polcon package."

"All right," said Quimby decisively, making the chop. "I'll buy it. With one proviso. Both suit and glasses have got to be ready before my announcement speech tomorrow. I want my appearance to be consistent."

"Can do," said Scalese, stepping forward with a tape measure to take Quimby's size. His assistant was there to record the measurements as Scalese spoke them.

"If we're through with dress, may we get on to *hair*?"

A handsome, fragile young man stood up and came toward the candidate, then circled him as he talked, focussing on Quimby's head.

"I'm due for a trim next week," said Quimby.

"Neck, fourteen," said Scalese.

"A trim, sir, will *not* do it," said the young man."I mean —I mean something *drastic* has to be done about that *hair*."

The young man was Roger Frangipani, an Hawaiian hairdresser. In earlier times, before everyone in America got so touchy, Roger Frangipani would have been described simply as a fag. But in the sensitized sixties, it became clear to many people—mostly do-gooder Democrats—that large groups of Americans had fallen into the bad habit of slurring, stereotyping, and shitting (so to speak) on other large groups of Americans. This was deemed destructive to the development of a true democratic society, and so committees were formed to defend everybody's right to continuous public admiration. Everybody wanted to be seen in a warm Norman Rockwell painting on the cover of *The Saturday Evening Post*. Everybody—not only black Americans—wanted to be beautiful. Magazines got published, for example, describing what terrific people Italians were.

Roger Frangipani and his friends were the beneficiaries

of this new, uneasy civility. Now that they had organized into the National Gay Community, now that they had glossy magazines and network clout, now that everybody in the country had come to understand Roger's destructive early relationship with his powerful mother and his utter reliability as a baby sitter or camp counselor or corporate attorney, it had become inappropriate to describe him publicly in sexual terms at all. And yet the word "fag" did not disappear entirely. It simply took its place—along with those other historic designations like "kike," "wop," "spick," "sheeny," and "coon"—in the lexicon of private American fury.

Roger kept circling Martin Quimby as though the candidate were a mannikin in a window. Quimby, who had not dealt knowingly with people like this in his civil engineering days, started to revolve warily, keeping an eye on Roger. It was kind of a ballet.

"Your hair—your hair—" said Roger, searching for an apt phrase.

"Please stand still, Mr. Quimby," said Scalese, who was trying to measure his inseam.

"Your hair is the unkempt hair of a *fisherman,*" said Roger.

"Watch it, Frangipani," retorted Quimby. "I *am* a fisherman."

"Inseam, twenty-nine," said Scalese.

"And I don't mind comments about the suit or the glasses," Quimby went on, "but my hair is *me*, for Christ's sake!"

"Well, we certainly can't grow it out in the back before tomorrow," said Roger. "Or do any *real* shaping. And the implants will have to wait until after the election."

"*Implants?*" echoed Quimby. "What the hell are you talking about?"

"It's a beautiful process," said Roger. "Only *slightly* painful. But the only thing that can save you for tomorrow is a wig."

"I reject the implants, and I reject the wig. You'll bear watching, Frangipani."

"Then what in heaven's name can we *do*?" asked Roger, turning to me.

"When I get up in the morning, I'll comb it," said Quimby, running his hand through his sparse gray hair. "That's what we'll do."

"It'll *never* work," said Frangipani, throwing up his hands and sitting down with a sigh of rejection.

"Sleeve, thirty-three," said Scalese.

Quimby was now looking at me skeptically.

"Is hair this important to the democratic process?" he asked me.

"Everything is important, Martin. Three governors and a senator won in 1980 on hair alone. Two of them were using hair to cover hearing aids."

"I'll be damned," said Quimby.

"And my first recommendation when I took on the late Governor Quimby was that he lose weight and have plastic surgery to remove the droops from his eyelids. They made him look bored."

"He *was* bored," said Quimby.

"That's true, but it's the job of a political consultant to show the candidate in his best light. So Polcon covers all bases. Nothing is left to chance. And that's why a person like Benson McClure is with us today."

Benson stood up, skinny and intense.

"Benson here knows more about recorded animal and human sounds than any man in the Western Hemisphere. His book, *The Tin Ear*, is a landmark in human communications. Benson—"

"I hope, sir, that you'll be able to set aside considerable time to work in my area of the campaign," said McClure melodiously.

"I'll do my best," said Quimby.

"I don't want to demean the value of any of my colleagues, but the fact is that I can bring your voice across to the people of New Jersey in a unique and compelling way. Your *larynx* is probably your biggest asset in this campaign, and I am confident that I can help people perceive you through it. The task: to put the sounds you make into a time frame. For time and sound, you see, can combine in an endless number of meaningful forms. This new vision of time-cum-sound is one of the most important concepts on the Spaceship Earth. It is the spiritual epoxy that holds the Global Village together."

"What's your conclusion, Mr. McClure?"

"That we should do a package of one-minute radio spots."

"I'll buy that," said Quimby. "And what about television? I assume we're going to do a slew of TV spots."

Alexander B. Christian stood up. He was a fat man who ran a brilliant film company from a crummy loft on West 46th Street, and he was considered to be one of America's leading producers of thoughtful, understated motion pictures—second only, perhaps, to Charles Guggenheim.

Christian's most famous film, the Oscar-winning *Chickadee* (1968), was often confused with the earlier W. C. Fields comedy, *My Little Chickadee* (1939). *Chickadee* was a delicate *cinema verité* depiction of how a handful of crumbs thrown to a hungry chickadee in Maine brought newfound happiness to a Yankee family of five—three of whom were crippled and blind. Adapted from a paean in the *Reader's Digest*, it was perhaps the most excruciatingly sensitive film ever made in America.

Everything about Alexander B. Christian appeared loud

and forceful. His blazing eyes. His upthrust red hair. His vivid green polyester blazer with buttons of shiny brass. But when he opened his mouth, his voice came out calm and circumspect, clashing with everything else about his appearance. No one I'd ever worked with (with the possible exception of Douglas MacArthur) was more adept at bringing the diverse threads of a meeting together with apparent innocence to produce the exact result that he wanted.

"I hope we can do some natural TV, Mr. Christian," said Quimby, growing enthusiastic. "I'd like you to show me to the people as I really am. Fishing on the beach, standing before Paola's plaque, painting my house, riding in my hot-air balloon—but, even in these moments, concerned about the difficult questions that face New Jersey."

"The beach is out, Martin," I interrupted. "The Kennedys ran America's beaches into the ground politically. And the balloon is out, too."

"But I own the most handsome hot-air balloon in New Jersey! It's my hobby—wafting. And she looks beautiful wafting over the Poconos in the early autumn sunlight."

"Martin, believe me," I said. "There are certain key words in politics. You cannot afford to be associated in the public mind with the concept of hot air. If we do a TV spot with you wafting—"

"The argument is moot," said A. B. Christian quietly. "I am recommending that we use *no* television in this campaign. I'll lose money, but nevertheless, that is what I recommend."

"But why?" asked Quimby. "I had it figured that film would be the only way we could reveal some of my best qualities."

"That's true," said Christian. "But unfortunately, there are no television stations in New Jersey. Our material would have to be beamed out of Manhattan or Philadelphia. No matter how skillfully we might reveal you, sir, eighty-eight percent of our audience could not vote for you. They don't live in New Jersey. Why waste the money?"

"But how will we reach the broad spectrum of New Jersey voters?" I asked.

"Direct mail," said Christian. "I recommend computerized, personalized, direct mail. Seemingly personal letters. Besides being useful, they're the latest political fashion."

"But there's a literacy problem, Alexander," I objected. "Many people here can grasp a TV spot better than a letter."

"I'll make the spots if you like," said Christian, shrugging. "But that's my recommendation. And my second recommendation is that Mr. Quimby's face not appear in *any* of our material, no matter what the medium."

"Wait a minute," said Quimby. "Shouldn't the people know what I look like?"

"It would only confuse them," said the television expert. "You have the most famous last name in New Jersey. I recommend that we put your face aside as we concentrate on your name and on the basic thrust of the campaign."

"Well, I'm glad we *got* to that," said Quimby. "Here we are, farting around about my suit and my hair and my balloon and my picture, and *nobody* has mentioned the basic thrust of the campaign."

There was a silence. Everybody turned to look at me. I hadn't had the time to think up a basic thrust, but I plunged ahead anyhow. Something would develop.

"As we move into action," I said, "I think we might profitably take a look at the 1966 Pennsylvania primary, when Milton Shapp ran for the first time for governor. That campaign used something that I think we can use, too."

I paused to light a cigar.

"The Shapp campaign used *wit*," I went on. "Given Mr. Quimby's particular personality, I think we can use wit to great advantage."

The experts nodded. This sounded more like it. Quimby nodded, but his face was noncommittal.

"I recommend that we bring in the chap who wrote those Shapp '66 radio spots. He was brilliant. He hit just the right note. One of his spots, for example, used the entire minute to extoll the virtues of the first governor of Pennsylvania. And it concluded with: 'If you liked William Penn, you'll *love* Milt Shapp!' "

Quimby laughed his loud laugh. He loved it. But suddenly his face went serious again.

"Wait a minute," he said. "Shapp lost that election."

"That's the one thing we'll do differently, Martin," I said. "We'll win."

"I still don't see the basic thrust, Quick," he said. "What the hell *is* it?"

He had me. I took a deep breath and began the next sentence without even knowing what the verb would be.

"Martin, let me put it this way. In order for a campaign to successfully interface with the people—"

"I wonder if I might interrupt," said a fluid woman's voice from the rear of the group. I had not seen Victoria come in, but there she was, standing tall and easy and luminous in a chrome yellow suede Sant 'Angelo safari suit with horn buttons. The entire room was electrified. Once again, her presence had taken me off the hook. Quimby got up, inadvertently knocking over his chair.

"And who is this young lady?" he asked.

"Victoria Woodhill, may I present the candidate, Martin J. Quimby."

Quimby, still not knowing what to make of her, went slowly to greet her. I thought for a moment he was going to kiss her hand.

"Victoria here," I said, "is the Polcon consultant in the area of intuitive politics."

"Well, well, Quick," he said quietly, beaming at her

lovely face, continuing to shake her hand, "you really *have* covered all the bases. What were you going to say, my dear?"

"Tom Quick has told me about you, Mr. Quimby," she said. "And I sense that you're very combative at heart."

"That's true enough—true enough."

"When Tom outlines the thrust of the campaign for us, I suspect that your combativeness is going to be an important part of it."

"I'll buy that."

"But Tom tells me that most successful New Jersey political careers have been built on attacking the crookedness of the incumbent. You can't attack the incumbent, Mr. Quimby. He's dead."

"Please call me Martin."

"So the question is there from the jump—*who* or *what* can you attack?"

Quimby nodded. I would have interrupted, but I didn't have the answer to her question.

"Most candidates, Martin, take the easy way out," said Victoria. "They attack tax loopholes or nursing home mismanagement or the cost of meat or Arabs or shiftless welfare mothers."

"I've heard them," said Quimby.

"But as a new kind of candidate, you've got a chance to make a new kind of attack. One that could raise a little hell and shake the people up. Shake 'em *good*!"

Everybody was nodding yes, and there was a pause as we waited for the concluding sentence.

"In running for governor," suggested Victoria, "why don't you attack the people themselves?"

Across Quimby's shoulder I could see the fun-filled, hell-raising light in her eyes. It was another of Victoria's hammerblows. Stunning. The experts waited for the client's reaction, but it took only a second for Quimby to see the pristine beauty of it.

"Attack the people of New Jersey?" he asked, relishing the idea.

"The people," said Victoria. "The voters. I think it'd be a new wrinkle."

"A wrinkle?" echoed Quimby. "It'll be a *bombshell!*" He took Victoria by the arm and brought her back to the center of the group. "I'll be damned. *Brilliant!*"

"You can start by just telling them to look around and see what a mess they've made."

"*Good* start!" said Quimby, chopping. "Then I can attack their subtle racism, their frozen minds, their gloomy lethargy, their overblown expectations, their belief that the State of New Jersey is a governmental wet-nurse!"

"How about their greed?" she asked.

"By God, I almost forgot their greed! Why, the greed of the rich is even more virulent than that of the poor."

"That's how they *got* rich."

Quimby suddenly took Victoria's hands in his and pulled her down a bit so he could kiss her on the forehead.

"*That's* the campaign, Victoria! And I want you as my campaign manager."

I could see several problems looming with that.

"Hold it, Martin," I said. "Victoria has never managed a campaign before."

"And I've never run," he said. "But with an idea like this and all you experts to back us up, we can't miss!"

"But there are some things you've got to know about me first," said Victoria. "I'm not all that experienced in political—"

"Nonsense. Your intuition is brilliant. No politician has ever attacked the electorate. That's perfect!"

"I hate to sound too traditional, Martin," I interrupted. "But at some point along the line, you'll have to get the people *with* you, not against you."

"True," said Quimby. "But my first job is to come to the

attention of the sixty-four percent of the New Jersey voters who have never voted in their lives because they don't give a hoot in hell about the state that is their home. My second job is to point out that people *always* vote for their own short-term, two-bit comfort if nobody takes the time to tell them that deeper interests are at stake. My third job is to make clear what those deeper interests are."

"Too cerebral for New Jersey," I said. "You might get away with it in Massachusetts or Oregon, but—"

"Horseshit!" said Quimby. He turned quickly to Victoria to apologize for using the word.

"It's all right," she said. "I've heard of horseshit."

"Good! Now, listen, Quick; if I can do those three things, the people will take their thumbs out of their mouths and *vote* for me!"

"One can only hope so," I said.

"What about the slogan?" asked Quimby. "Who's the slogan expert? Stand up, please."

"There are no slogan experts, Martin," I explained. "The slogan always grows naturally out of the campaign themes once we're under way."

"No time for that," said Quimby. "I thought one up driving over here with Al Divver. Go ahead, Al. Try it out on them."

There was a slightly pained expression on Divver's face, but he went ahead.

"Mr. Quimby's slogan is 'Rectitude with Latitude!' "

"There's an exclamation mark after 'latitude,' " said Quimby proudly.

The experts sat in shocked silence and looked at me.

"Well, it's rhythmic, Martin," I said. "But there are a lot of people in New Jersey who will not know what rectitude is."

"How about latitude?" he asked.

"They'll mix it up with longitude."

"There's something else," said Gus Schmiddle. "The

words are too long for a good bumper sticker—much less a button. Too many hard consonants as well."

"It's a bad slogan, Martin," I said.

"I like it," he said testily. "I want to use it."

For a moment it looked as though the issue of control of the campaign would come to a head right there.

"But it has one big count against it, Martin," said Victoria, laying a hand gently on his forearm. " 'Rectitude with Latitude' sounds like a slogan for Preparation H."

Quimby stood silent for a moment, shaking his head in abject admiration.

"Victoria. I had not looked at it from that angle. You're absolutely right! And I'm *glad* you're aboard!"

He put an arm congenially about Victoria's waist and beamed up at her.

"The slogan should be simply Vote for Quimby," she said.

"I'll buy that," he said, continuing to beam.

CHAPTER 15

THE MEETING finally broke up at the end of the day, and I turned the experts loose to begin working their various magics. As I followed Quimby and Victoria toward the door, Al Divver cornered me in one corner of the big J-Mart store.

"I like him," said Al. "He's a good man, but he's got two things ass backwards."

"What, Al?" I listened carefully to this timeworn expert.

"First, he's got to get rid of the Toyota Corolla. It's not just my own feelings about its weight. I tried to convince him that *nobody* campaigns for governor in a small Jap car. I got nowhere."

"I'll see what I can do."

"An' the second thing is worse. The Machine would *never* let him get away with attackin' the people!"

"He's not the Machine candidate."

"He's still got to know what he kin get away with."

"But wait a minute, Al. When a candidate can contact the people directly instead of going through a dying political organization, he can—"

"The Machine ain't dyin', damn it," said Al, with his side-of-the-mouth emphasis. "Only the guys who write *The*

New York Times think so. An' they've thought so for forty years. I tell yuh, Quimby *can't* drift too far from what the people expect. If he does, they'll rise up an' smite him. Jesus, Tom, they did it all the time in the Bible."

"I may be able to get him to go for the bigger car," I said. "Come to dinner with us and we'll work on him."

"But what about attackin' the people?"

"He'll never change that. He loves it."

The four of us ate at Maaden's, a heavy old oaken German restaurant in Newark that had been Douglas MacArthur's favorite place for hassenpfeffer. Over the sauerbrauten, I brought up the matter of the car. Al joined in with enthusiasm as we tried to persuade Quimby that he should let us rent him a big black limousine for the campaign.

"The Toyota will do," he said. "I feel at ease, campaigning in my own car."

"The vehicle is not impressive enough for a big entrance," I said.

"You gotta arrive in a big car, crunchin' the gravel," explained Al Divver. "People notice you then. Some of them think you're *already* governor."

"That's not an impression I want to give," said Quimby. "Even as governor, my car should be related to my achievement. Tell you what! If I have two great years in office, then we can lease a limousine."

"But you need it *now*," I said. "For campaigning."

"Nonsense. Jerry Brown campaigned in California in his '65 Chevy coupe."

"That's different," said Divver. "He was a Jesuit."

"You've got to trust our judgment on this, Martin," I said. "The right vehicle has always been important in American politics. There's a handsome red-and-blue coach still parked in the carriage house down at Mount Vernon. George

Washington wrote a letter to Isaac Brinton in Boston telling of how important that coach was to his victory."

"What do you think, Victoria?" asked Quimby.

"My mind's on something else," she said. "Something we'll have to get straight tonight. But why not go along with Tom on these first decisions? He knows more than either of us."

Quimby sat there, squinting at me for several seconds across a piece of sauerbrauten.

"All right," he said decisively. "I'll go for the limousine. I want a Mercedes just like yours, Quick—except all black. No hammered-pewter roof."

Al and I exchanged another glance. He turned back to Quimby with a small sigh.

"Governor," he said, "there's still something you don't understand. The Mercedes, like the Toyota, is a foreign car."

"What about it?"

"People who ride in foreign cars never get elected."

"Never?"

"Never," I said. "I've got the Polcon figures on it. John Gilligan lost in Ohio once because his wife drove a Volvo. And years ago, Bruce Lyman Wilbur lost in California because he drove an Hispano Suiza. What you need is a big black Avis Cadillac."

"That coach of George Washington's," said Quimby, cocking an eye at me. "I'll bet anything it was built in England."

"As a matter of fact, it was built in Philadelphia," I said. "By two brothers—David and Francis Clark."

"All right," said Quimby. "A black Cadillac with no padding on the roof, and with one of these gooseneck lights, so I can work on my speeches in the back seat."

Al Divver excused himself immediately. Delighted with

the decision, he said he had to go rent a U-Haul A-bar. I was happy, too. When a candidate is going to be tough to control—as Quimby would be—you have to win at least a few of the early arguments or pretty soon he is asking himself just why he needs a consultant at all. I plunged ahead.

"Martin, you've also got to buy the idea of a speech-writer. I want to bring in that brilliant guy who did the Shapp spots. His speeches are as touching as the third act of *Our Town.*"

"Nothing doing! No speech-writers. The things that come out of a candidate's mouth must also come out of his head. He's got to speak his own stuff. Like the Pope does."

"The Pope has a speech-writer."

"Why would anyone who's infallible need a speech-writer?"

I decided not to press it.

When we came out of Maaden's, Al Divver and my driver had completed their handiwork. The Toyota was locked to the rear of my Mercedes with the U-Haul A-bar, ready to be towed back home.

"Now when you get to Misty Harbor, Governor," said Divver, "just have Tom Quick's driver put that Jap car into the garage for the rest of the campaign. When you win, we'll sell it! My brother-in-law can get you a good price."

"Thank you, Al," said Quimby, shaking hands. "And God bless you—and goodnight."

The Mercedes slid through the cool September night down the Jersey Turnpike, then swiftly made the crossover to the Garden State. Quimby and I lit cigars. I poured three Courvoisiers from the brushed-aluminum bar that stood between the two rear-facing seats. Victoria and I toasted Quimby's candidacy, and he toasted us. Then he excused himself and went back to writing his announcement speech, chuckling at the fact that he was really going to blast them. After writing at high speed for a while, he took off his glasses, sat back, rubbed his eyes, and cradled his head on the German orthopedic headrest.

"I have to admit it, Quick. These big cars ride smooth as a ferryboat." He touched the switch on the gooseneck lamp, flicking it off and on a couple of times. "And the gooseneck lamps make them seem very *political*."

Victoria sat forward as if to interrupt, but Quimby went on remembering.

"I was in Washington one winter night years ago," he said. "Must have been about ten o'clock out in front of the Treasury Building. And you know who rode by in a black limo, lit up by a gooseneck light, reading a thick sheaf of paper? Robert McNamara. The whole Vietnam war was falling on its ass at the time, and there was this brilliant hard-nosed man from the Ford Motor Company trying to keep it all together by making the paperwork right. I wonder what ever happened to him?"

Victoria sat forward again. Her classic face was creased with concern. The quicksilver eyes had a message. She touched Quimby's knee lightly.

"Martin, you've *got* to know who I am."

"But I do know, Victoria."

"Not all of it. You don't know about me down at the bottom line."

Quimby caught the urgency in her face.

"Is this what we've got to settle tonight?" he asked.

"Yes."

He smiled at her gently, closed the writing pad, and sat back relaxed.

"All right, my dear. Who are you?"

"I better start at the beginning."

"Start wherever you're comfortable," said Quimby, holding out his glass. "I'll have a little more brandy—"

"If you listen carefully, Martin," I said, pouring, "you'll see that Victoria as a public figure in the campaign can wreck the whole—"

"It's her story, Quick, not yours."

Victoria plunged in.

"Have you ever heard of the Kawaiute Indians?" she asked.

"I have," said Quimby, as he lit up a Hav-a-Tampa. "Read about them in the *Reader's Digest* a couple of months ago. They're from Nevada, if I remember right. They've got a sacred lake out there—something like that."

"I'm a Kawaiute, Martin. Half Kawaiute and half black."

"That surely doesn't disqualify you."

"And it's called Thunder Lake. Its only source of water is the Reno River. For years, they've been taking out more and more water for irrigation, so the sacred lake is drying up. Ten years ago, my father got into an argument with a rancher about that—and killed him. Two years after that, my father was killed in a fight inside the Nevada State Prison in Carson City."

"I'm sorry to hear that, Victoria," said Quimby. "It's a sad tale, but it has nothing to do with the campaign. I'm hiring *you*."

"After he died, my mother took me back to Harlem. She took a job as a maid in Scarsdale, so I never saw her. I had my own key. And I spent all my time trying to figure how to get out."

"Of what?"

"Harlem."

"Well, it's not exactly a supportive home situation, as they say," said Quimby, "and yet I—"

Victoria laid everything on the line.

"Martin, do you know what I was doing when I was fifteen?"

"What, my dear?"

"Giving blow jobs on Eighth Avenue to northbound commuters in the rush hour."

Quimby maintained his equanimity, but his eyebrows shot up momentarily.

"You know what a blow job is?"

"I do, indeed," said Quimby. "But how did you get into that field? Were you subverted by a fast-talking pimp?"

"No. I never trusted pimps."

"Good. Good!"

"Even as a kid, I felt there was something wrong with a man who would drive a whole Cadillac covered with purple suede."

"Very sensible," said Quimby.

"I did it all on my own. I got my costume together after I saw a German Nazi hooker in an X-rated movie I sneaked into. Then one winter afternoon, I came downtown on the Lexington Avenue Express and walked over to stand on the corner of Eighth and Forty-third—in a black mini-skirt and high black platform boots and a black cape thrown over my shoulder. I was scared to death."

"Somebody picked you up?"

"Right away. He looked exactly like Billy Graham, but he wasn't quite so religious. He didn't even say hello. Just blurted out 'How much?' I blurted out 'Twenty-five,' and he bought me on the spot. Then he asked where the hotel was, and I found out for the first time that *I* was supposed to know the hotel. The only hotel I'd ever heard of in Manhattan was the St. Regis. But when I said the St. Regis, he got rattled and said what the hell, there was no time to start shopping around for hotels. He had to take his wife to a dinner party in Westport. How about if I just blew him right there in the car?"

"And all this time, the car is travelling up Eighth Avenue?" asked Quimby, leaning forward. I had the feeling that, swept up in the excitement of the story, Quimby was losing sight of the problem.

"That's it. As the light changed at Fifty-first Street, I lay down on his lap, threw the cape up over my head, and fumbled around there in the dark for his fly. By the time we got to Columbus Circle, he was finished. After the payoff, I grabbed a cab and rode back down Ninth Avenue to my lucky corner. By the time the rush hour was over, I'd made five trips with a gross of one twenty-five."

"It seems to me you could have charged more," said Quimby, considerately.

"You're right, Martin," said Victoria. "Inside of a month, I'd doubled the price. By then, I had my regular daily commuters northbound, and my regular cab drivers to take me back."

"You worked going *both* ways!" said Quimby with admiration. "No deadheading! Good planning, Victoria."

"In a single day, I could make nine round trips and go home with nine big bills."

"I hope you were frugal," said Quimby.

"From the jump, Martin. I blew the men, but not the money."

"*Excellent*! I understand that people in the sporting life can easily lose sight of the value of money."

"Not me. After buying clothes and paying my federal and state and city income tax, I put every cent into Control Systems, Inc."

"How'd you find out about a growth stock?"

"From one of my regulars. A black stockbroker with Kuhn, Loeb & Company."

"We've wandered away from the basic problem, folks," I said. "It's clear that with a heavy background like this, Victoria cannot possibly become your—"

"Let her finish," said Quimby. "It's a tale of great courage."

"I finally found out," said Victoria, "that even though the money was good, there was no future in it. There I was, providing a lot of pleasure for hot, moaning strangers, but where was it getting me?"

"A sound question," said Quimby.

"It was a chump job, Martin. That's what it was. And so one afternoon, I just quit. Walked off the corner and took a cab home. Three weeks later, I entered Vassar."

"Splendid!" said Quimby, his face beaming. "We are emerging on solid ground at last."

"I went in under this federal program that was supposed to shove disorganized blacks into the mainstream of American life," she explained. "Later, Congress killed it, but I had the cash to keep going anyhow."

"Did you graduate?"

"In three and a half years."

"What the hell are you worried about, Quick?" said Quimby. "My campaign manager is a Vassar graduate who has *made* something of herself. Nothing wrong with that. She may have a checkered past, but—"

"But my present is checkered too," said Victoria.

"Oh?"

"I'm a four-hundred-dollar call girl in Manhattan."

The enthusiasm on Quimby's crinkled face faded. He swirled the brandy in his glass. He puffed a couple of times on the cigar.

"So you went back into the sporting life?" She nodded. "But I'm sure you *tried* for something else after all that educational effort."

"Yes, Martin. But they'd refined my language in Poughkeepsie to where I could make two thousand dollars a day at Madame Danou's. Even with banks hiring show-and-tell blacks for the front window, even with Kuhn and Loeb hiring black women stockbrokers, *no* straight job could touch that kind of cash money."

"And you wanted all you could get, of course," said Quimby, nodding. "What American doesn't?"

"Right."

"But wait a minute," said Quimby, suddenly sitting forward. "You mean that you'd give up this remarkable sinecure at Madame Danou's just to manage the Quimby Campaign?"

"I would," she said. "But only now that you know who I am."

"You have all the facts for a decision, Martin," I said. "And it's clear as hell to me what it must be."

"Me, too," said Quimby. "I appreciate your honesty, Victoria, and I'll stand by the decision I made this afternoon. *You* are the campaign manager."

I exploded.

"For Christ's sake, Martin, what are you doing? How can we get any decent PR out of this? When the reporters ask where Victoria Woodhill came from, do we say she's been working in the highest-priced whorehouse in Manhattan—where it costs a hundred bucks extra for a golden shower?"

"I don't think we need that much detail," said Quimby thoughtfully. "But we'll tell the basic truth about Victoria or about you or me or anybody else in the campaign."

"And what's your version of the basic truth about Victoria?"

"Simply this. Ms. Victoria Woodhill has been engaged by the Quimby Campaign not because she's black, not because she's Indian, not because she's a beautiful woman with great legs, not because she's a three-hundred-dollar call girl. . . ."

"Four hundred—" said Victoria.

"Not because she's a four-hundred-dollar call girl. She's

been engaged as the campaign manager because she had the brilliant original idea upon which the campaign is based."

"I'll tell them," I said glumly.

"And you can add that we're an equal-opportunity employer. Anybody with any other idea that good gets hired, too."

We pulled up at Quimby's house on Dingle Street. I helped my driver unhook the Toyota, and he backed it into the garage. Quimby invited us all in for a nightcap, but as I stood at the curb looking at Victoria, snug and warm in the big back seat, I found my mind in its characteristic drift away from serious business. I told the candidate that we had to get back to the city, had to be up bright and early to guide the TV crews from Manhattan to Newark for his announcement speech.

"They don't know the way?" he asked.

"Not too well. They only come to Newark to cover riots. At those times they're guided by the smoke."

"We've *got* to get our own TV station," he said. "Victoria, please put that on the list."

"All right, Governor," she said.

Quimby touched the brim of his hat.

"Thank you both—and God bless you—and goodnight."

From the car, we watched him go up the lighted path through the stone garden. Next to the house, he paused, turned to one side, removed his hat, and stood there silently in the cool night.

"What's he doing?" Victoria asked.

"There's a little plaque there. A memorial to his wife."

The car moved out.

"I like him," said Victoria. "He can be funny, but he's serious underneath. Can he win?"

"You're the campaign manager."

"I say he can win."

"He's got the qualities to win," I said. "He's assertive, dignified, talkative, intelligent, funny, and humane."

"Isn't that enough?"

"It ought to be. But the question is whether those qualities are in demand in America. Could Thomas Jefferson win in New Jersey today? Would the people rally to him, or would they reject him as a slave-owning snob, a carpetbagger violinist from the South who danced faggy dances like the minuet and built that fancy house in Virginia he copied from a Dago castle? Politics is almost as much a mystery as religion, Victoria. You're going to find that out."

She thrust herself close to me, just as she'd done in the cab in Trenton.

"I'm scared, Tom. *I* can't manage a campaign. Why didn't you talk him out of it?"

"Because you didn't want me to. And because he didn't want me to."

"But *you* don't want me in the job."

"I know ten professionals who could do it fine. On the other hand, you might be better than any of them. You'll be more dedicated, anyway."

"How do you know?"

"None of them would be giving up two grand a day."

"But what if I screw up the whole campaign?"

"Stay loose, Victoria," I said. Gently, I started to rub the back of her neck. "Quimby knows what he's getting into. He doesn't know where he's coming out, but he knows what he's getting into. And there's nothing more to solve tonight."

"But I don't want to screw it up. I like him. And I like you."

"Remember what you told me to do when I got upset?"

"Yes. Get your mind off politics."

"Get your mind off politics, Victoria."

I kept rubbing.

"That feels good," she said.

"I know," I said.

There was silence. The car, whooshing northbound on the Garden State Parkway, was filled with powerful, evocative scents. Now, in the silence, there was time to notice them. The scent of the brandy, the faint scent of perfume, the animal scent of the yellow suede safari suit, the subtle scent of Victoria herself.

Still rubbing, I reached over and switched on the quadraphonic tape deck. The rich heavy music that Jackie Gleason used to record in Miami Beach filled the car. Gleason's saccharine musicians were playing "I'm in the Mood for Love." Quietly, I sang along, picking it up on the second eight bars:

Heaven is in your eyes
Bright as the stars we're under.
Oh! Is it any wonder
I'm in the mood for love?

"I'm *not* going to be upset," said Victoria, suddenly sitting straight hard bolt upright. "I'm *not* going to be stone down. For the first damned time in my life, I'm gonna have power!"

Why stop to think of whether
This little dream might fade. . . .

"Yes, Mr. Charlie," she said, with a hard glint in her eye. "I'm finally gonna have power that doesn't grow out of my fucking!"

We've put our hearts together,
Now we are one, I'm not afraid!

I thought that by singing and rubbing her neck I could move her toward the moment of entangling rapture that I had in mind. Doggedly, I hung in there.

If there's a cloud above,
If it should rain, we'll let it. . . .

"For a long long time," she said, "I've been looking for something with more—more dignity."

But for tonight, forget it!

"And no matter how you look at it, managing a political campaign is one step *up* from going down!"

I'm in the mood for love.

The record was finished. It had not worked its magic.

"Power!" said Victoria. She extended her hand to me with the palm vertical and the fingers bent backwards. We rocked palms and then executed a complex tribal handshake.

"Power! It's what my father always *wanted* and always missed. Power—power—*power*!"

"Victoria, you sound like the President of Consolidated Edison."

"Fuck me, Tom!"

Aah hah! She had not forgotten after all!

"Push the lighted green button, Victoria."

This time, she did. She lifted the panel and pushed the button. The green light turned red, and there was a low hum as seven concealed electric motors automatically began to reconfigure the rear compartment of the car—changing both its form and function.

Carrying the two of us, the big black seat flattened slowly to horizontal, then slid slowly forward to join up with the padded edge of the rear-facing seats.

"Lift your feet," I said.

The refrigerated bar slid forward into the driver's compartment. Concealed amber lights came up on a dimmer. A cranberry satin sheet and quilt were automatically drawn by thin sliding cables across the whole area of the newly formed bed. Two compressed pillows popped down out of a compartment in the roof, like oxygen dropping down in an airline emergency. At the same time, the quartzite crystals in all windows rearranged themselves, polarizing so that the windows became opaque from the outside. Now we could lie there and look up through the Star-Vue window in the roof and see the stars over New Jersey.

Victoria was instantly in the spirit of it. In a brief slithering shuffle, she had shed the suede safari suit and was wearing only a yellow bikini bottom about the same size as that big triangular French Guiana postage stamp. In a trice, that was gone, too.

"When you exchange affection, you have to be naked," she said. "That's your line from the Metroliner!"

"A total tactile experience," I said, getting naked myself. "But I hardly recognize you without your polka dots."

"Don't worry, Tom. I'll keep my boots on so you'll know me."

"I can scarce believe my good fortune," I said.

She rolled into my arms, then tickled my left nostril. It was great! We lay nuzzling each other, pressing corresponding parts together, murmuring low. But I noticed with concern that something that should have happened immediately wasn't happening. No matter what delightful things Victoria did, it didn't happen.

"Victoria, I have an announcement. For the first time since I was thirteen, I can't get it up!"

"What happened when you were thirteen?" she asked, with genuine interest.

"I lured Teresa Brent Sweringen into an empty apartment on East Seventy-Third Street, and then I got scared. Teresa was ready, too."

"Well, man, sometimes it works and sometimes not. Don't worry about it."

"What do you *mean,* don't worry? It's important to my whole way of life to have it come up on schedule."

She lay on her back, breaking into a long and happy laugh.

"Know what the trouble is?"

"What?"

"Secretly—*way* down inside—you're furious that I'm going to be campaign manager. Your joint just got the subliminal message. It's retaliating. It's showing me who's boss."

"Maybe it's simpler than that," I said, after a moment's thought. "Maybe the trouble is that I've never screwed a campaign manager before."

"Don't go away," said Victoria.

She disappeared from my line of sight, but it was easy to tell where she had gone. In a moment she was playing an old Italian game, very popular in sixteenth-century Pisa, though frowned on by the Church. Fellatio, it is called.

"Come to think of it," I said, "I've never done this with a campaign manager either."

Suddenly, things were looking up. I had been lying on my back through all this, with Victoria crouched down below. Then silently, without warning, she sprang up and forward like a shiny black feline, impaling herself with incredible precision upon me. No hands! And so there we were, once again balling affectionately in a moving vehicle! But this time, horizontally.

After sharing explosions, we lay quietly in each other's arms, looking through the Sky-Vue window.

"The Mercedes doesn't jiggle like the Metroliner," she said.

"It's a whole different kind of suspension," I explained.

"As long as we keep doing it in vehicles, Tom, we should try a bumpy back road on a Honda CB420L."

"You know Hondas, too?"

She nodded.

"The new CB420L has a front fork lock, an emissions control system, and brand new bootpegs. Just right for a fast ride I have in mind."

"You're licensed to drive a Honda?" I asked. The idea was beginning to sound pretty good.

"You're slippy in the head," said Victoria. "The *man* drives. The woman just crouches in front of him like a chicken on a rotisserie!"

"Age will not wither nor custom stale your infinite variety, Victoria."

"So I understand."

"And I want you to notice that we have *not* gone *pouf*!"

"So I understand."

We drifted into another moist, overheated kiss. When the steam finally cleared from the polarized windows, we were riding up Park Avenue. The Grand Central clock said midnight.

CHAPTER 16

THE FOLLOWING MORNING, a hard cold wind roared down from Canada, swept across Newark, and blew a two-week accumulation of sulfur dioxide and airborne particulate matter out into the Atlantic Ocean. The sun was bright in Newark, and it was a good break for us. With no smog, the television cameras set up in Military Park—a green space in the heart of Newark—would now be able to see our candidate.

A crowd of about six hundred people was gathered in front of the concrete bandshell where Wyncyncynski and Kabu Makabu and the mayor of Pemmican, New Jersey, had made their announcements the day before. All the Military Park regulars were on hand—senior citizens, unemployed people, truant children, salesmen, pushers, soapbox orators, and pretty Prudential Life secretaries on their coffee break. It was a good crowd for televising, with plenty of interesting faces—black and white—for the cutaway reaction shots that would help link the candidate with the people.

The bandshell was brightly decorated. Quimby had complained at dinner the night before that political campaigns had grown too austere, that they lacked the *hoopla* of a torchlight parade, that people didn't *festoon* enough anymore. So Victoria had come over at 5:00 A.M. with some volunteers and they had festooned all morning. Red-white-and-blue bunting ran everywhere. Clotheslines had been strung in parallel catenary lines across the opening of the bandshell, then hung with huge VOTE FOR QUIMBY posters that flapped in the breeze. The whole scene had a substantial, believable political quality—like a segment out of *Citizen Kane*.

The television film cameras that would capture Quimby's announcement speech were placed on a cast-iron pipe scaffold about sixty feet in front of the bandshell. By a quarter to ten, the TV crews—all set up, all ready to go—were lounging competently on the platform in their Hush Puppies, smoking, looking down on the crowd with the disenchanted faces so characteristic of their trade. These people had spent their lives finding the shallow, theatrical side of the news, cutting it up into one-minute segments, and passing it on in color to a violence-prone America. They had seen everything and they believed very little of it, and so they were a difficult bunch to electrify; but their very presence here represented a victory for us.

Video-wise, Martin J. Quimby had broken through. For the first time since the fourth Newark riot, New York crews were on hand for a New Jersey remote. For the first time since the execution of Bruno Richard Hauptmann, media people from Philadelphia had crossed the Delaware in their mobile units to cover an event in the Garden State.

At five to ten, right on schedule, the Misty Harbor High School Band tumbled out of a yellow school bus, formed up, struck up, and marched with meticulous zip to a roped-off area in front of the bandshell. They were under the direction of William ("Trombone") Lonergan, a Misty Harbor neighbor of Quimby's, and they were playing Lonergan's composition, "New Jersey Is the Only Place for Me." It was a stirring march with the trombones heavily featured in the trio.

At ten, right on the button, a new black Cadillac limousine came up State Street at high speed, wheeled sharply to the curb, and came to a halt with a faint squeal of rubber. It was a Divver maneuver—safe, but eye-catching. Before the big car had quite stopped, Martin Quimby had thrown open the rear door and his feet were touching the pavement. It was the same way in which the U.S. Secret Service arrives at a location, bringing a sense of taut commotion.

Quimby tossed his overcoat into the back of the car, adjusted his new hat, and headed directly across the grass toward the bandshell. The Misty Harbor Band played a soaring fanfare as he approached. There was a ripple of applause. Quimby smiled as he walked, clearly enjoying the hoopla.

I looked over at Sam Scalese. He was shaking his head negatively. Later I learned that he was happy with the glasses and the suit, but he did not like the hat. The new hat was Quimby's idea, and it was modern enough in shape. But Scalese felt, as did JFK, that hats have no place in the public arena. Scalese, who was devout, always buttressed this argument by pointing out that Jesus never wore a hat.

Victoria Woodhill, in a dark blue Thai-silk pants suit, greeted Quimby at the bandshell. Arm in arm, they went up the steps, crossed to the rostrum, and stood there between two flags—the American and the New Jersey. The band struck up again. I had asked Trombone Lonergan to play our national anthem at this point, but instead his group favored us with another chorus of "New Jersey Is the Only Place for Me."

Victoria stepped forward to the microphones. There was

a surge of applause and the shriek of wolf-call whistles, but Victoria stood there just as cool as she'd been while dancing in the PATH station. After the commotion had died down, she said simply:

"Ladies and gentlemen, may I present Mr. Martin J. Quimby of Misty Harbor—Independent candidate for Governor."

Quimby stepped forward, took off the hat, laid it to one side, grasped both sides of the rostrum firmly, and looked out across the crowd, sizing them up while they settled down. He was not smiling now. His aviator glasses had gone partly dark in the sunlight, and as he stood there, crustily confident in the new suit, I saw something that I had not seen before. Up on the platform, he seemed to be an echo of Truman—Harry Truman with slightly flared pants.

"Ladies and gentlemen, my first task is to introduce the handsome young woman who was kind enough to introduce me. May I present Victoria Woodhill, who will be the manager of the Quimby Campaign."

Victoria smiled, waved, got another big hand and more whistles. Quimby bowed slightly toward her, and continued:

"Miss Woodhill, and people of Newark. I have come here to Military Park with a single purpose—to announce my candidacy for the governorship of New Jersey in the election just four weeks from Tuesday, on November fifth. I am sixty-five years old, sound of body, clear of mind, and without political tarnish. I am running for this office out of a sense of duty, of hope, and of fun. I expect to win. But win or lose, I'm going to have a *pisswhacker* of a time!"

Even in a linguistically liberated America, it was a startling word to put into a formal political announcement. The TV networks would blip the word "pisswhacker," of course, but Quimby's ebullient, chance-taking spirit would shine through the blip. Now he paused with just the trace of a smile, as his live audience shuffled uncertainly, not knowing quite what to make of this man. Quimby was having a pisswhacker of a time already.

"Last week," he went on, "an alleged Mafia figure, a Mr. Joseph ('Big Greeny') Buzzini, testifying before a Senate investigating committee, took the Fifth Amendment a hundred and seven times. The first time he took it was in response to the question: 'Mr. Buzzini, what state do you live in?' Though he is in fact a resident of Tenafly, Mr. Buzzini flatly refused to admit that he lived in New Jersey, saying that such an admission might tend to incriminate him.

"My fellow residents," Quimby went on, chopping at the rostrum to make his point, "*that* is the crummy estate to which New Jersey has now fallen! We call it the Garden State, but for God's sake, look about you. Just take a minute and look! *Look*! It's no wonder that Big Greeny Buzzini was so embarrassed. You have let your entire polity fall into a state of disrepute, disrepair, and disgrace. Shame! *Shame*! *Shame*!"

A smattering chorus of boos arose from the audience.

"Don't boo *me*, for God's sake! I'm offering to run for the *governorship* of this situation. And I'm here under the protection of the First Amendment to the Constitution of the United States. In case you're not familiar with it, the First Amendment allows every kind of free speech in this country, except for the hollering of 'Fire!' in a crowded theatre when there is actually no fire. Let me remind you also that I am not discussing matters that can be solved by mindless booing in a public square. So while I'm speaking, please *shut up*!"

The crowd fell dead silent. He went on:

"Every political campaign in the history of the United States has been nothing more than an expensive exercise in kissing the voter's ass. And the voter, as a result of over two centuries of anal coddling, thinks he is pretty hot stuff. He or she has no idea at all of what a narrow, ineffective, uninformed, self-centered oaf he or she really is. And the politicians, once they are in office, continue to be of no particular value to the democratic process. Most of their speeches consist of simply deploring the conditions they deplored to get elected. This is getting us *nowhere*!

"The Quimby Campaign is going to be different. I'm going to level with you. I'm going to assume that *no* governor elected on November fifth will be powerful enough to overcome your ignorance or overpower your greed or erase your ancient racial hates or force you to create a civil human community. That's *your* job. And I say you haven't been doing it."

A few people cheered, but the new surge of booing was loud and menacing. Quimby seemed unimpressed by either. He turned around to look at Victoria, seated near him. She was smiling with absolute ease, enjoying the tension that he was creating. She winked at him.

"The problem of a stupid populace is not a new one in the United States," he went on. "Back when the country was getting started, it was the cause of a big fight between Alexander Hamilton and Thomas Jefferson. Hamilton did not trust the people. He trusted only his classy friends. But Jefferson said that he knew of no safer repository of the ultimate power of the society than the people themselves. Then he added—and get this: 'If we think the people unfit for the task, the remedy is not to take the power from them, but to inform their discretion through education.'

"Well, there you have the guts of the Quimby Campaign, folks. Win or lose, in those many areas where I think you are unfit for the task, I plan to inform your discretion if it's the last Goddamned thing I ever do!

"It is in this constructive spirit that I earnestly solicit your vote. Thank you."

Trombone Lonergan led the band back into "New Jersey Is the Only Place for Me," thus covering up the smattering of applause and the chorus of boos. Quimby put on his hat, took Victoria by the arm, and they left the bandshell to cross toward Divver and me at the car.

The crowd was clearly unsettled by the speech, but the TV people, moving their equipment quickly from the scaffold to their mobile vans, were delighted. They had discovered a volatile man who violated dreary political predictability, a theatrical man who was just right for their punchy kind of news.

From the roof of one of the mobile units, a TV director gestured to his driver to follow Quimby and Victoria as they walked through the crowd. And so the cameraman on the roof caught another unique moment when a squat and furious man—with red neck, white skin, and blue collar—rushed out of the crowd at Martin Quimby, his beefy hands held before him in a ring as though to strangle the new candidate. Quimby saw him coming. He stepped ahead of Victoria, waited until the man was upon him, then lifted his leg gracefully, pivoted his body a hundred and eighty degrees, and caught the man square on the chin with his heel. It was a piece of flawless karate. The beefy man went down. Victoria started to applaud. She was joined by others.

As the man got up, Quimby stood his ground, facing him, elbows cocked. The man seemed undecided about continuing the attack, and at precisely the right moment, Quimby said calmly:

"The First Amendment deals with *peaceable* assembly, you jackass!"

Dropping his posture of defense, Quimby took Victoria's arm, and they continued calmly toward the car. The crowd made way for them, falling back, murmuring with respectful surprise.

I got into the car, feeling that it was an appropriate moment to get the hell out of there. Divver was in the driver's seat with the engine running. But Quimby would not be rushed, nor did Victoria seem anxious. He helped her into the limousine, and then before he climbed in, he paused, turned to the people, touched the brim of his hat, and said quietly:

"Thank you—and God bless you—and good-day."

Quimby slammed the heavy door and dropped into the back seat with a smile.

"I'll have a Michelob," he said.

I took a can from the bar refrigerator and handed it to him.

"American politics is sure rough and tumble," he said, laughing, popping the top.

"Your kind is," I said.

"You can raise hell even better than my father!" said Victoria with admiration.

"What'd you think?" Quimby asked me, sitting back and taking a drink.

"The karate was brilliant, but the speech was too long," I said. "I thought we agreed it would be only one minute."

"I couldn't swing it in a minute."

"But now you're in the hands of TV film editors. If it'd been a minute, they'd have to run it whole."

"On the other hand," said Al Divver over his shoulder, "if you'd gone *another* minute, they'd have lynched you."

"Nonsense," said Quimby. "Lynching is illegal in New Jersey."

"Did we get any votes?" asked Victoria. The campaign manager had turned to the central issue of the campaign.

"I'd say we got a maximum of forty votes," I replied. "But we did solve the publicity problem. Look!"

I pointed through the small back window of the limousine. Two television mobile units were following us. One from WNYC and the other from Philadelphia.

"I thought they were here just for the announcement," said Victoria.

"They were. But with speeches like that one, they'll stay right on Martin's tail through election night."

"Free television!" shouted Divver happily. "The best kind. Makes people think you're already governor."

"Martin," I said, "I want to take all the money budgeted for our paid TV and put it into a handsome, conservative brochure. Muted-color photography. High-quality stock."

"We already have a brochure coming out," said the candidate.

"That's a political brochure, with you attacking the issues as well as the people. This second one will be a *personal* brochure. Quimby the man—Quimby the neighbor—Quimby the Presbyterian—Quimby the jogger—Quimby the fisherman. It'll hardly mention the election at all."

"What the hell for?" asked Quimby, cocking his head to one side.

"With the free television coverage we're now going to get, we must somehow put out the word that Martin J. Quimby is not as volatile as he seems on the evening news. Our subliminal brochure will say *very* quietly that down underneath, Quimby is really a civilized human being."

"Christ, Quick, you want to wreck the campaign?" said Quimby, sitting forward. "That's not the kind of thing we *tell* people. That's what we let them find out for themselves."

"While you're *attacking* them?"

"Precisely," said Quimby. "That's the beauty of Victoria's idea. They'll gradually come to see that there is *merit* in my attack. If we can lower their bloated expectations while we increase their understanding of"—

"There's not enough time for such a big shift in public attitude," I said.

"Truman did it."

"But he had almost eight years in the White House to do it," I said. "And most of that warm admiration for Truman's toughness didn't develop until after he was dead."

"We can't give them that much time," said Quimby. "I can take a week to get their attention by being loud and indignant. Then, without changing my pissed-off posture *one scintilla*, I can begin to throw in the constructive ideas—and come out a statesman. You'll see."

"What's the next stop?" asked Divver.

Victoria looked at the schedule.

"The Ira Minskoff Sintered Metal Works," she said. "Just outside Metuchen."

"Seventeen minutes away," said Divver, picking up speed, "and a *great* plant for politicking."

"Why is that, Al?" asked Quimby.

"The place has good natural light, Governor, and talkative workers. Also, refreshments for everybody in the candidate's party and the TV crew. I think Mr. Minskoff is a frustrated politician."

"And what do they manufacture?"

"Sintered metal rotors for automobile distributors."

"The plant been here long?"

"Minskoff's grandfather got their first contract from Charles Kettering of General Motors in 1912."

"Who was Charles Kettering?" asked Victoria.

"The inventor of the self-starter," said Divver.

"And just what is sintered metal?" asked Quimby.

"Governor, I'm damned if I know."

CHAPTER 17

IT BEGAN as a regular political plant visit, the candidate walking down the aisle between huge pieces of machinery, nodding, smiling, shaking hands, asking total strangers for their support on November 5. It was the kind of a tour that has been done a half million times since the inception of television. The television crews had followed us into the Minskoff plant, but they were instantly bored by the predictable scene. They did not even bother to turn on their lights or cameras.

At Sintered Metal Press No. 32, Quimby stopped for a longer chat. He held out his hand to the pale woman running the press, but she ignored it and went right on with her work. Quimby was unfazed.

"Good afternoon, madam," he said. "My name is Martin J. Quimby. I'm running for governor of New Jersey, and I feel that when a man gets up in the morning and goes down to a plant to talk to the workers, he'd better know what he's talking about."

"Get lost, crumb," said the lady, glowering.

The TV lights and cameras came on instantly. Quimby

took a step closer to her and turned slightly for a better angle.

"Good afternoon, madam," he said. "My name is Martin J. Quimby. I'm running for governor of New Jersey, and I feel that when a man gets up in the morning and goes down to a plant to talk to the workers, he'd better know what he's talking about. I'm here to earnestly solicit your vote."

"Fat chance," she said with a sneer.

"Would you repeat that, please, madam?" he asked, as camera No. 2 zoomed in on her for an angry close-up.

"I said, 'Fat chance.' "

"Fat chance what?"

"Fat chance that I'd vote for you, Quimby."

"In that case, may I ask which of the other twenty-two candidates you *are* voting for for governor?"

"*None* of 'em."

She was about forty, tall, skinny, drawn, and her upper left incisor was missing. She gave the impression of having spent her early years in Appalachia.

"May I ask your name, Ms.—"

"You spell it H–A–I–G–H–T. An' you say it 'hate.' Martha Haight."

"And you're here working with sintered metal, eh?" he said, trying to strike a hopefully congenial note.

"That's what the sign outside says, buster."

"Just what *is* sintered metal?"

"How the hell should I know."

"Now, Ms. Haight, as I understand you, you're planning not to vote for *anybody* for governor on November fifth?"

"You got it."

"And yet one of the first duties of a citizen is to—"

"Don't tell me about my first duties, buster. My first duty is to survive in this damned stinkin' job."

"But it would only take five minutes to vote. Why not?"

"Because I've never voted in my life. An' because votin' is nothin' but choosin' between crooks."

Quimby bridled.

"Now hold on, Ms. Haight. I'm no crook. I'm a civil engineer, and honest as the day is long."

"Don't tell me," she said. "You're in politics. That means you're a politician. That means you take kickbacks from defense contractors. That means you got three million stuffed in a shoe box or a Swiss bank. That's what that means."

Quimby smiled. But only with his mouth. His eyes were grim.

"Ms. Haight, none of what you're saying is true. And furthermore if you can—"

"Don't 'furthermore' me, buster."

With a single expletive, she switched off the big press, and stepped angrily around a box of finished rotors to face Quimby. She towered over him.

"Why you comin' in here anyway, Quimby? Cuttin' into my piecework time—suckin' up to me—usin' *me* to make you look good in front of your damned cameras—usin' *me* to help you take over the state so you kin get your kickbacks—"

"Now, hold on, Ms. Haight. We can't let you bug out of your role as a citizen in such a mindless, shortsighted way. If you don't like the New Jersey state government, you can vote to change it."

"I wouldn't piss on it!"

Quimby turned calmly to address the camera. He was now framed in a tight close-up.

"Obviously, a case of political disaffection. We find it all over New Jersey these days. And yet it would be wrong as a candidate to promise Ms. Haight here too much. Even if we could deliver the goods, her sour heart may be beyond legislation."

"Don't tell me I've got a sour heart, you little crumb." Her face pushed back into the frame. It was a classic TV confrontation.

"Don't be embarrassed, ma'am. Millions of Americans have sour hearts. Maybe *most* of them. The Industrial Revolution has not brought the universal happiness that James Watt predicted."

"I don't have to listen to this."

"Karl Marx saw the sour heart as an economic problem," he explained. "Jesus saw it as a religious problem. Darwin described it as a survival problem. Freud as a neurosis. But I think they all would have agreed that it is not socially productive for the State of New Jersey to be permanently saddled with the bitter gall of your discontent."

"Why, you little—"

"The state *can* help you, Ms. Haight, but in the end, you'll have to find the bluebird of happiness for yourself."

"I wouldn't piss on the bluebird of happiness."

Quimby moved even closer to her, speaking a shade more confidentially.

"Ms. Haight, elect *me* governor, and we'll meet you halfway with some remedial programs."

"You sound like the plant psychologist," she said disdainfully. "*Another* jerk-off. What would you try to remedy in me?"

"I don't like to give a snap diagnosis, but I'd say that your whole life needs remedial work, madam. Your whole life."

"*I* don't need the work," she shouted at him. "It's *New Jersey* that needs the remedial work. All you'd try to do is get me adjusted to my dismal surroundings."

Quimby returned her shout, even louder.

"The state needs fixing too, lady, but for God's sake quit your *whining*! It's enough to drive a candidate crazy!" Then he quickly composed himself, putting a gentle hand on her shoulder. "Excuse me for shouting, Ms. Haight, but you really pissed me off there for a moment." He turned to Victoria. "Victoria, will you please read the list of women's programs we're considering for the Quimby Administration. I think Ms. Haight may find them of interest."

Victoria stepped into camera range, flipped open her big loose-leaf campaign-plan book as the cameras swung and zoomed in on her.

"Women's counseling, rape counseling, sex therapy, hot-lines, halfway houses, family planning, encounter groups, retirement counselling, vocational rehabilitation—"

"Notice *that* one, Ms. Haight," interrupted Quimby.

"—abortion counselling, day care, alternative education, marriage encounters, assertiveness training, peer counselling, human-potential groups, self-help groups on the pattern of Alcoholics Anonymous—and special services for the dying."

"Thank you, Victoria. Now, Ms. Haight, somewhere in all those services, I think we can find something—*some one thing* that will improve your life. Right? And if you could just bring some faint sense of affirmation to making a choice—"

"How you gonna pay for all that bureaucratic crap?"

"With some carefully considered new taxes," said Quimby.

"That *I'll* have to pay!" she shouted at him.

"Of course you'll pay your share." Quimby was shouting again. "This is the third richest state in the Union, and yet taxwise, it is—"

"More taxes?" she said, in abject disbelief. "You'd have the *nerve* to pile more *taxes* on this place?"

"I would. There's no sense my kidding you on that."

"An' there's no sense my kiddin' you either, buster," she said, fixing him with her grimmest glare. "Not only would I not vote for you—I wouldn't piss on you!"

Quimby raised his arm across his face to ward off the bitter concluding phrase, but she shouted it anyway. Then she wheeled back to her machine, hit the button, and it began to thump out sintered parts. Quimby stood quietly for perhaps half a minute, watching her at work. The cameras kept turning. Quimby's mood became quieter for the wrap-up.

"Thank you for your attention, Ms. Haight." He turned to face the camera. "One of my aims in this campaign is to lower the expectations of the people in terms of what the state can do for them. Clearly, that is not a problem for Martha Haight."

He turned back to her at the machine.

"Nevertheless, I want you to know that I came here constructively to earnestly solicit your vote."

"You muffed it, Quimby," she shouted over the noise of the big machine. "Get your ass out of here."

"Thank you—and God bless you—and good afternoon."

The campaign team was shaken by Quimby's first individual encounter with a Jersey voter. But Quimby was philosophical about it. He said simply that you couldn't win them all, that Ms. Haight was simply a vote we'd do well not to count on. Then he forgot all about her as his mind shot ahead to the next thing on the schedule.

"We want to go to Scottsboro Houses," said Victoria to Divver.

"Twenty-three minutes," said Divver. "Everybody sit back and relax. This could be a big one."

Scottsboro Houses was the name of an apartment complex planned and financed by a group of blacks in a grimly marginal section south of Passaic. Back in 1960, a whole square block had been demolished here with the idea of building a modern school to replace the worn-out Public School No. 27 that had been standing across the street since

1895. The new school, it was said, would provide quality education for everybody, including the blacks who were pressing in from the west. But the white world being what it is, they never *quite* got around to building the new school. This meant that the rocks and bricks that littered the vast vacant lot were used for years as ammunition to break the windows of the old school, driving it further and further toward decrepitude. Stoning the school was a popular local game, like stickball in Manhattan.

Then in 1975, some black interests with Detroit money bought the block and announced the construction of Scottsboro Houses, a low- to medium-income high rise. The white interests, an intensely ethnic group, whose faultlessly neat brick houses stood just beyond School No. 27 to the east, sued to block the construction of the Houses. These property owners were confident that the matter could be squashed in the courts if they persisted long enough, particularly since those were the days when Richard M. Nixon was peopling the Supreme Court with civil propertarians who would defend the nineteenth century well into the twenty-first.

Yet it didn't work out that way. Now, more than a decade later, this was the day that the hundred and fifty-sixth injunction would expire, the day that construction was at last to begin. The white interests, vocal and bitter, announced a major confrontation for 1:00 P.M.—the hour at which the injunction would die. As in the hundred and fifty-five earlier confrontations at this site, there would be shouts, threats, broken heads, and perhaps even a death or two. But unlike those clashes, this one would be led by two gubernatorial candidates—one on each side. Sal Wyncyncynski and Kabu Makabu.

On this opening day of campaigning, it became clear that Martin Quimby would be a politician who, like FDR and Huey Long and Mao and Governor Altgeld, gravitated naturally to the vortex of a hard issue. And loved it. As we arrived at the site, the battle lines were already drawn in medieval fashion. The shouts and the threats had begun. There were also lewd gestures being thrown across No Man's Land by men carrying hopelessly provocative posters. Stuff like Fuck You, Whitey! and Get Your Black Ass Out of Town! (As in a political campaign, some of the letters were reversed.)

On our left, a big Caterpillar M-27 bulldozer began slowly to move toward the chain-link fence that surrounded the building site. This was the vehicle that was supposed to dig out the foundation hole. Kabu Makabu's followers were strung out in a broad V behind the machine, jeering. In the prow, as advertised, Makabu himself was chained to the top of the scraper blade of the big yellow monster.

On our right, about a hundred and fifty feet from the advancing bulldozer, stood the defenders of the fence and the neighborhood—with Sal Wyncyncynski chained to the fence. The black men behind the bulldozer were outnumbered—as always in America—but still they moved ahead, jeering as loudly as the ethnics who stood with their backs against the fence. There were about a hundred police, ready to dispense their own forceful brand of justice, but the chief was already on public record as not liking either side's lawlessness and disorder.

Quimby leaned forward and told Al Divver to ram the Cadillac over the curb, to drive right between the opposing forces, and stop. As the heavy car lurched across the rough ground, Quimby took a new bullhorn out of a Hammacher Schlemmer box, and when the car stopped, he leaped out, vaulted to the hood and then to the roof—all in one graceful motion that would have been a credit to a man half his age. Both blacks and whites were waving and shouting to get the damned car out of the way. But even though the black limousine stood directly in the path of the bulldozer, Divver did not move it. He was taking his orders from the candidate alone. The giant Caterpillar kept coming right at us.

Quimby bent down over the open door and shouted:

"Get Victoria out of the car, Quick!"

I helped her out. She had exactly the right distracting influence as she stood there with her hands on her hips, looking first at the one group, then turning to look at the other. The bulldozer stopped. The shouting diminished. The big yellow machine was about twenty feet from us, and Quimby pointed directly to the operator.

"Will you please turn off your engine," he said in a calm tone. His voice on the bullhorn carried easily. The engine sputtered to silence. "Please turn off our engine, too, Mr. Divver," said Quimby. Divver did. But he stayed at the wheel.

"I realize that you're all anxious to get on with the business of kicking the shit out of each other," said Quimby to the crowd. "But I'd like to take advantage of the fact that we're all here to make a short political speech. About two minutes."

He paused. There was a kind of stunned silence over the field.

"My name is Martin Quimby. I'm a candidate for governor on November fifth. The young lady standing next to the car is my campaign manager, Victoria Woodhill. I have come here specifically to disassociate myself on this issue of Scottsboro Houses from my two opponents who are already on record. Mr. Makabu on my left, chained to the bulldozer. And Mr. Wyncyncynski, on my right, chained to the fence." It was as though he was introducing two fighters in a ring.

"We don't have to listen to you, asshole!" shouted a voice from the distance.

"That's true," said Quimby, "but can you reserve that judgment until you've heard what I have to say? You have no basis whatsoever, mister, for calling me an asshole. We've never met. And what difference does two minutes make? You'll probably be in the hospital for two weeks when this is over."

The man was silent.

"Of course, Mr. Makabu and Mr. Wyncyncynski may want to speak in rebuttal to me, but that's their decision, not mine. So let me begin by complimenting them. In their present roles as leaders of narrow, angry, pissed-off factions of our broad society, they are ideal. But *not* for governor. You know why? Because they are here to bring out the worst in you. The politician who does that does not wind up governing a state. He winds up running a zoo."

Quimby paused as though waiting for the idea to sink in.

"A good governor does not ask his followers to beat up the opposition," he went on. "A good governor knows that any American community rests on *one* very fragile idea—the idea that—"

"Cut the highflown horseshit, Quimby," shouted a gravel voice from the crowd. "Are you *for* Scottsboro Houses or against it?"

"I'm for it, mister, as long as no more than two hundred additional people get killed before it opens. I'm for it because it conforms with the law and because it's taking longer to rebuild this region after Riot Number Five than it took to rebuild all of Europe after the Second World War. But the way that we treat each other is just as important as what we get done."

There was a long pause. Nobody shouted. It was so quiet now that Quimby could continue without the bullhorn. His voice carried easily, and he turned slowly to include everybody.

"You're not only wrecking each other here today, my friends. And you're not only wrecking Scottsboro Houses.

You're wrecking the proposition. Lincoln talked about it years ago—'the proposition that all men are created equal.' Listen, we are not united by race or nationality or geography or religion in this country. As a matter of fact, most of the time we hate each other. And that's why the proposition is so precious. It's the only thing that holds us together."

The candidate turned back toward his heckler.

"If you think this is highflown horseshit, mister, you're dead wrong. Because this country is a goddamned miracle, that's what it is! A bunch of lawyers and merchants sat down in Philadelphia in the summer of 1787 and wrote out a loose-fitting document that has made all of you standing here in this field the freest men on the planet. Dumb, maybe, but free! And if you keep wrecking the proposition as you'll do when we drive away now, New Jersey is eventually doomed, and your freedom is doomed—no matter who becomes the governor."

Suddenly, there was a sound of one person applauding. It turned out to be Victoria, leaning against the big front fender, smiling up at him, clapping loudly. It was a gesture of genuine support from the campaign manager.

"Martin, that's *beautiful,*" she shouted up to him. "Did you just make that up?"

"No, Victoria. I've been mulling over this problem ever since Hubert Humphrey spoke to the 1948 Democratic Convention. But I'm not through." He turned back to the crowd. "Think about it, gentlemen. I don't mean right now, because you'll be too busy attacking each other. But in the hospital—or on some quiet summer evening—think about it. Think about it for maybe as long as a *minute*. Maybe you'll get a new thought on this old subject, and that would be good. Most people, you see, go all the way through life without getting a single new thought on *anything*. And that's why they remain shortsighted, angry, childish victims from the cradle to the grave. But you don't have to be a victim *all* your life. Your own head—and your own heart—can get you out of that category any time you want.

"It is in this constructive spirit that I earnestly solicit your vote. Thank you—and God bless you—and good afternoon."

Quimby tossed the bullhorn down to me, stepped onto the hood, then vaulted to the ground. In a few seconds, we were all back in the Cadillac, and Al was driving us out from between the roaring, shouting factions as they closed in on each other. Clearly, Divver saw it as a kind of getaway.

"What's the next event?" asked Quimby.

"A bingo game at the Guild for the Jewish Blind," said Victoria.

"That sounds a little more restful," said Quimby.

We looked through the back window. One TV mobile unit was right behind us, but the other had stayed to cover the burgeoning confrontation and riot. The bulldozer was pushing over the chain-link fence. Small figures were pummelling each other. Cops were clubbing.

"You were so *damned* good," said Victoria sadly. "Why didn't they understand you?"

"They understood," said Quimby. "But just because a man understands something, that doesn't mean he believes it. What'd you think, Quick?"

"It's not going to be your average campaign, that's what I think."

"Does Polcon, Inc. have any statistics on the number of nobodies in New Jersey?"

"No. We've never tried to develop any figures in that area. Be very difficult to define. Why do you ask?"

"Well, as you look at the fight back there, you can see that one of the big jobs of the Quimby Administration is going to be to get the nobodies off each other's backs. They could get together on a lot of issues, if they could only see how much alike they are."

"That's not easy, Martin."

"Nothing is easy. But as it stands now, when a man is a nobody, the most important thing he can find is somebody who's more of a nobody than he is. It's not good for the democratic process."

"But you can't devote the whole campaign to nobodies," I warned him. "We'll have to keep in mind the people with power, too."

"That's right," said Quimby. "Remember them as you do the scheduling, Victoria. People with power and with money."

"All right," said Victoria, who was making some notes in the campaign plan book. "But I've always thought that people with power can screw a community as fast as those without it."

"Faster," said Quimby. "Somehow they have the idea that their money and their background and their prestige and their position and their mobility and their connections make them special—set them apart."

He sighed as he sat back and popped the top of another Michelob. It was as though the scope and the intricacy of the campaign had come home to him for the first time.

"The only person more troublesome than a nobody," said Martin Quimby, "is a somebody."

CHAPTER 18

MARTIN J. QUIMBY (IND.) had kicked off his campaign with smashing effectiveness. In a single evening, he exploded into national prominence. His Military Park announcement, his joust with Ms. Martha Haight, and his Scottsboro Houses speech were run back-to-back on NBC News that night, taking up five-and-a-half minutes of nationwide television prime time. That had never happened before. CBS-TV gave him six minutes, and then at the end of the program, the network's new resident gray eminence leaned forward on his low, invisible desk, folded his hands, looked sharply upward at the camera from underneath his mobile eyebrows, and devoted the entire one minute and forty-seven seconds of his commentary to Quimby:

"Back in April of 1924," he said quietly, "the late H. L. Mencken, who was known as the sage of Baltimore, wrote this about democracy: 'Its greatest defect is that it forces every candidate for office, even the highest, into frauds and chicaneries that are wholly incompatible with the most elementary decency and honor. In proportion as he is intelligent and honest,' "Mencken said," 'his candidacy is hopeless. Facing a mob, he is compelled to adapt his views, willy-nilly, to their changeable and illogical superstitions and delusions. Worse, he is compelled to fit these views, at the same time, into the prejudices of the professional politicians who now surround him and into the notions of self-interest of the rich rogues who stand behind *them.*'

"Well, it is clear tonight that at least one of the twenty-three candidates, in the race for the governorship of New Jersey, does not fit the Mencken description. He is Martin J. Quimby, and his candidacy, which exploded across the state today, is unfettered and unpredictable. He is an Independent if there ever was one! His campaign manager is a black woman as inexperienced as he. His one credential is thirty years of work as a civil engineer. And his tactic is a slashing verbal assault on those citizens who Mr. Quimby believes take no responsibility for the well-being of the Garden State.

"Quimby is not simply campaigning," said the gray eminence. "He is Blondin, walking across Niagara Falls on a swaying wire with each foot in a wooden bucket, mesmerizing the crowd. There will be many, of course, who hope he falls in the drink. There will be others who hope that he makes it to the other side and actually takes over the reins of government.

"Quimby's success or failure will be made clear on November fifth. Meantime, something else written by Mr. Mencken in that same year of 1924 surely *will* apply to this remarkable campaign:

" 'The chief merit of democracy,' "said the sage of Baltimore," 'is that it is incomparably humorous and thrilling. It may be clumsy, it may be swinish, it may be unutterably incompetent and dishonest. But it is never dismal. It is never *absolutely* a bore.' "

Throughout the whole campaign. Quimby continued to magnetize the media. He attracted almost as much attention as a presidential candidate. Two weeks before the election, he appeared on the cover of *Newsweek*. That same week, campaigning over western New Jersey in his red hot-air balloon, he was on the cover of *Sports Illustrated*. The week before the election, he was scheduled for the cover of *Time*, but he was pushed off at the last moment by the explosion of the first Laotian atomic bomb.

The continuing national story all through October was the contentious Quimby. Every day, he was out on the campaign trail, shouting to be heard above the din that he had himself created. And whenever he momentarily moderated his position or spoke more quietly or dealt with somebody less wildly exotic than Ms. Martha Haight, the news cameras were simply turned off. TV news directors show us the world as a vastly simplified theatre, without nuance, without shading. They were not going to tamper with the unique public character that Quimby had created in his opening speech. They would hold him to it all the way.

Quimby was a brilliant, tireless campaigner. I'd never before seen a candidate schedule, and then make, thirty appearances a day—from a Communion breakfast with a group of Weehawken barbers at 6:30 A.M. to a spot with Johnny Carson on the "Tonight" show nineteen hours later, at the end of a Falcon jet ride to Los Angeles. And even at the dead-tired end of the day, he had the energy to explode indignantly and volcanically on cue. Part of the key to his great scheduling success was Al Divver, who knew the name of every public character in New Jersey and knew also exactly how long it took to get from any point in New Jersey to any other point.

Yet all was not well. On the Friday before Tuesday's election, I recommended that Quimby quit campaigning for half an hour, and come meet with me at Quimby headquarters. He didn't want to break the rhythm of his schedule, but I told him it was critical. At three o'clock, Al Divver delivered him to my office, which had been partitioned off in a corner of the J-Mart store. I hadn't seen Quimby in six days.

"You look great, Martin."

"I feel great, but I don't have any time to fart around. There's two thousand people waiting for me in Paramus."

"Martin, there are three American activities where the final answer arrives on schedule and with crushing finality. You know instantly whether you've made it or not, and there's no going back to fix anything."

"What are they?"

"A political campaign, opening a musical comedy at the Winter Garden, and taking off for the moon."

"What's the point?" asked Quimby.

"The point is that in these activities *all* the mistakes must be removed in advance. The next-to-final Polcon poll is in, Martin. The final one comes down from Hartford tomorrow. You've created one hell of a lot of hoopla along the campaign trail. The PR has been brilliant. Victoria has worked like a veteran. But we are still deficient in one major respect."

"What's that?"

"Votes."

"I've come up in the polls—"

"Sure, but not enough. After all our efforts and all the nationwide excitement, you've moved up only six percentage points in the past two weeks."

"You don't know these crowds like I do, Quick. I tell you, I'm ready to peak. When I finish the whistle-stop tour on Monday night, I'll have the most—"

"We can't depend on your intuition, Martin. The fact is that William Spavin has also come up six points, campaigning from the dayroom of the Clabberville State Hospital for the Insane."

"But I've magnetized the media. It's a media society! I can't lose!"

"That's a typical campaign trail delusion. The fact is that you *can* lose if you don't get enough votes. So I've asked you here to make a recommendation."

"Have you cleared it with Victoria?"

"Of course."

"I thought she'd be here."

"She's over at Bruce headquarters," I explained, "trying to get Myrtle Bruce to withdraw in your favor. She already got Virginia Smith to withdraw, along with that sewer commissioner of Asbury Park."

"Excellent."

"But not enough. I recommend that for these last four days of the campaign, we cancel the whistle-stop tour and move immediately into minicam videotape, making some instant TV spots. We need a complete mood change."

"*What?*"

"You will visit a gentle Mennonite farm housewife, and we'll make a spot out of it. You'll visit your grandson down in Flugel County and make a polluted-river spot with him. You will take some teenagers through the Jersey Meadowlands, explaining that all improvements there could create more money for the school system of the state. You will go to Jungle Land as an ordinary happy tourist. You will—"

Quimby was furious. His chop gesture was modified into a heavy pounding on my desk.

"For God's sake, Quick, what are you *doing*? My campaign is a substantial entity. It is not some fake thing that I can put on and take off like a Nixonian viewpoint. It's—it's *me*! And I knew it was me the moment Victoria suggested it."

I flipped open the computer print-out, and the sheets cascaded down to the floor.

"Look at the figures, Martin. Recognition Factor, ninety-eight percent. Credibility Factor, ninety-three percent. Fragmentation Factor, eighty-nine percent. Affectional Factor, thirty-one percent. I'm advising you professionally on the basis of my experience that if we could increase your Affectional Factor, we might just stand a chance. Otherwise, forget it."

"What the hell is the Affectional Factor?"

"It says that only thirty-one percent of the people perceive you as a well-rounded person, capable of love and affection."

"Horseshit."

"I'm not saying it's *true*, Martin. But as the result of the campaign to date, it's the way people see you."

"Now listen to me, Quick—"

A tremendous crash of breaking glass shot through the headquarters. I leaped around the desk, but Quimby got to the office door ahead of me. We looked across the expanse of the big converted store, over the heads of the frightened, crouching volunteers to where a huge plate-glass show window had been shattered.

"Son of a bitch!" I said. "Another one."

At the same moment, Victoria burst through the front door, frightened but furious.

"I got the license plate," she shouted. "New Jersey BPR two-five-five! Take it down, somebody. New Jersey BPR two-five-five. A green Ford with two honky pricks in it! Joey, call nine-one-one—nine-one-one. Get the cops over here!"

One of the volunteers picked up what looked like half a brick and handed it to Victoria. She headed directly across the big room to my office, telling everybody firmly to get back to work, holding her fright until she got inside. And then there was a flood of tears in her eyes and she started to shake.

"Oh, Tom, I'm stone down and scared—scared. Martin, I'm glad you're here. Are you all right?"

"I'm fine," he said.

I held her to me. Quimby took the brick from her hand, unwrapped the note that was taped around it. He unfolded the paper—lined paper that had been ripped from a schoolkid's notebook. In blunt pencil was the spooky, spiky half-printing, half-writing, of the potential loon:

> Quimby:
>
> It is your kind of skum that is wreking this state. Stay out of the office of Gov. Stay out of trenton. Get yoreself elected and you will here from me again with a hell of a lot more than this. You will here from me with a assful of buckshot.
>
> George L.

Victoria was still trembling, but Quimby remained unshaken. He smiled at me.

"This must be one of the people who doesn't see me as a well-rounded person, capable of love and affection."

"Martin—" said Victoria, catching her breath, "Martin, in the past four days—there's been—well, there's been something *awful* here—"

"Take it easy, Victoria," said Quimby. "Come on, sit down."

"About twenty crazy letters like this have come in."

"Through the window?" he asked.

"Martin, *please.* Don't laugh at this."

"Matter of fact, it *is* the second one through the window," I said. "I've tried to tell Victoria that it's not necessarily a groundswell. The whole thing could be done by the two guys in the green Ford."

"They'll bear watching," said Quimby.

"I've taken the letters to the Newark police," she said, "but all they say is that they're working on it."

"All right," said Quimby. "They'll work on the notes; we'll work on the campaign. When you stir people up, some of them love it, some of them hate it, and some of them go ape. But a candidate can't be responsible for the mental health of everybody in New Jersey. It's enough work to get elected."

"Did—did you hear Tom's recommendation?"

"Yes, and I didn't buy it."

"You know what *I* recommend? Cancel the tour, go back to Misty Harbor, and stay home until election day."

"Victoria, that's the first crummy suggestion you've come up with," said Quimby. "I thought you were a hell-raiser at heart."

"So did I. And I was—until that first brick came through the window three days ago. And then I—I got afraid for you, Martin. I want you to *win*. I don't want you to lose—or get hurt by some slippy-headed crazy."

"Victoria—Victoria. Listen. Nothing bad is going to happen to me that can be *prevented*. The whole story of American public life proves that. Lincoln, Garfield, McKinley, Jack Kennedy, Bobby, Martin Luther King—my God, they even took some pot shots at genial old Jerry Ford."

"That's why if you change the tone of the campaign, Martin—" I said.

"Listen! If I change the campaign or cancel the campaign, it would say to the people—both the sane and the insane—that I'm afraid. Well, the fact is that I'm not afraid. So I'm not changing anything." He put on his hat. "I'm going over to Paramus now and give them hell."

"You can understand our concern," I said, holding his overcoat for him.

"And I appreciate it, Quick. I do, indeed. But if you'll excuse me now, Al Divver is waiting. And come see me off at the station in the morning, will you? My historic whistle-stop tour across the State of New Jersey is going to be a smash!"

"We'll be there," said Victoria, giving him a kiss on the

cheek. "I'm sorry we didn't leave enough room in the campaign for the Affectional Factor."

"Don't worry," said Quimby. "I predict that when the final poll arrives tomorrow, it will show Martin J. Quimby climbing—climbing—outstripping the opposition—*surging* into the lead!"

"One can hope so," I said. "And we do, Martin."

He paused at the door to turn back.

"I want to thank you for getting me into this, Quick. I'm going to get more than forty percent of the vote on Tuesday. I'm going to *love* being governor. And I'm going to be *very* good at it."

CHAPTER 19

NEXT MORNING at seven-thirty, we saw the candidate off on his final swing, with Quimby waving and doffing his hat from the back platform of the "Quimby Special" as the train pulled out. Neither Victoria nor I matched his ebullient mood, but we tried not to let Martin see that. After breakfast at the Newark Hilton, she left with Divver to see if she could persuade Six Fingers Tarantina to withdraw in our favor. She was carrying our campaign plan book and our latest computer print-out to prove to Tarantina how badly he was doing, but I did not think it would be persuasive. I told her she'd have better luck with Mr. Spavin or Smokey Carson.

I spent half the morning stewing in the office, partly about Quimby's safety, but also about what my next move would be if the final poll showed that Quimby would lose—and then he did. This produced nothing but anxiety and a headache. The final poll, being run off on a leased computer in Hartford, was supposed to be on my desk at 10:00 A.M. When it had not arrived by eleven, I decided that it was time for some action, that—win or lose—I was going to get something out of all this effort. I pounded on my desk and left for Manhattan.

Half an hour later, I entered the House of Harry Winston on the corner of Fifth Avenue and 55th Street. The private Winston cop nodded vaguely to me as he unlocked the triple doors. I had been there three times over the past fourteen years, and the same cop always opened the doors.

I asked for Mr. Schlemmer, and in a few minutes, my Dutch diamond expert came out of the back room, smiling, dipping his cueball head in a slight European bow when he saw me.

"Ahhhhh, Meester Quick! I did not expect to see you again. Velcome back."

"Hello, Mr. Schlemmer. How are you?"

"Fine, fine. Und how can I help you?"

"I'd like a square-cut diamond engagement ring—nine or ten carats, say."

"Not another one!" he said, smiling and making a clucking sound of disapproval. "My friend, I thought that you had sworn off."

"Mr. Schlemmer, don't talk yourself out of a sale."

He did a refined Dutch chuckle.

"But don't you remember?" he asked.

"Remember what?"

"What you told me one day after your third divorce—standing in front of Atlas at Rockefeller Center?"

"What did I say?"

"You said that a man und a woman get along just beautiful—up until the time the man buys the woman a can opener. Then the trouble begins."

"That's true, Mr. Schlemmer. But sometimes you just can't help yourself. Sometimes you find somebody so special—so great!—that you just go for the fourth can opener! There's no way out."

Schlemmer shrugged an acceptance, took a velvet tray

with half a million dollars' worth of diamond rings from the bevelled glass case, and I held them, one by one, up to the light.

"Take your time," said Schlemmer.

As I continued to look them over, he leaned confidentially on the glass case with a question.

"Und may I ask if she is another from Vassar?"

I nodded, and Schlemmer looked slightly pained.

"Und did you consider," he asked, "that you might have a little better luck at another institution?"

"No," I said. "But the new Mrs. Quick is not a white Presbyterian. She's a black American Indian."

"Und so perhaps *that* will make the difference?" he asked, his eyebrows shooting up in surprise. "You have known her long?"

"Five weeks Tuesday."

"Hmmmmmmm. You will want her initials in the ring along with the T. J. Q.?"

"Of course. Her name is Victoria Woodhill."

He started to print her name on a white pad, then suddenly looked up. "Wait—wait. I am remembering something from my naturalization examination down on Church Street. Victoria Woodhill! That was the name of the first woman ever to run for president of the United States."

"That's not exactly right, Mr. Schlemmer. The woman you're thinking of was Victoria Claflin Woodhull. In 1872 she ran for president on the Free Love ticket."

"Und lost," said Schlemmer.

"Yes," I said, "but single-issue candidates have never done well on the national level."

"I didn't know that."

"But I'll tell you something else, Mr. Schlemmer. If *this* Victoria ever runs for the job, she'll win!"

Back at Quimby headquarters, with the tabulations of the final poll spread out before me, I called in my secretary to dictate a wire. My secretary was no longer Emily, but a pleasant Rahway housewife, Mrs. Irma Remsen. Mrs. Remsen, an old-line do-gooder Democrat, had volunteered for the campaign, but she was so solidly reliable that I quickly put her on the paid staff. She smiled constantly and typed with machine-gun accuracy.

(Actually, I still missed working with Emily, but I had not been able to persuade her to leave Manhattan. Partly, it was because of her disappointment in me, of course; but Emily was also strongly committed to her friends. In dim, narrow bars on First Avenue she knew a spectrum of showy young men and women with identical hair. They drank odd drinks, sniffed a white powder, talked an oblique argot, and appeared in Bloomingdale's ads with their slim, stylish hands on the hips of each other's fifty-dollar English saddle-cut jeans. Emily said that friends like this could not be duplicated anywhere in New Jersey, and I think she was right. We parted amicably. I gave her a powerful recommendation, and she went to work for a trendy little no-load mutual fund that operated out of a town house in the East 70s.)

"This will be a full-rate telegram, Mrs. Remsen, going by Western Union to Martin J. Quimby, *The Ferdinand Magellan*, Delaware and Lackawanna Railroad."

"*The Ferdinand Magellan*?" she inquired.

"It's an old observation car that the Chesapeake & Ohio rents for campaigning. FDR used to use it all the time to travel to Hyde Park."

"Perhaps some of Mr. Roosevelt will rub off on Mr. Quimby."

"Anything would help, Mrs. Remsen. The final poll is not good."

"They don't come any better than FDR," she said with a smile of remembrance.

"That's true. Tommy the Cork once said that FDR was a nonrepeating phenomenon."

"I only saw him one time in person," she said. "At the Delaware Water Gap, cutting a ribbon. But I heard him forever. I was twenty-four when he died, and he had been President for half my life."

"That's interesting, Mrs. Remsen."

"And you know, whenever Roosevelt spoke, it was springtime. He would reach out and embrace you with that voice, and no matter what he said—"

"Mrs. Remsen, can we reminisce after Tuesday? I have to get this out fast."

"Of course, of course—"

"Dear Martin," I began. "Let me begin by saying some good things. The PR on the campaign has been brilliant. You have turned out to be the best campaigner I have ever worked with. I also report that Victoria spoke so winningly this morning that Smokey Carson threw in the towel and joined with us. Tarantina is still holding out, and I think will continue to do so. Paragraph.

"You were right also to persist on your chosen track. I am sure that thousands of voters have by now seen through your abrasive words to the real you, a man who really does have a dream for New Jersey. Paragraph.

"But in spite of all the excitement and the hoopla, Martin—"

"This is going to be an expensive telegram," said Mrs. Remsen, who was economy-minded around the office.

"—but in spite of all these good things, Martin, we have simply not been able to convert the excitement and the hoopla into votes. The hard fact is that, according to the final Polcon poll that is now on my desk, we are going to lose this election. If we continue doing for the next two days what we are doing now, we will lose. It will be a runoff between Makabu and Wyncyncynski. Paragraph."

"That's crushing news," said Mrs. Remsen. "Crushing—"

"So, Martin, we have to do something else. We need what a former mayor of Detroit calls a 'roarback.' That is, we must drop some surprising bombshell on the candidates who still oppose us. By dropping it on Monday, the last day of the action, they will have no chance to reply. I don't know what the roarback is at the moment, but I will let you know as soon as I think one up. Whatever it may be, it is our only chance. Best, Quick."

All through Saturday and on into the evening, Victoria and I had the headquarters staff brainstorming and skull-beating in search of a roarback. It was an exhausting, aggravating, unsuccessful procedure, and it wasn't until one o'clock Sunday morning that I called off the fruitless search and sent everybody home.

Back at UN Plaza, Victoria and I soaked in the Levantine marble tub for a couple of hours in warm oil of *goan*, and now, at 4:00 A.M., we lay on top of the electric quilt on the huge bed, gazing up into the ceiling mirror. I mentioned to Victoria that this would be the first time we would exchange affection without travelling somewhere at high speed in a moving vehicle. Such had been the mobile scheduling pressure of the campaign. Victoria sat up in fake surprise.

"If we're not going anywhere, why is the bed jiggling?"

"I turned on the Magic Fingers," I said, pointing to the coin slot on the night table. (I had purchased this neat device from the Holiday Inn Christmas Catalogue.)

"Turn the Magic Fingers off," she said, taking my hand

and beginning to kiss my fingers one by one. "Yours are enough."

And so they were. Victoria fell gracefully back across me so that my fingertips could go nowhere but to her breasts—two examples of soft sculpture that would put to shame the entire collection on the fourth floor of the Whitney. Though we were knowing companions by now, I always touched Victoria Woodhill with a sense of awe. Not reticence, but awe. Everything about her looked so neat and worked so smoothly and felt so right. It really was awesome to lie there, touching the very tip of one breast and seeing the coffee-colored nipple of the other one emerge like the nose of a kitten poking its way into the world. There was such an ambience of beauty about her that the savoring had no end. She was a Mobius strip of pure pleasure.

We began to kiss with an amiable ferocity, as though we had not seen each other in years. Then I began to kiss Victoria in a whole host of places. She started to moan, as she had long ago on the Metroliner, while I slowly kissed my way down the bronze curve of her back, came to a smooth cleft, kept going, and finally arrived at a place where Victoria turned from bronze to pink. Then I heard her voice, as from a far distance, saying the old magic imperative sentence once again.

But a little while later, while I was perhaps ten seconds from a particular kind of Paradise, Victoria's thrusting and Victoria's moaning suddenly stopped. She twisted her head to look back up at me.

"I've got it!" she shouted happily.

"What?" I asked.

"The *roarback*!"

"*Victoria*! This is one hell of a time to talk politics!"

But Victoria would not be deflected from her primary role as the manager of the Quimby Campaign. From her position on all fours, she sprang away from me with the sound of a cork leaving a bottle. And then she was pacing the floor, clapping her hands in naked delight with what she had just conceived.

"Listen, Tom. Just listen to this!"

I lay back on the bed with a sigh. I was unfulfilled. I was disgruntled. The flare had gone out of my nostril.

"What a wrinkle—what a *wrinkle*!" she kept repeating.

I bunched a pillow up under my head, sighed again, lit a cigar, and picked up my drink.

"This better be absolutely terrific, Victoria."

"It is. Listen: the roarback is to have Martin J. Quimby get *married* on Monday afternoon—and to introduce his new bride to all New Jersey on the Quimby Telethon on Monday night! That will win it!"

"Married to whom?" I asked.

"Me."

I spluttered the drink just the way Oliver Hardy used to do when Stan Laurel would hit him with a large wooden mallet.

"I know it sounds a little slippy in the head," she said, still pacing and putting her thoughts together, "but just let me make four—"

"For Christ's sweet sake, Victoria," I said.

"—just let me make four quick points. That's all. Four points. Point One: Your polls show that people think of Quimby as half-a-man because he doesn't understand affection. He marries me, and that takes care of the Affectional Factor. It shoots from thirty-one percent to ninety-two percent overnight."

"For Christ's sweet sake, Victoria."

"Point Two: We've heard all along that Quimby is a shade too old—that he should be settling down instead of trying to stir things up. With me on his arm, he'll seem a lot younger to everybody—including himself."

"For Christ's sweet sake—"

"Point Three: The marriage will help him over the race barrier!"

"For Christ's sweet—"

"It's true. It's *true*! Kabu Makabu's people will see it as just another rip-off by Mister Charlie, but they'd never vote for him no matter what. The older, sentimental people —black and white—will see the marriage as a symbol of the healing of those old frictions Martin is always hollering about. And Point Four—"

"Quimby will never buy this. Never!"

"Why not? He likes me."

"He loves you, Victoria. So does every man who lays an eye on you. But Quimby's much too conventional for a bombshell like this. Much too square—much too straight—much too devoted to the late Paola—much too—"

"Wait a minute, Tom—"

Victoria paused with the naked, legs-apart stance that I remembered from the governor's office the day that Divver walked in on her. She laughed the low, sinuous laugh.

"Let's let the candidate speak for himself."

I sat up, squashing the cigar, looking at her. The big trouble was that Victoria's roarback, like all her other stuff, was indeed terrific. It was the only thing that could possibly put Quimby over the forty percent mark. It was the only thing that could possibly carry me to my secret position as the Lieutenant Governor of New Jersey. And yet, as frequently happens in the entertainment media as well as in life itself, things had subtly changed. There was a time a few weeks before when I wanted nothing more than the financial shelter of that unsung office in Trenton. But I had become a victim of rising expectations. Now I wanted something *more*. I wanted Victoria Woodhill. I wanted her officially. The Harry Winston diamond was resting in an ormolu drawer across the room, and the plan was to make Victoria *mine*, for Christ's sweet sake, and not Martin Quimby's! Anything else was, as Churchill used to say to Rudolf Hess, unacceptable. I sprang off the bed and took her in my arms.

"Baby, let's run away to South America!"

"You haven't heard Point Four. Point Four:—"

"I did a campaign in Paraguay last year," I went on fast. "I was very big in Paraguay, and I got an offer from Ecuador just yesterday. Let's go,Victoria. Braniff Flight No. 802 out of JFK arrives in Quito at four this afternoon. I'll start packing."

"Point Four:—"

"Forget it. Politics is so *easy* down there. Political consulting is a snap. You'll love it! There are no caucuses, no primaries, no voting machines, no constituents. Nothing! All you do is take a few polls to count up the armament of the opposing junta. The rest of the time, you make love!"

"I'm *not* going to South America, Tom. I'm just getting started in North America."

"Your roarback is splendid," I said, holding her close. "Splendid like everything else you've dreamed up. There's only one thing really wrong with it."

"What's that?"

"*I* want to marry you."

"You?"

"Me."

"*You*?"

"Me."

"That's jive you just made up right now."

"No. I've got the Harry Winston ring and everything."

"Nooooooooooooooo—"

"Don't sound so shocked, Victoria."

"But I *am* shocked. You've kept saying all along that—"

"I know. I know. That I'd never again get entangled.

That all I wanted to do was carom off women like a well-aimed cue ball in a massé shot on the billiard table of life."

"That's *exactly* what you've been saying."

I said nothing for several seconds, then spoke very quietly.

"Victoria, we've been so busy with sex and politics since the day I rescued you that I've never really said what I wanted to say. I love you, Victoria. That's what I've wanted to say. I love you."

She turned away from me and went to the huge plate-glass window that looked south across Manhattan. She stood there looking out, her hands low on her hips, and then she spoke very quietly, too.

"Nobody's ever said that to me before, Tom."

"Come on."

"No. I mean it. Not that way. Not quiet and easy like that. I wonder why—"

"I can tell you. Because you put out so much pure sex, Victoria, that it gets in the way of *everything*. Your blazing passion is like a firestorm on the sun—with flames leaping up a quarter of a million miles into the air. It obliterates everything—even love."

"Point Four:—" she said, turning around, coming back toward me with a smile. "Point Four: My proposal to Martin is what's called a 'marriage of convenience.' They used to have them all the time in the fifteenth century."

"Oh?"

"I learned about them at Vassar. People used to marry just to hold the kingdom or the duchy together. We'll marry just to bring a Democratic and Independent majority together."

"And then?"

"Martin will understand this, of course. After he's safely the governor, then he and I can quietly drift apart until—

pouf!—a friendly divorce. The divorce rate in New Jersey is high enough so that it can't possibly hurt his career. Nobody will even notice."

In a trice, the future lay bright and clear and solid before me. I slipped into my shorts.

"Come on, baby. Get dressed. We've got to find the *Ferdinand Magellan.*"

"But it's four-thirty in the morning."

"Yes, and Martin is out somewhere in the wilds of northern New Jersey. But I want this item on the morning AP wire."

"We've got to do one thing first," she said, taking me by the hand.

"What?"

She dropped back onto the bed with a bounce and a rich laugh, stretching full length in the shape of a delectible, soft letter X.

"Finish," she said.

"Boss!"

I slipped out of my shorts. Victoria rolled over, dimmed the lights, and then closed on me like one of those Chinese rattan finger traps.

The only time I ever got west of Eighth Avenue as a child was one summer when I was sent to my mother's second cousin's farm in Kansas. There were two tornadoes while I was there: one in the day and one in the night. An orgasm in concert with Victoria Woodhill is like a Kansas tornado in the night. Fright is replaced with pleasure, of course, but the externals are pretty much the same.

It starts as a kind of distant, wondrous tremble. You can feel it coming. You can hear it coming. It *keeps* coming. And there is nothing you can do about it but ride it out—ride it out all the way—hanging on for dear life! Finally it is upon you, swirling, roaring across you, shaking the bed, shaking the house, shaking the earth, shaking the sky itself. Exhilaration is sucked into the tightest vortex on earth. And then whammo!—it is gone! *Somewhere*. Nobody ever knows. You sit up groggily, running your hands over your body and the body of your panting companion, checking for any damage that might have been incurred. And you wonder if you could *ever* put up with anything like that again. The answer, of course, is Yes. At the very first opportunity.

CHAPTER 20

FOUR HOURS LATER, on a brilliant autumn morning, we were riding with Quimby in the parlor lounge at the rear of the *Ferdinand Magellan.* The gracious old car moved along a single Lackawanna track through the bright-colored leaves of an eastern hardwood forest, making the old graceful click-click, click-click sound.

I sat in a mohair chair, drinking a Manhattan on the rocks, looking at the old burled, scrolled woodwork and listening to Victoria. Perched on the edge of a table in a striking light green pongee pants suit, she smiled with delight at Quimby as she described her roarback, proposed marriage to him, and began to lay out her four points.

Martin J. Quimby was stunned by the scheme. He sat in an overstuffed chair of buffalo hide, his feet on the matching ottoman, his eyes wide behind the aviator glasses. Martin's face showed shock and surprise, but I could see that it also held traces of slavering anticipation. Even before he spoke, it was clear that my self-serving prediction about his unwillingness to go along with the idea was dead wrong. Quimby was ready. And when you came right down to it, why not?

Just before the critical Point Four, the candidate held up a hand, then sprang lightly from his low chair to kiss Victoria. It was not the usual peck-type kiss that is exchanged between people who have a chasm of time between them. This was a kiss that bridged the chasm, and when it was over, Quimby already appeared younger. There was no real reason for my hand to be shaking as I took another belt of my Manhattan, but I noticed that it was. Quimby's hands, however, were not shaking. They were firmly locked around Victoria's supple waist as he summoned speech.

"Victoria—Victoria! I accept your superb proposition! Never—never in my wildest flights of fancy did I think I would deserve or possess a—a magnificent woman like yourself."

He kissed her again. I had never seen Martin so truly touched, so truly wound up, so truly uncool.

"That's something like what Thalberg said about Garbo," I remarked, taking another drink.

"Will you excuse us, Tom?" asked Quimby politely. I nodded, and he took Victoria by the hand and led her out onto the observation platform, where they stood together for a long time, chatting, smiling, laughing, holding hands, enjoying the autumnal beauty. I thought I might notice a change in Martin when she got to Point Four, but he remained as ebullient as ever out there.

I rang a tasselled cord, and the steward appeared. I told him I wanted to stop at the next station to put a story on the AP wire and alert the networks. He said that the next town was Bailiwick, New Jersey, a scheduled stop on the tour. I ordered another drink. Quimby and Victoria were still out on the platform as we pulled into Bailiwick.

Bailiwick, New Jersey, is a lovely little town so incredibly out of the way that it still has an Esso station. A sedate group of ten Bailiwickians, including the mayor, had come down to the station to hear the candidate speak. The mayor had arrived in a Stutz with a chain drive.

The speech began with Quimby's regular harangue, and then he moved on to the rural issues he'd put together for the whistle-stopping. But his old abrasiveness was toned down and at the end of the speech, when he came to introduce his campaign manager as the woman he would marry tomorrow, the toughness had vanished from his voice. He spoke with warmth and with awe.

"I realize that there is a forty-two-year difference in our ages," said Quimby. "But age has nothing to do with true affection. True affection can fracture the rigidities of time, for it is, as Theodore Roosevelt once said, the wonderful cement that holds the whole world together. I earnestly solicit your vote—and your wish for our happiness. Thank you for coming down to listen to me—and God bless you—and good-day."

I was standing down on the tracks with the audience, watching their reaction carefully. These rural New Jersey folk—plagued by sagging railroad service, stunned by soaring inflation, victimized by an endemic cultural lag—would they approve this black-white, May-September marriage? Three of the ten were negative and suspicious. They turned and walked away. But the other seven Bailiwickians, including the mayor, came forward to shake hands with the candidate and Victoria, and to wish them well. If that ratio held across the whole population of the state, we were in clover.

A plaque at the entrance said that the Bailiwick railway station had been designated as a national historic site. In every respect, it was. The three employees—ticket seller, news vendor, and telegrapher—were all wearing their sixty-year pins from the Delaware and Lackawanna Railroad. I nodded to the ancient news vendor, who was lighting a Sweet Caporal and reading a copy of *Collier's*. I crossed the spacious room to give my story to the Postal Telegraph man. As I wrote it out with a soft pencil on the faded blue-and-white pad, he would take each page, pull down his green eyeshade, and click it out to AP headquarters in Chicago. He had a good fist.

The message said:

WHAT HATH GOD WROUGHT? MARTIN J. QUIMBY (IND.), CANDIDATE FOR GOVERNOR OF NEW JERSEY, ANNOUNCED THIS MORNING TO A WHISTLE-STOP AUDIENCE IN THIS SMALL NORTH JERSEY COMMUNITY THAT HE WOULD MARRY TOMORROW.

HIS BRIDE WILL BE VICTORIA WOODHILL, THE YOUNG WOMAN WHO HAS BEEN SERVING AS THE MANAGER OF HIS INTENSE, CONTENTIOUS CAMPAIGN. MR. QUIMBY IS 65. MS. WOODHILL IS 23. IT IS HIS SECOND MARRIAGE AND MS. WOODHILL'S FIRST. HIS FIRST MARRIAGE ENDED WITH THE DEATH OF THE LATE PAOLA LO BRUTTO QUIMBY, WHO WAS FOR MANY YEARS THE PRESIDENT OF THE MISTY HARBOR GARDEN CLUB.

THE COUPLE PLANS TO JOURNEY TOMORROW MORNING TO MISTY HARBOR, N.J., IN THE FERDINAND MAGELLAN, THE PRIVATE RAILROAD CAR THAT HAS CARRIED THE CANDIDATE ON HIS FINAL RECORD-BREAKING WHISTLE-STOP TOUR. THE WEDDING WILL TAKE PLACE AT NOON IN THE MISTY HARBOR PRESBYTERIAN CHURCH. AFTER THE RECEPTION, THE BRIDAL COUPLE WILL RETURN TO THE OLD ROCOCO RKO THEATRE IN NEWARK FOR THE FINAL ELECTION-EVE TELETHON, "ASK QUIMBY." THE THEATRE IS SCHEDULED FOR DEMOLITION LATER IN THE WEEK.

THE COUPLE PLANS TO MAKE THEIR HOME IN TRENTON.

It was an understated piece of PR, but it worked. When we got back to Newark late Sunday evening, five thousand people were waiting at the station for a glimpse of the candidate and his intended wife. There was a pandemonium of affection for them. Clearly, we had struck a responsive chord. And it was only the beginning. Just before noon on Monday when our train pulled into the Misty Harbor station, there were twenty-five thousand people on hand to greet the happy couple. An unfettered roar of welcome went up as Quimby and Victoria stepped out onto the observation platform to smile and wave.

As the roar continued, I began to pick out familiar faces in the sea of cheering humanity. Everybody was there. Dick Tuck was there. Joe DiMaggio was there. Charlie Bulotti was there. So was Truman Capote. So was Bill Cosby, surrounded by kids. So were the Norton Zelvers of Menlo Park and Halston and Phil Rosenthal and Carol Channing and John Glenn and John Denver and Meredith Burch and Angie Dickinson and Tom Wicker and Doots Carr and Dinah and Walter Hickel and Steve McQueen. *Everybody*! Even Eli Bleisch. It was neat. The cheering did not stop, and it was accompanied by the strong beat of the Misty Harbor High School Band playing, predictably enough, "New Jersey Is the Only Place for Me."

A little later, when Trombone Lonergan tried to march his group right into the Presbyterian church for another go at the song, I objected. It was then that Trombone confessed to me that he had spent sixteen years and seven thousand dollars trying to get four state administrations to make his stirring composition the official state song of New Jersey.

"But now," he said, with a wild ray of hope in his eye, "if we can just drum it into Quimby's head and then he gets elected, my song may stand a chance at last!"

"But not in the church, Trombone," I said. "Why not set your band up at the Misty Harbor Hilton? You can alternate with the rock band at the reception."

"*Bellissimo*!" shouted Lonergan. "We'll do it! But which rock group did Martin invite?"

"Passaic Abbatoir."

"It figures," said Lonergan. "They're his favorites."

"Apparently," I said. "It was one of the great surprises

of my life to learn that Martin J. Quimby is a heavy-metal rock freak."

"How about you, Mr. Quick?"

"I'm more partial to things like 'Moon River.'"

"We'll play it for you! And thanks a lot."

Handing me a Xeroxed copy of the inspirational lyrics to "New Jersey Is the Only Place for Me," he was gone.

The wedding in the handsome old stone Presbyterian church turned out to be as tasteful as any jostling public event can be. As at the old gangster funerals in Chicago, the people pushed forward and the cops crushed them back.

I was the best man, of course, and had rushed back to Harry Winston's that morning to get the ring with which Quimby would marry Victoria Woodhill. The whole matter was quite confusing to Mr. Schlemmer. He was not his jovial, twinkling self. Though he was concerned that I might want to come back later and return the engagement ring, I think that in his methodical, racist, Dutch Reform mind, he was glad to hear that I was not linking up officially with a non-Caucasian.

Victoria would be given in marriage by her old friend from Whoopeeton, Belton Waco Jones. Belton showed up at the church in a soft beige suede suit that had obviously been tailored in Texas. I thought he looked fine, but Sam Scalese shook his head negatively. He whispered that the lapels were too wide and the pants too narrow. And the chocolate-colored leather patch just below the right shoulder—designated to take the thrust of the butt of a shotgun in the bush—it was far too theatrical for Sam's taste. Just before the ceremony, Scalese sidled up to Belton and reminded him to take off his Stetson before they started down the aisle. Belton agreed and thanked him kindly.

I had arranged for a large press table to be placed down near the pulpit. Behind the pencil reporters was a battery of twelve film and television cameras. The minister, brilliant at PR, had distributed Xeroxed copies of the entire service so the cameramen could switch on for coverage of the pivotal moments.

I counted forty-three people covering the event. On the TV side, not only were there cameras from the three networks, PBS, Westinghouse, and Metromedia, but it was the first time in history that an American social event had been covered by SovTel, the Russian TV news agency. (SovTel had been personally accredited by the President just the week before, after the *New York Daily News* had inexplicably been invited to open a bureau in Leningrad.)

At high noon, Victoria and Belton Waco Jones started down the aisle, summoned by the clarion call of "Here Comes the Bride" on the mighty Wurlitzer organ. They were both smiling, easy, happy, but nobody was looking at Belton. Victoria wore a dress of the softest white wool, and she came to a halt before the minister in the single shaft of sunlight that came through the windows high above. What a remarkable sight!

I was standing to one side with Quimby, holding the ring on the tip of my little finger. Quimby was wearing a new charcoal suit with a faint pinstripe, a suit that Sam Scalese had run up from scratch in just five hours. Quimby and I smiled at each other. For the first time in the whole campaign, I thought this incredibly self-confident man looked just a shade nervous. But the chips were down, and the cameras were rolling, and Martin J. Quimby did not falter.

The ceremony went off gracefully to the whirr of the cameras. When it was over, Quimby turned to give his bride a kiss. It was not just a symbolic or *pro forma* kiss for the media either. It was a big long one—so long, in fact, that the whole congregation finally broke into applause. It was the first time I had ever seen a reporter applaud anything.

Even the dour cameraman from SovTel was clapping. So was his soundman. Then the organist soared into the recessional at full volume. I thought I recognized the melody. Sure enough, it was "New Jersey Is the Only Place for Me."

The wedding reception was planned for seven hundred campaign workers, but when Quimby and his wife arrived at the Misty Harbor Hilton—driven by a happy Al Divver behind the motorcycles and sirens that he loved—Quimby threw the doors of the party open to everybody. It was just like Andrew Jackson arriving at the White House in March of 1831 and throwing open the doors so that the plain people of America could come in and have a piece of the 285-pound Victory Cheese that stood in the East Room.

The Hilton manager was furious. He had planned meticulously for only seven hundred. But the party was an ear-splitting success anyway, with plenty of food, plenty of booze, a revised budget, and an endless stream of music as Trombone Lonergan's band alternated with the intricate, loud, hard-rock tapestry provided by a stoned Passaic Abbatoir.

As I stood amiably next to Victoria in the receiving line, she leaned over to whisper in my ear.

"I have to pull your coat to something, Tom."

"Is it something neat, Victoria," I whispered, "or a bombshell?"

"A bombshell."

I took a Manhattan from a passing tray.

"Yes, baby?"

"You remember on Saturday when Martin and I went out on the observation platform just before we pulled into Bailiwick?"

"I do. It was a critical moment."

"I had to tell him right there that this was going to be a marriage of convenience."

"That was Point Four. *Of course* you had to tell him."

"But when we got out there, Tom—when we got out on the platform, and I looked at Martin beaming up at me, and when I listened to what he said—well, he was so damned happy that—"

"What'd he say?" I interrupted.

"He said that it was all a dream, but that he was going to live it like it was real life, and that I was the one who would make his golden years *truly* golden."

"And so," I said flatly, "you couldn't bring yourself to tell him about Point Four."

"That's it."

"Son of a bitch! It's a bombshell, all right." I took a long belt of the drink.

"But he was so tender and happy and—and *vulnerable* that I couldn't disappoint him."

"Tell him now! It's not too late!"

"If *he* had proposed to *me*," she whispered, "it would have been easier to—"

"Tell him *now*! He's not vulnerable. He's a tough old civil engineer."

There was a long interruption while we had to greet a raft of excited guests who had begun to stream excitedly through the reception line, shaking hands, getting names wrong, kissing Victoria.

"Victoria," I whispered when the first batch had passed on, "if this is really going to be a legit marriage—"

"Oh, we'll drift apart," she said, trying to reassure me. "But I can't be mean about it, Tom. It'll have to be a *natural* drift. It'll take longer—"

I looked over at Quimby. He winked at me in clear anticipation of what was to come that night after the big telethon. It was clear that Martin J. Quimby had not the slightest intention of drifting anywhere.

"I would say his maximum drift is going to be about six

feet," I said glumly. "Victoria, it's clear that we've gone *pouf*!"

More guests came by and we lit up our smiles to greet them. Then she took my arm gently and spoke in a whispered rush, explaining things to herself as well as to me.

"But look at it this way, Tom. If I *had* laid Point Four on him, and the wedding hadn't come off, and his Affectional Factor hadn't gone up the way it has, and then he didn't get elected, and *you* didn't get elected either—well, that would be stone down for your brilliant house-of-cards plan, wouldn't it?"

"Take it easy, Victoria. I understand. I understand."

Actually, I didn't. Movies out of the thirties are full of jilted lovers saying that they understand, when, in point of fact, they haven't the faintest idea of how come they've just been walloped right between the eyes with a two-by-four. That was me, standing there dazed in the reception line. I did the only thing possible. It's the same thing that people do in incurable wards every day. I looked on the humorous side.

"Victoria," I said with a big smile, "not since Woodrow Wilson collapsed in his fight for the League of Nations and Mrs. Wilson took over the whole executive branch of the United States government have I seen political loyalty carried so far!"

"I'd do that with New Jersey if Martin got sick," she said.

"And you'd do a hell of a lot better job than Mrs. Wilson," I assured her.

She smiled, but there was also a passage of sadness over the classic face.

"Say, there's one thing I haven't done!" I said, with continuing fake jauntiness.

"What's that?"

"Kissed the bride!"

"That's right."

I put down my drink, turned Victoria to me, took her lightly by the shoulders and gave her a chaste kiss, one appropriate to the situation. It was nothing at all like the enmeshed kisses we had exchanged in the Mercedes or on the train or in that executive jet or in the *Boston Whaler* on the Secaucus River or in all those other moving, jiggling vehicles that had carried us affectionately through the busy campaign.

"Oh, Tom—" she said.

"Oh, Victoria—" I said.

"I just thought of something else," she said.

"Oh, no."

"We never did buy that Honda CB420L."

We turned back to greet another surging mass of wedding guests. It would be a substantial task to pry Victoria Woodhill Quimby out of my mind forever. I noticed that I had one of my headaches and also that Trombone Lonergan's band was playing "I Cried for You."

CHAPTER 21

WAITING at the Newark station to cheer the newlyweds on their way to the RKO Theatre for the final event of the campaign were sixty-eight thousand people—by official police count. Behind the Misty Harbor High School Band, we rode away from the station in the dusk, with Divver at the wheel of a four-door Duesenberg convertible provided by a machinery millionaire who had come to regard Quimby as the savior of New Jersey. It was the last remaining open sedan—a phaeton, I think they used to call them—left in all of Newark.

Quimby and Victoria sat up on the rear of the back seat, waving with all the assurance of English royalty. I rode up front with Al Divver, who sensed the depth of my depression and tried to cheer me up with the news of the great size of the crowd. When that didn't work, he offered me a cigar and called my attention to the fine workmanship on the carved English walnut dashboard of the Duesenberg.

"The first American car with a tachometer," he said, pointing to the dial, which was as big as a saucer.

"Very interesting," I said.

"Why are we bullshitting this way?" he asked quietly.

"Tom, I want you to know that I'm sorry about what happened between you and Victoria."

"Do you *know* what happened?"

"A good driver knows everything," he said. "You have my condolences and my congratulations."

"Congratulations?"

"Sure. Victoria is a great gift to lay on the altar of democracy."

"That's sure as hell true."

"An' I have great respect for your forbearance and generosity."

"Thanks, Al." I saw no reason to explain that Point Four had gone awry.

"But can all this nuptial hoopla be translated into votes?" he asked.

"I'm damned if I know," I said. I turned around to look up at the ecstatic candidate and his wife. "I've never before been involved with an election that carried such a sensuous emotional wallop."

"But it'd be a shame for you to lose Victoria and then lose the election, too."

"That's sure as hell true."

"An' I want you to know that my condolences cover both them contingencies."

"Thanks, Al," I said.

The Quimby telethon, produced by A. B. Christian even while he questioned its effectiveness, would run live for two hours, and it would be beamed back into the state from both New York and Philadelphia stations. The program was called "Ask Quimby," and the format was simple. The stage of the old, doomed RKO Theatre was festooned with red-white-and-blue bunting. Quimby and Victoria would sit in comfortable Eames swivel chairs at stage center. A few feet away—in a fixed Eames chair at a telephone console—

would sit a smiling, high-speed conversationalist from San Diego. This man was J. Peter Weems, who ran the fastest talk show in the West. He had been flown in to do the same thing here, to take unscreened telephone calls that flowed in from citizens all across New Jersey, to chat with them for seven to ten seconds, then to pass on to the candidate so that they could ask their question. The voices on the phone would be heard clearly throughout the theatre. Questions from the phones were to alternate with questions from the theatre audience, and the clearly unrehearsed quality of the whole thing was designed to give it an unexpected, anticipatory, nervous edge.

I had stolen the idea for "Ask Quimby" from the most successful American political television program ever put on—with the possible exception of the Checkers speech. It was Hubert Humphrey's 1968 Election Night Telethon from Los Angeles (ABC–TV), produced on the last night of his remarkable campaign against the man who was then the former Vice-President of the United States, Richard M. Nixon. "Ask Humphrey," the show was called. As a friend of the skilled people who produced it, I dropped in on a couple of their wildly chaotic rehearsals, and at one point I suggested that the program should be called "Ask Hubert." The chairman of the Democratic National Committee overruled this suggestion, saying that it was a time for formality rather than folksiness.

"Ask Humphrey" was the event that capped the unprecedented surge in the last two weeks of the '68 campaign, a surge that brought Mr. Humphrey to within a twentieth of one percent of victory. Many experts later said that had the program been extended for another half hour, Hubert Humphrey would have been elected president of the United States, and many things would never have happened. (All those leading Nixon Administration figures would never, for example, have left their substantial jobs at Disneyland for the fragile, bungling criminality of the Nixon White House.)

There was, however, one big difference between "Ask Humphrey" and "Ask Quimby." "Ask Humphrey" was star-studded. In the Humphrey telethon, the questions were not only answered by Humphrey and a relaxed Ed Muskie (whose smiling urbanity peaked that night and never quite returned to the same level again), but by a slew of fifty dedicated Democratic movie and television stars, who occupied a long double dais on the stage. With sangfroid and aplomb—and even with accuracy—people like Burt Lancaster and Buddy Hackett and Nancy Sinatra were fielding questions from all across America, questions about open housing and monetary policy and Haiphong Harbor—then talking them over with Humphrey as he ranged about the stage. They were taking the pulse of America, and doing it without even using the seven-second tape-delay circuit that lets crazies be cut off the air before their profanity comes on; it was a classy, courageous production.

When "Ask Humphrey" was over, I went into the control room to offer my congratulations to Robert Squier, the cool producer who had pulled the whole thing together in seventy-two hours. While there, I quietly lifted the roster of stars from the console of the director, an electronic Barnum named Sidney Galanty. I still had that list in the Polcon file.

In proposing "Ask Quimby," I had recommended that Martin invite this same constellation of stars to Newark to do the same routine in his behalf. I figured that at least half of them, intrigued by Quimby's heavy national publicity, would accept.

"I'll buy the program idea, but I won't buy the stars," said Quimby.

"Why not? We've got the money. It would give a neat lift to the end of the campaign."

"But why would anybody look at me when they can look at Nancy Sinatra—or Paul Newman?"

"The stars will get more people to tune in in the first place."

"Sure," said Quimby. "To look at *them*. I can't compete with those big, expensive faces, Quick."

"Humphrey did," I said, remembering his lively performance with admiration. "He was wearing his electric blue suit with two vents in the back."

"I remember the suit," said Quimby, "but for God's sake, Quick, use your head. The man was the *Vice-President* of the United States. He had been the Mayor of *Minneapolis*. In 1948, he had galvanized the Democratic Convention with his stand on civil rights. In 1960, he had gone up against Jack Kennedy's father's bank account in West Virginia. In 1965, he had appeared on the cover of *Life* with *Lyndon B. Johnson* on the adjacent horse! He was a celebrated, beloved, garrulous American!"

"You're celebrated, Martin," I said.

"But still basically *unknown*. This is no time to go up against Burt Lancaster—or Buddy Hackett, either."

"So we do the telethon with just you sitting on the stage?" I asked.

"Me and J. Peter Weems and the cameramen. We'll do just fine."

I lost the argument, but went ahead with the program anyhow. I figured that we'd get a decent enough political-type rating, but nothing that could compare with "Kojak." Then came the roarback and the wedding and everything changed. There was a chair for the bride on the stage now, and everybody in New Jersey would be tuning in to size up the new Mrs. Quimby. Our Arbitron dial in the control room showed, even as our program began, that we were out-pulling everything else on the air, except a National Geographic Special that dealt with human fecundity in the tropics.

Martin Quimby had the time of his life on "Ask Quimby." Like FDR, he was an explainer at heart, and he sat there, sipping a Michelob, smoking a Hav-a-Tampa, smiling great crinkled smiles at Victoria, and answering everything bluntly. From the beginning, the candidate gracefully made his wife an integral part of the program. Many of the questions were answered by both of them. Sometimes they talked back and forth, searching for an answer. And Victoria handled the many questions directed to her—questions that had a much wider span than marriage or homemaking or whether she planned to have children or if she subscribed to *Ms.* Victoria even talked about her work at Mme Danou's in an easy, straightforward way! It was a critical moment. I had a feeling that the needle on the Arbitron dial would drop to zero. Instead it went up at this point—as more viewers tuned in—and it stayed up. Victoria Woodhill Quimby was turning out to be a compelling public figure.

Quimby took his characteristic stand on the issues, promising very little, even talking at one point about blood and sweat and tears. There were questions on unemployment, education, welfare, medicine, abortion, open housing, defense, inflation, foreign policy, transportation, energy, the environment, and, of course, the death penalty. There were also questions about blacks, chicanos, Puerto Ricans, Indians, and caucasians. Many of the identical questions had come up on "Ask Humphrey" years before, for the fact is that the big gut issues don't change much over time. (The Middle East, for example, has been a big gut issue for over two thousand years.)

"Big issues are important, of course," said Quimby,

toward the end of the program, "but we don't have to shake the world, folks. Let's try to get some agreement on smaller issues too, and maybe rebuild a little confidence in the process of state government. Without your confidence, your state government isn't worth a hoot in hell."

He was asked from the theatre audience to describe one such smaller issue.

"Sure," said Quimby. "Let me give you a modest example. If elected tomorrow, I shall propose to the New Jersey State Legislature a bill to have the owner of an urban or suburban dog carry a plastic container to clean up after the dog as he or she takes him or her for a walk through the streets. Now that is a perfectly *reasonable* piece of legislation—a banner to which, as George Washington once put it, we can all confidently repair. In our sanitized society, there is no reason at all why one man or woman should have to step in another man's or woman's dog's shit."

The crowd roared its approval. Victoria and Quimby held hands and smiled at each other. The Arbitron needle jumped higher. It seemed as though Martin Quimby had found an issue on which the citizens of New Jersey might come together at last.

At three minutes to nine, the floor manager gave J. Peter Weems the three-minute signal. Weems turned off further questions and asked Mr. Quimby to bring the telethon to a close.

Quimby thanked Weems for his fine work, then turned easily to the camera with the shining red light. His old contentiousness was there, but now it was muted by Victoria's presence and by his own aura of confidence.

"As the campaign draws to a close," he said, "I want, first, to thank all of you who have worked for me—and believed in me. I've learned a lot in these few weeks. I've learned that a man does not run all alone for an office. He cannot win all alone. And if he gets elected, he cannot govern all alone.

"In particular, I am indebted to Victoria Woodhill Quimby. My wife has thought up the three main ideas on which the campaign has been based. I wanted you to know that."

He swung his chair around, leaned over to kiss Victoria, then turned back to the camera.

"I hope, of course, that I do win tomorrow and do become the Governor of the State of New Jersey. But I want you to know right now tonight that—win or lose—this campaign has been the best thing that has ever happened to me! Even though four bricks were thrown through the windows of Quimby Headquarters, I have had a *pisswhacker* of a time!

"If I am elected tomorrow, we will all proceed modestly, walking together, stumbling at times, but getting up again and trying to find a constructive and humane path for *all* our citizens. In a democracy, as I have pointed out, we are irrevocably linked to the stupidest man or woman among us—that angry, poor, frustrated slow learner of any race or sex or creed who is always ready to drag us back toward the chaos of his or her own limited vision. And yet that person is one of us—in fact, that person is *most* of us—and we cannot in good conscience push him or her off the Great American Ferris Wheel.

"But *can* we inform the discretion of our sour-hearted citizens? In this grimy, urbanized society, can we find a constructive and humane part for everybody? Can a state government be of any *real* service to somebody like my angry friend, Ms. Martha Haight of the Ira Minskoff Sintered Metal Works just outside Metuchen? Frankly, I don't know.

"But I know that we must try. We must try at long last to create a community. We must have the guts and the energy and the humanity to begin anew. The Quimby Administration, like all others, will have shortcomings. But it will not be short on guts or on energy or on humanity."

The audience broke into what the *Congressional Record* describes as "prolonged applause."

"I urge you to go to the polls early tomorrow," Quimby said, "and I earnestly solicit your vote. And as you stand there in line waiting to vote, stand there with some pride, will you? For the line you stand in is a long and honorable one that stretches back for over two hundred years through the whole story of America. Washington stood in that line. So did Jefferson and Andrew Jackson. So did Abraham Lincoln and Elizabeth Cady Stanton and Eleanor Roosevelt and Ethel Waters and Joe Penner. That line, in fact, is the only place that we have *all* come together. Every single damned one of us! Terrific!

"And when you get to the head of the line, just step inside the green curtain and vote for Quimby—and Quick!"

That was it! The opening gun in my quiet campaign! I looked at my watch. One minute to nine. As the TV program ended with a final rousing chorus of "New Jersey Is the Only Place for Me," my campaign was beginning in a more muted way. By now, two thousand volunteers were gathering in local Quimby headquarters all across the state. In one hour, they would begin to fan out, to spend the entire night searching for those cars that had the VOTE FOR QUIMBY bumper sticker. In the morning, thanks to the color-perfect match of Schmiddle Litho, Inc., each would be converted into the long sticker with the new message.

At the same hour, unionized billboard pasters would go to work on twelve hundred adjoining billboards in every part of New Jersey. The VOTE FOR QUIMBY signs had been posted earlier—on the day that Martin had opened his campaign. Now, on this final night, the right-hand billboards would be emblazoned with—AND QUICK! This was the most expensive part of the operation. The billboard pasters were on triple golden time.

As the audience poured out of the old RKO palace for the last time, there was a faint whirring sound in the night sky. The people looked up to see the Goodyear blimp suspended over Newark. We had chartered it for these two nights, and as it floated slowly along, it lit up with the slightly cryptic incantation that they had just heard inside:

VOTE FOR QUIMBY—AND QUICK!

My name was unknown. My policies were unstated. My speeches were unspoken. But I was in the right place on the ballot, and my name was blinking in the sky over New Jersey. I was in the race to stay!

CHAPTER 22

ON ELECTION DAY, November 5, when the citizens of New Jersey got up, the QUIMBY-QUICK message assailed them from everywhere. It was part of the aural environment as well as the visual. Our last money had been budgeted by Victoria for a slew of ten-second radio and television spots—the only media buy that we made.

On radio, Quimby's now-familiar voice said:

"It's election day, folks. Get yourself down to the polls right now. Vote for Quimby—and Quick!"

The single television spot had no narration at all. It consisted of a single shot, beginning on the VOTE FOR QUIMBY billboard, and then zooming back during the ten seconds to include the adjoining—AND QUICK!

It worked. The whole campaign worked. At 4:00 A.M. the following morning—nine hours after the polls closed, six hours after the CBS computer predicted that he would win—the other seventeen candidates conceded the victory to Martin J. Quimby (Ind.). The last telegram to arrive at the Quimby hospitality suite in the Newark Hilton was a surly concession from Sal Wyncyncynski, who vowed to continue his private vigilante patrols as an outpost against Quimby's dangerous left-wing-homo-pinko-commie policies.

The suite was on the top floor of the Hilton. I went over and looked out the window. High up in the sky, the Goodyear blimp had got the message. It was now blinking:

QUIMBY WINS—AND QUICK!

Martin's total vote was 40.02 percent. There would be no need for a runoff. He was victorious! According to that 1973 Polcon survey, a person in my ballot position should have received 86 percent of Quimby's vote. But it didn't work that way. I actually did better than Quimby, getting 50.31 percent of the *total* vote. There was no explanation for this, but when you win, no explanation is necessary.

There were hundreds of calls and telegrams of surprised congratulations. The waiters were calling me "Mr. Lieutenant Governor" when they brought me drinks. But I did not feel a surge of unfettered delight. Like the Bible, my victory had happy parts—I had indeed won; and it had sad parts—I had lost Victoria in the process. Yet I did start to feel a little better after the visit of Rocky Bettenhauser. I had not seen Rocky since the day he tried to fire me in Trenton. He arrived at the suite just after the Wyncyncynski telegram to ingratiate himself with Quimby and me. I should have been, like Winston Churchill, magnanimous in victory. It would have been sensible and politically sound. But I just wasn't up to it. Instead, I greeted Rocky with a broad smile, shook hands warmly with him, and told him loudly to go fuck off.

At 4:15 A.M., it was time to go greet the loyal well-wishers and campaign workers across the street in Quimby headquarters. Quimby and Victoria and I rode down alone in the elevator to the lobby. It would be the last time for many days that the Governor and I would not be surrounded by eager people who were glad that we had won—and wanted something.

Leaving the elevator, we were taken in hand by a cadre of New Jersey Turnpike troopers. Having left their Harleys outside the lobby, they'd formed a wedge for us so that we could push our way through the boisterous crowd. Just before the push began, the lead trooper, in white helmet, blue uniform, and black boots, stepped up smartly to Quimby and saluted. Quimby responded by touching his fingers to the brim of his hat.

"Governor, I'm Captain Hanson of the Fourth Division, Motorized."

"Good evening, Captain."

"We're here to escort you to Headquarters, but before we start, I wanted to give you and the Lieutenant Governor your Golden Lifetime Passes on the New Jersey Turnpike."

He took two rectangles of golden plastic out of his shirt pocket, handing one to Quimby and one to me. Our names had been engraved on them. They looked like flashier versions of the American Express Executive Card.

"Thank you, Officer," said Quimby. "But how'd you turn these out so fast?"

"We had one made for each candidate, Governor. We've already destroyed the losers."

"And you mean, Captain Hanson," asked Quimby, "that even if I'm defeated four years from tonight, I'll *still* be able to ride free on the Jersey Turnpike?"

"Yes, Governor. It's a genuine Lifetime Pass for you and the missus."

"Damn," said Quimby, happily dropping the card into his wallet. "I *knew* it was right to get into politics."

As the push began, I slipped my Golden Lifetime Pass into the breast pocket of my new, conservative Scalese suit. The piece of plastic was the first hard evidence of my accession to power.

The Quimby headquarters was festooned beyond belief. Behind the podium was the largest picture of Quimby I had yet seen. Quimby and Victoria mounted the platform. I followed them, but stood just a shade to one side out of the main beam of the limelight. The crowd roared incessantly. Quimby tried to quiet them for a while. I expected him to grab the mike and bellow at them to shut up, but he did not do this. The responsibilities of the office were becoming clear. Now he had to act like a governor. So he just stood there beaming, holding Victoria's hand, and beaming some more until, finally, when he was all beamed out, the crowd simmered down.

"My friends, the best way I can thank you is to make the shortest speech of the campaign. It is a great feeling to win, of course. It is infinitely better than losing. And yet when the shouting and hoopla are over, when the parade has passed by and the Goodyear blimp has returned to Lakehurst, we are all left sitting in our New Jersey living rooms with a slew of real problems. How do we face them? In Act Four, Scene Three of a play of his called *Julius Caesar*, William Shakespeare put it this way:

> 'There is a tide in the affairs of men
> Which, taken at the flood, leads on to fortune;
> Omitted, all the voyage of their life
> Is bound in shallows and in miseries.
> On such a full sea are we now afloat,
> And we must take the current when it serves
> Or lose our ventures.'

"My friends, on such a full sea is the government of the Garden State now afloat. We shall take the current when it serves. We shall not lose our ventures. With history the final judge of our deeds, we shall move forward, working out the destiny of this historic American state. We shall move forward with a strong and active faith. And we shall gain the inevitable triumph, so help us God!"

A great cheer welled up from the group. I could see tears on the faces of many of the campaign workers. As a matter of fact, I unexpectedly felt one coursing down my own cheek. And when the great swirling noise had finally subsided, Quimbly said simply:

"Thank you—and God bless you—and goodnight."

CHAPTER 23

NEXT MORNING, Governor-Elect Quimby announced that there would be many more than the two traditional New Jersey Inaugural Balls—the one in Newark and the one in Trenton. He was arranging to have smaller editions of the Inaugural Ball in every firehouse across the state. Martin wanted everybody to be able to go down to the firehouse and get into the spirit of the new Quimby Administration.

The schedule for the night of January 3—Inauguration Night—called for the Governor and Mrs. Quimby to leave the Newark Ball at 11:00 P.M. and to stop at four firehouse balls on the way to Trenton. At 11:55 they would arrive at the big Trenton Ball, and at midnight, Mrs. Penelope Potter, the venerable Registrar of Candidates, would propose a toast to the new Chief Executive and Mrs. Quimby. This scene would be carried on TV to all the firehouses, of course, and everybody could raise a stein of congratulations to them.

Everything was on schedule. At about ten after eleven that night, our cavalcade was travelling south at high speed on the New Jersey Turnpike. The night was clear and cold. In the lead car, with his siren wailing and his red-and-blue light twisting and flashing, was Captain Hanson, the New

Jersey trooper who was now on permanent assignment to guide and guard the Governor.

Immediately following Hanson's blue cruiser was a brand-new Cadillac 120 Limousine, purchased that morning by the New Jersey Department of Motor Vehicles for the Governor. Al Divver was at the wheel. Quimby and Victoria, having danced radiantly at the Newark ball, were relaxing in the back seat. The scheduled turnoff from the turnpike was Interchange 13, and we would make our first appearance at the Pikeville firehouse.

I was following the Cadillac in the Mercedes, and strung out behind me were half a dozen Cadillacs and Lincolns containing a raft of Democratic hangers-on who were anxious to get in on the ground floor of the Quimby Administration. I sat alone in the big back seat under the gooseneck light, trying to memorize the second verse of Trombone Lonergan's stirring march. Quimby's first public act as Governor that morning had been to designate it as the official state song. Martin already knew all four verses, and I didn't think the Lieutenant Governor should be left moving his lips uncertainly every time the Governor stood up at a speaker's table and called for the state song.

I glanced up at the speedometer which was mounted next to the tape deck above the bar. We were passing through the city of Elizabeth at eighty-two miles an hour. Though we were in violation of federal law, we had the approval of the New Jersey Turnpike troopers. I looked back down at the lyrics, and then suddenly the whole back of the car lit up with a bright silent orange light. The sound of the explosion came a moment later—a monstrous blast from a vast oil refinery up ahead, off to our right. A bright gash of flame blazed from the base of one of the great cracking towers—a structure perhaps twenty stories tall. There were three or four more explosions, lighting up the whole refinery like daylight. High up at the top of the tower, the huge red neon sign that said HUMBLE winked twice and went out.

Then, as a maelstrom of flame kept pouring out of the rupture at the bottom of the huge tower, the whole structure began to topple. It was a piece of slow-motion film. The path of the fall was directly toward the turnpike, and you could tell from the arc that the monster would indeed smash onto the road. Slowly, it picked up speed.

My driver slowed up, uncertain about the timing—not knowing whether to stop or to hit the gas and make a screaming run for it. Half a second later he hit the brakes for a full, screaming emergency stop as the great structure inclined more and more toward us. I was thrown hard into the rear-facing seats, but kept my eye latched on Quimby's limousine. The angle of the big Cadillac's body changed abruptly. The rear dropped down hard over the back wheels and the long shiny hood rose up as Al Divver decided to make a run for it, pushing the huge engine all out.

It didn't work. The top of the great black tower came down with a thundering crash on top of the Quimby car. The steel H in HUMBLE cut away the entire rear quarter of the big vehicle, as though it had been placed on a chopping block.

The Mercedes was at a dead stop when the tower hit the road two hundred feet ahead of us. My driver pulled hard to the left, and we shot into the wide median strip and around the wreckage. On the other side of the tower, I could see the crippled Cadillac careening uncontrollably down the road, the body dragging, sending up a shower of sparks. As it finally ground to a stop, we were also coming to a halt right next to it.

Victoria was in the severed car, holding on to the velvet assist cord, her face pinned in a silent scream. Quimby was simply not there at all. Hanson's cruiser, having made a screeching U-turn, came to a stop. I waved him on back to the fallen tower, shouting Quimby's name. Al Divver, in shock but apparently not hurt, had already opened the door on Victoria's side and was trying to lift her out.

There was a huge welt on Victoria's forehead, and her foot was trapped under the footrest. Divver and I together were able to raise up the twisted metal bar, so I could lift her gently from the car. It was not until then that I saw the long diagonal gash in her silver dress and the long gash down the same line across her back. Suddenly there was blood everywhere.

Hanson's cruiser came screaming back from the fallen tower. He looked out the window, his ruddy face now a pasty gray.

"Sir, I'm sorry to report to you that Governor Quimby is dead."

"All right, Hanson, turn on your siren and get us to the Elizabeth Hospital. Mrs. Quimby is badly hurt."

"Yes, sir, but I suggest that someone stay here, Governor, in order to—"

Al Divver ran toward the cruiser and jumped in.

"Damn it, Hanson," he hollered, "turn on your light and move out!"

As my driver sped after Captain Hanson's cruiser, the entire wreckage of the tower burst into flame. I looked back. The wreckage of the Cadillac was burning. The whole surface of the road was burning. Roaring again through the night, I lay Victoria across the seat and ripped off my shirt to press it along the gash, trying to stop the blood. It was a pathetic gesture. There was no way to stop it. She lay with her face turned to one side, and she seemed to want to say something—but no sound came out. I knew that if we didn't get there fast, she'd be lost.

Blood-soaked, I waited in the emergency waiting room with Al Divver. A nurse came up with a hospital gown.

"Governor, you might be more comfortable if you put this on while you wait."

"Why, yes. Thanks."

As she took my blood-stained coat, I slipped into the gown, thinking how odd it was for a total stranger to suddenly come up and call me "Governor."

"I'm sorry about Governor Quimby," she said quietly, tying the gown up the back. "I really liked him."

"I did myself," I said. "He was—he was a good man."

A doctor came out of the treatment room and guided me a little way down the hall so we could talk.

"She's alive, Governor, but we can't tell yet how badly hurt."

"Why not?"

"We've stopped the bleeding, but before we can do anything else, we must replace the blood she's lost. You have to know that I've placed Mrs. Quimby on the critical list."

"I'll wait here until we know more," I said.

"That may be several hours."

"Makes no difference."

As the doctor left, another man appeared at my elbow, calling me "Governor" and flashing a credential embedded in plastic. "Excuse me, Governor," he said. "I'm Special Agent Charles Edwards, FBI."

I took the wallet and inspected the card closely.

"How the hell did *you* get here, Mr. Edwards?" I asked.

"We were tailing your cavalcade, Governor. We've had word in the past few days that Governor Quimby may have been in danger."

"Oh?"

"I have two agents with me here at the hospital. One will guard you until further arrangements can be made, and—"

"What kind of arrangements?"

"—and the other will be posted outside Mrs. Quimby's door here at the hospital."

I was still having trouble putting all this together, but Special Agent Edwards seemed to have it all worked out.

"I strongly recommend that you skip the rest of the evening and go immediately to the executive mansion in Trenton, where it will be easier to guard you."

Victoria was now wheeled out of the treatment room. At a nod from Special Agent Edwards, another agent followed her stretcher as it moved slowly down the hallway.

"I'm going to stay here at the hospital until I can talk with Mrs. Quimby," I told him.

"But there's a task you should begin immediately, Governor," said Edwards.

"If that's true, then I'll begin it here."

"I recommend that you open a state investigation tonight into the death of your predecessor to see if there is any possibility that this was an assassination."

"Wait a minute, Mr. Edwards. That's an odd suggestion. Did you see the accident?"

"From a distance, yes. We were the last car in your cavalcade."

"Well, I was right on top of it. I can't believe that the whole tower was blown up with the express *aim* of having it fall on Governor Quimby's car. Is that what you're saying?"

"What I'm saying for certain, Governor, is this: When a new and abrasive Governor is killed on his Inaugural Night, when his victory margin was two one-hundredths of one percent of the vote, and when specific threats had been made against him, then it is simply our duty to investigate the possibility of foul play. The situation is basically ominous."

"But for that tower to fall on Martin Quimby's car by *design*," I persisted, "you would have to have—you would have to have a computer-controlled explosion, an airborne observer clocking the exact speed of the Cadillac, a saboteur who knew the exact strength and structure of the tower. It would be the most precise assassination in American history."

"Don't be misled by the precision of what actually happened, Governor. The tower could have fallen a quarter of a mile ahead of the Governor's limousine, halting all southbound traffic, and in the resulting flames and confusion, the Governor could have been shot from a slow-moving car in a northbound lane. A perfect target. A perfect situation for a getaway."

"All right, Mr. Edwards," I said. "I'll order the investigation."

It was my first act as Governor. Within an hour, still wearing the hospital gown, I was meeting in the hospital conference room with the FBI man, the head of the New Jersey State Police, and the Chief of Police of Elizabeth. The official investigation was under way.

At 3:00 A.M., they offered me an empty room, and the same doctor came by to recommend a sleeping pill. Unlike most people who live anxiety-ridden lives, I had never taken a sleeping pill. But it worked.

And yet I might as well have stayed awake, for my dreams that night contained everything. My head became a big kaleidoscope as the recent world floated, happily and sadly, in and out of focus.

Martin floated in and out—and Victoria—and Horace Quimby lying dead on the marble steps—and Mr. Schlemmer nodding his head over the diamonds—and the PATH station—and bricks that kept coming through the windows of both the campaign office and the House of Harry Winston—and Mrs. Remsen weeping while typing furiously—and pieces of Quimby's historic announcement speech—and Victoria suddenly frightened—and the *Ferdinand Magellan* going click-click, click-click—and Quimby roaring with laughter as the red brocade curtain in the RKO Theatre slowly descended—and the two men in the green Ford whom I had never seen as they kept getting away over and over and over again—and Victoria and I walking on the shore of Thunder Lake on the Kawaiute Reservation—and the smashed, cut-up Cadillac—everything—

I even dreamed that I was the Governor of New Jersey. It was profoundly upsetting. Jesus H. Sweet Christ, *I* was the Governor! In all my elaborate scheming for the unsung job of Lieutenant Governor, it had never occurred to me for a moment that I might turn out to be the Governor. But now that elegant office with the soft green walls—that was *my* office.

I woke up drenched in sweat. It was morning. I sat up wondering if I could really *be* a governor. I knew everything about politics, but nothing about government. I would have to settle down immediately and dig in. I would have to read the New Jersey Constitution again, this time searching for its substance and not just seeing if it could be broken down into radio spots.

Al Divver entered the room, carrying a suit on a hanger.

"Good morning, Governor," he said. "It's time to leave—for Trenton. I brought you a suit from UN Plaza. Nice place you got there."

"Thanks, Al."

"It'll take us thirty-seven minutes to drive to Trenton."

Al was his businesslike self, focussed as always on what needed to get done and how long it would take to drive to the scene of the action. It was somehow reassuring. He was helping to put the catastrophe into the background.

"How's Victoria?"

"About the same, Governor. But they think she'll survive now."

"I want to see her before we leave."

"She's sleeping." He paused, sizing me up. "We can't do much for Victoria, Governor, but there's a hell of a lot to do in Trenton.

"Let's go, Al," I said.

In just a few minutes, we were wheeling at high speed out of the hospital grounds. I rode up in front with Al, and we got waved through the toll booth on the Turnpike without even showing the Golden Lifetime Pass. By eleven o'clock in the morning, I was embroiled in a fight with the legislature. There was a powerful move afoot to repeal the legislation that had made the controversial state income tax into a permanent tax. The legislature wanted that. I did not. By noon, I had been entirely swept up in the job and was threatening a veto. The complex, embedded, contentious history of the state had fallen upon me, and there would be many times in the months ahead when I would wish I had the congenial, hard-bitten counsel of Martin J. Quimby, A.S.C.E.

Victoria survived. She remained in the hospital for a month, and at the end of each day, Al drove me back up to Trenton to see her. But she seemed not the same person. She was quiet, withdrawn. Her eyes had lost the glint of fun. For much of the time, we just sat silently together, holding hands. One day she said quietly to me that I just did not understand the real meaning of mourning. And perhaps she was right.

On the day that Victoria was released from the hospital, Al was waiting out front to bring her to Trenton. But she slipped out a side door and disappeared. Divver was furious with himself, and he wanted me to put out an all-points bulletin. But I told Al that there would be no APB. Victoria had a right to disappear if she wanted to. And down deep,

I was not too worried, for I thought I knew where she had gone. Back home. Back to Nevada. A few times in the long, muted hospital visits, Victoria had spoken about the death of her father and the Kawaiute rites of mourning. They were not over quickly. Only after the earth had travelled halfway around the sun would a Kawaiute time of mourning be over.

The official state investigation into the death of Gov. Martin J. Quimby went on for four months. The FBI stayed on to assist the state police and the local police.

There were the spiky, threatening letters to look into. There was a spate of early rumors and telephone calls to be followed up. There were speculative articles by spiritualists and ESP people. But nothing led to anything concrete.

At the site of the death out on the Turnpike, the scene was restaged again and again for motion picture experts and time-and-motion engineers and ballistics experts and explosives experts. It was Dealey Plaza all over again. But even after months of investigation and work, nothing led to anything concrete.

And so, as with the investigations of all American assassinations, this one started intensively, was pursued exhaustively, and finally petered out inconclusively. I brought it to a close.

On the third of June, six months to the day after Quimby's death, I was at work at the big desk in the Governor's office. I had no appointments listed because I was preparing to make another attempt to push a reasonably coherent school bill through the cantankerous legislature. I wanted it. They did not. (The new Governor was not doing too well with the legislature, but that was nothing new in New Jersey.)

With no announcement, the big double doors swung slowly open, and Victoria was standing there. She was wearing the Ghirardelli Chocolate suede coat and she looked magnificently her old self.

"Hello, Governor," she said quietly.

"Victoria," I said, standing up slowly, my eyes pinned on her as she came into the room and then paused.

"I'm back."

"Boss! How was home?"

"I needed to be there for a while."

"I know. Did you go down to Thunder Lake?"

"That was part of it. I had to go there."

"I know. But I'm glad you're back, Victoria."

"How are you doing, Tom?"

"Not bad. I've become almost as contentious as Quimby!"

"Are you going to become a great political leader? The FDR of New Jersey?"

"I hope so. But it's too early to tell."

"That was the worst night of my whole life, Tom," she said after a pause.

"Mine, too."

Then her eyes lit up as she broke into the old bronze symmetrical smile—the smile of a goddess. "Can't we—can't we move a little closer to each other?" she asked.

"We can," I said.

The Governor's office was big enough so that we could rush to each other and kiss as people used to do at the end of David O. Selznick movies. We did just that. It was not the same as ever. It was better. Absence had indeed made the heart grow fonder.

My appointments secretary, Mrs. Remsen, came to see why the double doors were unexpectedly open. Seeing what was going on, she discreetly closed them.

"Will Al Divver burst in on us?" asked Victoria.

"No. My instinct told me to give him the day off. He's at Monmouth Park."

I helped Victoria off with her coat.

"Would you like a drink?" I asked, heading for the historic rolltop desk.

"I think I'll try a Manhattan on the rocks," she said with the low laugh.

I rolled back the top, and then I turned to look at Victoria again. She was seated on the big leather sofa and her head was inclined toward me as it had been in the cab in Trenton that day so long ago. As I came over to hand her the Manhattan, Victoria reached up and very gently tickled my left nostril. That did it. The drinks remained untouched. But not us. With Woodrow Wilson looking disdainfully down upon us from the north wall, we drifted happily into the warm timelessness of love.

CHAPTER 24

DURING my first couple of months as Governor, after Victoria had disappeared and while the assassination investigation was still going on, the word got out that at the end of each working day, I would sprawl on one of these big leather sofas and talk for an hour or so into my SONY, getting this tale on tape.

People asked me if I was writing myself a campaign biography—one of those political puff pieces as fragile as the paper around an Italian macaroon—and I told them no. What I was working on, I would explain to them, was an unembellished memorial to my good friend, the late Gov. Martin J. Quimby (Ind.). Quimby had gone too quickly from the New Jersey scene—and from my own life. He was too good a man to lose so abruptly. He had qualities, it seemed to me, that were worth remembering and passing on, though, of course, no book could ever delineate those qualities as well as Quimby himself in action as the Governor of this state.

I also knew, of course, that this would be a report on me—a report on who I am and how I came to power. In this respect, I wanted to be equally straightforward, so that if it ever did get used as a campaign biography, it might actually help people to judge me on the basis of the Truth, the whole Truth, and nothing but the Truth—so help me God. And now, to be honest about it, I am hoping that it *does* become a campaign biography—and in a very big campaign.

For consider my position as of this writing:

My name is Thomas Jefferson Quick.

I am fifty, healthy, and without political tarnish.

I am the Governor of the third most densely populated state in the nation.

I am one of the biggest vote-getters in the history of that state.

I will shortly switch from Ind. to Dem.—emerging as a pivotal Democrat.

I have actually rammed a state income tax *increase* through the New Jersey legislature, the revenue from which will go for education, so that fewer people who cannot read at all will graduate from our high schools.

I strongly resemble one of the most captivating and charismatic presidents in American history. Yet I have made it to this point on my own.

I plan in another six months to marry the most remarkably handsome and liberated woman in the state—Victoria Woodhill Quimby. We hope to have two children, conforming to ZPG.

At a ceremony last week, the newest rest stop on the New Jersey Turnpike was officially named for me—The Gov. Thomas Jefferson Quick Rest Stop. So, in a modest way, I have already become a historic figure—in the same league with Walt Whitman, Clara Barton, Woodrow Wilson, Molly Pitcher, Richard Stockton, Thomas Edison, Joyce Kilmer, Grover Cleveland, John Fenwick, William B. Halsey, James Fenimore Cooper, Vince Lombardi, and Alexander Hamilton.

So, everything considered, it seems to me that I have a neat chance—a better chance than almost any other American—to get the Democratic nomination for vice-president when the Democrats hold their next convention in Miami. (Maybe even the mantle of the presidency if the other thirty-seven Democratic hopefuls falter in the primaries.)

If nominated, I shall act as my own political consultant, making no charge for my services. I shall sign the Common Cause creed and the sacred oath of the Fair Campaign Practices Committee.

If elected, I shall attempt to thrust a real sense of civilized responsibility upon all the people of this country—East and West, North and South, rich and poor, old and young, black and white, straight and gay, smart and dumb. I will be hardheaded about our nation's future, but I will be hopeful, too. I shall try to bring the fragile idea of fairness to the government of the United States of America, as I am now trying to do in New Jersey. It is possible, as Martin J. Quimby once said in a tirade in Tenafly, to make the government fair, even when fairness has not yet touched the hearts of all the people.

I earnestly solicit your vote.

Thank you—and God bless you—and goodnight.